THE GILDED TALISMAN

NINA GATES

BOHÈME ÉCLAT
PRESS

ISBN: 979-8-9932132-0-0 ISBN: 979-8-9932132-1-7 ISBN: 979-8-9932132-2-4

Library of Congress Control Number: 2025920651

BOHÈME ÉCLAT
PRESS

ALSO BY NINA GATES

The Roses of Ainsworth Manor

Be an Artist (or Just Live Like One)

The Elegance Code

BOHÈME ÉCLAT PRESS

CONTENTS

ONE

VENETIAN NIGHTS

T HERE ARE LIVES THAT unfold in straight lines—neat, predictable, each piece clicking into place. Hers is not one of them.

She can quote poetry, paint a portrait, recite the periodic table, and restore a Renaissance altarpiece with a steady hand. She knows the difference between Greek and Roman intaglios, can order dinner in four languages, and has weathered more relationships than she cares to count. Now she works on contract in the world's most renowned museums, tucked away in secluded restoration studios, coaxing color back to damaged canvases and repairing time-worn antiquities.

Some call it indecisive. Maren Bennett calls it curiosity. But sometimes she wonders if all these fragments will ever add up to something whole.

Nevertheless, like her famous parents, she is known for solving mysteries. Perhaps that's why, the day before he died, her father sent a text:

"Come to Venice as soon as possible—trust no one."

The next message was even more cryptic: a coded note she still hasn't been able to decipher.

Venice is a city of mysteries. She wonders what her father might have found here and whether it played a part in his death. Though the police quickly dismissed any suggestion of foul play, she had wanted to see for herself and go through his personal effects carefully before sending them to her mother in New York. When his remains were returned and the memorial service held, she finally felt ready to travel to Italy. She tied up the practical loose ends in her first three days, but she is not quite ready to leave. If her father uncovered anything of consequence, perhaps some trace remains in the winding alleys and frigid November piazzas where he walked. Sometimes she can feel his presence, and it is enough just to be here and remember him.

Tonight, in the city of masks, shadows drape over marble and water like a velvet cloak. Fog rolls low along the winding canals, blurring the line between solid and spectral. Lamplight battles the darkness earlier each day, casting reflections that shimmer then vanish into black water. As she crosses Saint Mark's Square, the ancient stones beneath her feet speak of winter.

Maren steps into the stillness of Saint Mark's Basilica. As often as she's seen it, she is never prepared for the majestic blaze of gold arching seventy feet above her head. More than 85,000 square feet of glimmering gold tiles, enough to blanket a football field and a half—tell an epic tale set in place by countless hands spanning eight centuries.

"Look down," says a woman standing nearby—perhaps a docent, or maybe just another seeker. "At first, it's only a patchwork. But every stone has its place. Follow the blue-green marble." She traces a serpentine path in the air, her finger hovering above a vein of seafoam tiles that curve toward the altar.

"It's a map if you know how to see it."

Maren studies the floor. Interesting, she thinks. The marble is a riot of color and shape, but the sea-green tiles do stand out. Like a river frozen mid-current, they invite her toward the apse. She follows until the flow comes to an abrupt, unsatisfying halt. Inexplicably, the river of tile simply vanishes into a stone wall, leading nowhere after all.

She looks around, searching for an explanation. There is only a small relief of a winged lion in the center of a circle, carved into the wall at eye level, its features worn smooth by time. Behind her, much higher, are life-size marble statues of the saints, watching over her from their ancient perch above the nave. Maren turns and smiles encouragingly at Saint Mark and Saint Matthew. "Hey guys, I could use a little help here." They offer no reply, staring down serene and impassive, guarding secrets they have no intention of sharing.

Her thoughts drift to her own life, the scattered tiles she's gathered: moments of joy, heartbreak, accomplishment, friendship, and more than a few unexpected detours. She realizes how often she's pressed her face too close to the mosaic, unable to see the pattern.

She lifts her eyes again, awestruck by the shimmering gold ceiling. Of course, she thinks: thousands upon thousands of tiny, gleaming tesserae, each essential, but none meaningful alone.

The pattern appears only when you step back.

Outside, she pulls up her collar against the icy wind. The square is deserted except for a man standing in the shadows beneath the arches. He meets her gaze, silent, then sets an object on the stones, murmurs something to himself, and walks away.

Curious, Maren crosses to where he stood just a moment ago, and bends to pick up a ring. At its center sits a vivid turquoise cabochon set in gold, encircled by a starburst of diamonds. This central motif rests atop a deep blue tablet flecked with gold. She wonders if the stone is lapis lazuli. The square tablet is bordered on all sides by pavé diamonds, with four emerald baguettes set at the four points of the compass: one indicating North, one pointing South, one East, and one West. As she turns the ring in her hand, it catches the lamplight and scatters it in every direction.

She hesitates, then slips it onto her left hand where her engagement ring used to be. The gold band is cold, but fits perfectly. It begins to vibrate faintly against her skin, as if stirred to life by the same ancient current guiding the river of mosaic tiles inside the Basilica. It is lovely, yes, but also strange, too intricate to be mere ornament.

As she settles the ring on her finger, Saint Mark's Square seems to tilt, and she feels a wave of dizziness. Reality feels subtly altered. Now the lapis stone is unexpectedly warm, almost pulsing in time with her heartbeat, as if the ring is attuning itself to her.

When she looks up, the stranger is gone.

She shakes her head, tells herself it's just the cold night air, but the feeling persists—a low, electric awareness that something has changed. Maren wonders if the woman was right. Maybe some maps are written in stones.

TWO

MIDNIGHT BLUE

A WEEK IN VENICE and she found nothing. No clues. No answers. Only more questions about her father's death, swirling beneath the city's foggy surface. Just as she was preparing to fly home, a note arrived at her hotel, unsigned and enigmatic, accompanied by a single ticket for the Orient Express to Paris. The handwriting was unfamiliar, the message brief: *Paris holds what Venice could not.* She hesitated, but the hope of understanding her father's fate, the lure of a trip on the fabled Orient Express train, and as always, the restless pull of the unknown, were impossible to resist.

Maren boards the Venice-Simplon Orient Express beneath a pale midmorning sky, stepping up to her carriage from the platform at Venice's bustling Santa Lucia Station. More than just a train, the Venice-Simplon is a living legend. Steeped in glamour and intrigue, it's a moving monument to another era. Its name recalls the original Orient Express, the famed line that once linked Western Europe to the temptations of the East. The completion of the Simplon Tunnel in 1906 opened a new chapter of the legacy, carving a path from Venice to Paris that became synonymous with romance, elegance, and adventure. In the 1920s and 30s, the train's sapphire blue carriages whisked aristocrats, spies, and celebrities across borders with decadent ease—a moving stage for both real and imagined drama.

She enjoys a glass of champagne in a monogram-etched flute, and marvels that every moment on board seems orchestrated with the devotion of a well-rehearsed symphony. Service is discreet but omnipresent. Silent hands refill your glass, replenish your cabin, and transform your berth.

In her compartment, with its brass fittings, polished wood, and velvet-cushioned banquette, it's easy to imagine Agatha Christie's famous detective peering through these very windows. Her steward, Patrick, explains that while she is at dinner this evening, her day lounge will be transformed into an intimate nighttime retreat, with a delightfully comfortable bed and pressed white sheets. There's even a pretty cotton robe, which she is invited to take home. He shows her the reading lamp, her call button, and padded hangers for her clothes. There are French soaps, toiletries, and starched, monogrammed hand towels in her water-closet.

Later, Patrick pokes his head into the open cabin doorway and offers a refill on her champagne.

"Of course!" She says, "Why not?"

She smiles up at him as he finishes pouring, then shifts on the banquette to look out the window at the passing scenery. She thinks about Paris. She has been to Paris many times, but Ethan had not. They had planned to make this trip together someday, back when traveling the world was a shared dream. Ethan is a corporate attorney who measures life in billable hours; he said he admired her range of interests, then suggested that when they married, she might stop "collecting skills" and start doing something that really matters.

When he decided he wasn't ready to settle down and broke off their engagement, the life she'd planned vanished in one wretched "we have to talk" moment. Soon afterward, Ethan announced his engagement to someone else, and she had to face the truth: it wasn't that he didn't want to marry. It was that he didn't want to marry her. That realization shattered whatever confidence had remained.

How quickly things change. It is astonishing, really, how life can turn in an instant. Sometimes a single decision is all it takes to set the world spinning. She wonders whether getting on this train bound for Paris will alter the course of her life. Probably not, she thinks, and lets the idea fade along with the landscape beyond her window. At least she will have a good story to tell. She gives herself a toast: "Here's to stories. Preferably with complimentary bubbles."

Not long ago, Maren's days followed the steady rhythm of museum hours and the orderly processes of restoration work. She has a lovely apartment near Dupont Circle in a gorgeous old Beaux-Arts building, three elegant rooms with high ceilings, elaborate moldings, and her bohemian mix of books. She has filled it with grand old portraits in oil and mismatched but comfortable furniture, yet she is rarely there. Most days she is at the museum, thriving on the logic of careful examination and the satisfaction of solving problems with a skillful hand and a sharp eye.

The end of her engagement brought an odd, painful free-dom. With no one waiting at home, she could lose herself in her job and let work fill the empty spaces. But even that comfort feels altered now, shadowed by her father's death.

Her father, Jim Bennett, specialized in recovering stolen art, work that was both interesting and lucrative. He and Maren occasionally even found opportunities to collaborate. Most recently, he had been in Venice, investigating a piece of jewelry—a necklace—for her mother. Dr. Elaine de Beaumont Bennett is an art historian with a lifelong fascination for the legendary 16th-century talisman necklace called simply, Rox-elana.

Maren knows very little about the mysterious necklace. She's aware it disappeared during the fall of the Ottoman Empire, surfaced briefly in Venice in the 1920s, and then vanished again. Her mother has always been intensely private about this hobby, sharing little beyond the occasional stray anecdote or a clipped article left on the kitchen table. Maren is left piecing together fragments. Never the full story, only hints and half-answers.

For centuries, the vast network of trade routes known as the Silk Road crossed Central Asia, connecting East and West. It's easy for Maren to imagine a precious talisman necklace being swept along those routes, making its way between the great trading cities of Istanbul and Venice.

Did her father discover something about the jewels in Venice? Maren wonders if she'll ever know.

At 6 o'clock, Maren makes her way to the bar car. Fleeting friendships are struck over pre-dinner cocktails around a glossy baby-grand piano. She is quick to laugh, a willing conspirator in stories traded with fellow escape artists. Carriage 3674 is alive with conversation and the rustle of evening finery. In this jovial hour before dinner, the elegant vagabonds are happy simply to be aboard. United, if only briefly, by the pleasure of the voyage.

She is gracious, of course. Her mother's daughter in every gesture, every thoughtful word. Though she loves France, and there is a certain French poise in the tilt of her chin, she has never truly called it home. Her mother, a Parisian beauty, left it for love, marrying an American and crossing an ocean. Her family often tells Maren that she has a trace of her mother's European allure woven into the fabric of her being.

Dining on the Orient Express is a ritual. Multi-course feasts are crafted from local ingredients sourced from artisan producers along the route and served beneath crystal chandeliers in luxuriously appointed dining cars. At dinner, she is seated in a comfortable grass-green velvet armchair, directly across from a silver-haired gentleman. They are each at their own table, yet perfectly aligned as if by design. After a few exchanged glances, they both laugh and agree it would be far more sensible, and much more fun, to sit together. He stands and introduces himself as Alistair Edwards.

She rises as well and extends her hand. "Maren. Bennett."

"How do you do, Miss Bennett," he says as the headwaiter slides Maren's chair in for her. "First time on the Orient Express?"

His accent is distinctly British, and, Maren muses—quite posh.

She smiles, swirling her wine. "It is. It's also my first time heading west by rail. Do you ever find you're more comfortable departing than arriving?"

He laughs, warm and knowing. "Ah, well, it's the departures that make us who we are, don't you think?"

"Perhaps," she concedes, glancing at the window where the hills blur past. "Or maybe it's what we choose to leave behind when we go."

He nods, as if understanding more than she says. Then, as she reaches for her glass, his gaze lingers on her hand.

"That's a remarkable ring," he observes, his tone casual but his eyes intent. "Such a curious arrangement of stones—lapis, turquoise, diamonds, emeralds. Not a combination you see every day. Jewels like that often carry legends. It must have quite an illustrious past."

As he speaks, Maren feels a faint, almost imperceptible vibration where the ring rests against her skin; subtle. She pauses, uncertain whether it's a warning or simply the ring's way of marking someone who notices too much.

He hedges, seeing her hesitation. "Perhaps some answers are meant to be revealed in time."

"Honestly, I know nothing about it. It was a recent... gift. I haven't had the chance to learn its origins."

The sensation fades, replaced by a sense of watchfulness, as if the ring is settling, still learning her boundaries and how she reacts to the world around her.

He studies her for a moment, then offers a small, almost satisfied smile. "Sometimes the most intriguing stories are the ones we unlock ourselves." He raises his glass in salute, as if acknowledging some unspoken understanding between them.

She lifts her glass as well. "To reinvention then," she echoes.

He leans in surreptitiously. "To second chances."

She laughs, the sound surprising her with its ease. "Or third. Or however many it takes."

He grins. "I've always preferred the scenic route anyway."

Dinner is delicious, and their conversation meanders from favorite cities to books and current events. Maren feels the disappointment that she did not find what she sought in Venice, but she doesn't dwell on it tonight. Instead, she lets herself be carried by the rhythm of the train and the promise of adventure ahead.

After all, she thinks, the chance to escape the sadness that has settled around her is reason enough to keep moving forward. Later, in the bar car once again, the pianist plays "Someone to Watch Over Me," and she sings along. Alistair gives her a smile, joining in, and soon the rest of the lounge is swept up in the song.

She is on the most beautiful train in the world, and Paris awaits. She has visited her grandparents, aunts, uncles, and cousins in France before, but Paris has always felt like her mother's city, a place seen only through borrowed memories. Tonight, with music and merriment all around, Maren hopes that one day Paris will feel like her city too.

THREE

PARIS

S HE ARRIVES WITH A single bag and a well-loved copy of Colette. On her finger, the blue ring is a silent companion, oddly reassuring and, at times, almost attentive. There are moments when she can swear it responds to her mood or the energy of a room, as if it's studying her.

Alone in Paris. The phrase is a kind of passport. One stamped not by customs, but by the heart. Winding through the crowd at Gare de l'Est, her old leather backpack over one shoulder, she thinks about what this journey might bring. Perhaps it's an opportunity to discover who she is; not as a fiancé, or a girlfriend, or a daughter, or someone defined by her job. For once, she wants to know herself outside the roles she's always played.

Paris greets Maren like an old accomplice, gifting her a bright, crisp morning at a café near Place des Vosges in Le Marais. Once a marshy outskirt turned aristocratic enclave, the neighborhood now mixes medieval streets, grand mansions, and chic boutiques in an easy, lived-in elegance. Ethan used to joke that she probably orders the same breakfast every day no matter where she is. Maren shrugs to herself. I have to admit he was right.

"Un café au lait, s'il vous plaît, et un orange pressé."

The waiter nods, already scribbling. Clearly, he's seen my type before: Creature of Habit, International Edition. Well, she thinks, at least I'm predictable.

She enjoys the warmth of the sun on her face as she eats an almond-scented croissant, idly browsing yesterday's Le Monde. An article in the arts section catches her eye: an upcoming exhibition of Ottoman artifacts at the Musée Carnavalet, just a short walk away. She folds the paper, marking the article with her spoon, and reads about a special lecture on the role of talismans and ceremonial jewels in the Ottoman court. Maren's interest is instantly piqued. Normally, she stays at a little hotel on the Champ de Mars, but perhaps later this afternoon she will find a place here instead.

These thoughts remind her that she hasn't spoken to her mother in a week. Feeling slightly guilty, Maren sends her a quick text: In Paris for a few days, took a train from Venice. All is well. She does not add that the train was the Orient Express, or that the sudden trip is courtesy of a mysterious benefactor.

Her relationship with her mother has always been laced with a kind of awe and a bit of distance. Though Maren admires her deeply, she's never felt quite in her mother's league, in beauty or brains. Maren had more in common with her father. The way they both delighted in obscure details, their ability to find humor in almost everything, and their easy way of talking to each other. Which just makes her miss him all the more. When he died, she lost her father and her best friend too.

She wonders if he had ever investigated the Talisman for her mother before, or if this had been a new challenge, one that had stumped even him, the world-famous art sleuth. She wishes she could send him a message too, even if only a text: In Paris, chasing secrets. Back soon.

A short time later, she walks with no destination in mind, and by noon, she is lost by design. Narrow brick streets. Hemingway's ghost. Baker's laughter. Ladurée. Flower stalls fill the air with the spicy scent of autumn greenery.

She passes boutiques displaying cutting-edge fashion and designer shoes, and Maren thinks, some amazingly daring lingerie—but she hardly glances inside. Clothes have never interested her much. She prefers the comfort of worn boots, one of her mother's old sweaters, and the anonymity of a simple black pea coat. In another life she imagines, as the breeze tousles her cropped hair, she might be the kind of woman who slows down to window shop, but today bookshops and galleries call to her more than clothes.

In the Latin Quarter, a blue door stands open. Her favorite bookshop in Paris, a place she has returned to since her first childhood visit with her parents. The proprietor greets her with a nod, as if he's been expecting her. She takes her time browsing, tracing the spines of classic French novels, familiar with their gold-leafed titles. She selects a small book with a cranberry-red cover, L'Éclat de la Bohème, and pays for it at the counter.

As she turns to leave, the bookseller stops her. From a drawer beneath the counter, he produces a folded map, its edges soft. The arrondissements, meaning literally "encirclements" in French—the city's districts—are inked in faded colors, and a single route is traced in red.

"For your journey," he says, eyes kind, sliding the map across the counter. "Paris is a labyrinth. It helps to know where you've been and where you might go next. Pour la chance."

She smiles. She believes him.

The ring tingles a little as she tucks the map into her coat pocket. On impulse, she picks up a pencil. Inside the cover of her Colette, she writes a brief note in French, an encouraging line for the next wanderer:

Ce que tu cherches est en train de te chercher.

What you seek is seeking you.

She pauses a moment, reading back the well-known words of Rumi, the 13th-century poet and mystic. Then she smiles and says, "I hope so."

She slides the book across the counter to the proprietor and steps into the street. Today, if there's an itinerary, no one has shared it with her. There is only the city, and the odyssey, and she is her own companion. Maybe she's never truly alone, she thinks. Maybe she's simply singular.

FOUR

INVITATIONS

S HE STEPS OUT OF the bookshop, squinting in the afternoon sun; the map tucked safely in her coat pocket. Passing a cafe, she smells the caramel-rich scent of coffee, and a waiter chalks the day's specials onto a blackboard. At the next bridge over the Seine she pauses, withdrawing the map and holding it up to the light. The paper is soft from years of folding; the ink faded but still just legible. A red line winds across the city from the Gare de l'Est train station to the cafe, the bookshop, and finally to a spot marked with a small, careful X. She traces her path with a fingertip and finds her place on the map. Strange. How could anyone have known my route today? Even I didn't know it.

She wavers, but an instinct urges her onward, and the ring on her finger is warm. That has to be a good sign, right? Maren thinks.

Following the map, she turns down a narrow street, walking faster now. The shops she passes are filled with treasures from another time. Windows with gilded names hand-lettered on the glass display old clocks, antique mirrors, and portraits whose eyes seem to follow her. At the end of the block, a gravel courtyard is half-hidden behind an elaborate wrought-iron carriage gate and the branches of a massive chestnut tree. Why is it that the merely rich want to display their houses to one and all, while the truly wealthy hide theirs behind so much ironwork and shrubbery it takes a minor act of espionage just to find the front door? She gives a little lopsided smile, checks her map, then her phone, and drops a pin just in case she needs it to get back.

The gate is Art Nouveau, quintessentially French, with lyrical whiplash curves and, at its center, the monogram RG in gilded script. Next to it, a smaller pedestrian entrance stands invitingly open—a porte piétonne, her mother once called this type of gate. Sliding the map back into her pocket, she steps through the portal.

The courtyard lies still except for water burbling and splashing somewhere in an unseen fountain. She breathes in the intoxicating scent of rosemary, and a few pigeons scatter as she crosses to the door of a stately Haussmann mansion. Its imposing facade of cut Lutetian limestone and wrought-iron balconies is everything she loves about classic Parisian houses. She imagines the house has been here at least since the days of Napoleon III, when Paris was modernized and reshaped into wide boulevards. There is no indication of who lives here, only a brass knocker in the shape of a sun on a massive oak door.

Maren's hand hovers over the knocker. She pauses, suddenly unsure of herself. Is she really meant to be here? Or is she making a fool of herself, crossing an ocean and following this trail of mysterious messages? Still, she can't ignore the sense that something important waits just beyond this door. She knocks.

For a long moment, nothing happens.

Then the door opens a crack, and a woman in a blue dress and white apron peers out, her eyes sharp and assessing.

"Bonjour," the woman says briskly. "You're early. Come in."

Maren steps inside and stops short. "Wow," she breathes. The entry hall is breathtaking with black-and-white marble floors, soaring ceilings, and ornate plaster moldings. At the center, a large circular table stands on carved and gilded lion's paws, supporting a blue-and-white Ming vase overflowing with roses, lilacs, lemon branches, and tuberose, flowers plainly out of season. The air is suffused with their scent, layered with the warmth of beeswax polish. This isn't a house, Maren thinks. It's a lifestyle.

The woman in the starched blue uniform closes the door behind her.

"This way, mademoiselle."

The maid leads her through double doors into a refined sitting room in pale blue and gold. Silk taffeta curtains in the same airy blue, pool like ball gowns at the windows. Maren admires the tall glass panes of the porte-fenêtre—French doors, as they are called in English. They frame a view into another courtyard, this one private, enclosed by a high wall adorned with espaliered pear trees; their branches tracing symmetrical patterns against the stone.

Near the fireplace, where a cheerful blaze wards off the afternoon chill, a pair of armchairs angle toward a low table. On it sits an antique sterling tea set, each piece engraved with an ancient Ottoman scroll pattern. Mounted atop the teapot's lid is an unusual carved stone. It is deep blue and flecked with gold: lapis lazuli, a perfect match for the stone set in her ring from Venice.

The maid gestures for her to have a seat, then settles into the chair opposite, pouring tea into fine Sèvres porcelain cups. The delicious aroma of bergamot curls upward with the steam, mingling with the faint perfume of flowers drifting in from the hallway. Maren tries to contain her nerves and lowers herself into an armchair, the silk brocade upholstery surprisingly cool beneath her hands.

"You have been—" the maid pauses, choosing her words with care, "invited here by Madame Geneviève-Hélène Sévigny d'Orleans Girard, Marquise de Saint-Clair. Madame Girard has summoned you for a matter of great importance. Rumors have surfaced in Istanbul about an artifact long sought by Madame Girard. A jeweled Ottoman talisman necklace. She believes this may be the same necklace your mother has studied, and that you, with your background in art and your family's history, are uniquely suited to recover it."

She sets the teapot down. With a small, formal gesture, she slides a cream-colored envelope across the table. Its heavy paper sealed with a disc of metallic gold wax, pressed with a sun just like the door knocker.

"Madame regrets her absence today and the necessity of such secrecy, but wishes you to have this."

Maren picks up the envelope, hands trembling, and breaks the seal. Inside she finds a ticket for the Orient Express to Istanbul, an elegantly engraved invitation to a ball, and a bank cheque for 50,000 euros, drawn on the venerable Banque Courtois. For a moment, she is too stunned to respond.

She has been aware of the ring's presence since she knocked on the door, but now it vibrates so insistently that Maren reaches to adjust it on her finger. The maid regards the ring with interest before continuing, "All expenses for this journey will be covered, and when you succeed, there will be a handsome reward."

"May I ask... why me? Why is Madame Girard going to all this trouble and expense to bring me here and send me after her artifact? I'm an artist, not an investigator. I'm just—"

The maid meets her gaze, her eyes kind but direct. "You are Maren Bennett. Daughter of James Bennett and the venerable Dr. Elaine Bennett. Your mother has spent a lifetime studying the artifact. Her work is known and respected, even among those who would rather it remain lost. Because you are American, you are least likely to be suspected, and most likely to succeed. And you, mademoiselle, have inherited her insight as well as your father's tenacity."

Maren's voice is quiet. "My father is dead. He died in Venice investigating this necklace. If it is the same one."

The maid inclines her head, her expression grave. "Yes, mademoiselle. Madame Girard believes it is. But your father's legacy—and you—are very much alive."

Maren places the envelope on the table, the weight of the invitation and the cheque suddenly heavier. "So, it's not just about my skills. It's about my parents."

"It is about you, Miss Bennett," the maid replies, her voice firm. "You are the bridge between the past and the present. Madame Girard trusts that you will see what others cannot, and go where others would not dare."

"I'd like to help, but Madame Girard has hired the wrong Bennett. It's my mother who is the expert on this piece."

The maid's eyes soften, and she nods.

"Madame Girard is well aware of your mother's expertise," she replies. "She has searched for this artifact for many years and has consulted with your mother several times. She and your mother both agree that it is you who must undertake this journey. Your mother's work laid the foundation, but it is your insight and courage that will see this through."

Maren picks up the envelope again, her thumb tracing the edge of the golden seal. She had seen very little of her mother after the funeral, both of them adrift in their separate grief. The thought that her mother, so formidable and exacting, would entrust her with something this important is both daunting and oddly comforting. Maren feels an obligation to help, but she is equally drawn by her growing interest in the very subject her mother has guarded so closely. Now, the need to understand pulls her forward as much as duty. She hesitates, searching the maid's face for any sign of doubt.

"My courage?" Maren repeats, almost to herself. "I'm not sure I see what they do."

The maid offers reassurance. "Sometimes, we only discover what we're capable of when we step into the unknown."

Maren sinks back into the armchair, the silence broken only by the occasional crackle of the fire. The significance of the moment presses upon her. She senses a door has opened, not just in this grand house, but in her own life.

"Madame said you might protest," the maid adds, a smile touching her lips. "She asked me to remind you that the greatest adventures begin with a simple 'yes.'"

FIVE

COUTURE

Madame Girard's maid stands up and smooths her apron. "And now you must go, mademoiselle." She says it softly, but there is an undercurrent of authority in her voice. "An appointment has been made for you at Madame's request, at Dior couture. Madame Girard is a very important client of the house. They will of course, extend you every courtesy. When you have chosen your gown for the ball, please select anything else you require."

Maren puts on her coat. She senses that declining the wishes of the Marquise de Saint-Clair is not an option, and anyway, she may need a few things if she is to rub shoulders with the glitterati in Istanbul.

"How should I contact you?"

"Do not concern yourself with that, dear. Madame Girard will be in touch. In the meantime, enjoy your stay in Paris. A hotel has been arranged for you as well. Monsieur le Chauffeur is available while you are here."

Maren reaches out, intending to shake the maid's hand, but instead finds herself swept into a gentle, unexpected embrace. The maid's arms are surprisingly strong, and for a moment, she feels a warmth she has not known in months. Maren blinks back sudden tears. The kindness, so simple and authentic, touches something deep inside her.

She gathers her bag and steps into the courtyard, where a black Rolls-Royce Phantom idles, purring. Its chrome grille and the Spirit of Ecstasy hood ornament catch the afternoon sun, blinding her for a moment. Madame Girard's silver-haired chauffeur waits beside the car, tall and dignified. On the lapel of his flawlessly tailored suit is a small stylized sun embroidered in gold thread. Obviously the Girard signature. She looks up at him, startled to see a distinguished man she recognizes. "You were on the Orient Express."

"Mademoiselle Bennett," he says as he opens the rear door with a graceful bow and the hint of a smile. "Edwards. At your disposal."

For a heartbeat, she hesitates. Madame Girard must have sent him to look after her on the Orient Express from Venice. "I don't suppose it was a coincidence that we met on the train?"

Edwards does not answer but presents her with his card. It is light blue and engraved with a golden sun. It says only, Alistair Edwards, with a phone number.

She stands at the edge of something new, exciting, and frightening. She looks up at Edwards for a moment, then takes a deep breath and slides into the sumptuous vanilla interior. The car door closes with a dampened, decisive click, sealing her fate.

As Edwards pilots the car away from Madame Girard's elegant house, Maren stares out at the city. Had he followed her in Venice? Does Madame Girard know something about her father's death? Maren has so many questions. With a sigh, she decides to simply be present today and pay attention.

She looks around the cabin, running her hands across the leather seat, marveling at the richness. Even her armrests are heated. She had heard that Rolls-Royce employs active noise-cancelling technology and extensive soundproofing in its cars, but she's pleased the interior isn't completely silent.

The gentle churn of the engine creates a soothing rhythm that calms her nerves as Paris slips past the windows.

The car glides to a stop in front of the House of Dior on Avenue Montaigne. Edwards steps out, opens her door, and hands her backpack to a doorman in a dove-gray coat who has materialized out of nowhere.

A petite store associate greets her just inside the door. "Bienvenue, Mademoiselle Bennett. We've been expecting you. If you'll come with me, s'il vous plaît? You speak no French, yes?"

"No." Maren stammers, immediately flustered. "I mean, yes—oui, je parle français."

"Ah, bon. Excellent." The associate nods briskly and sets off at a pace that leaves Maren scrambling to keep up.

She ushers Maren up a curved staircase and into the couture salon on the second floor.

The room is awash in shades of ivory. A splendid crystal chandelier makes rainbows on the parquet floor, inlaid with a subtle compass rose. Looking down at it, Maren realizes that the eight-pointed star on a compass rose is not unlike what she had assumed was a starburst on her ring.

The attendant anticipates the question. "It is Dior's compass rose, Mademoiselle—a tool for navigation that, to Monsieur Dior, symbolized a spirit of exploration."

"C'est fascinant." Maren says.

"Even today, we embrace Monsieur Dior's passion for adventure." Then, glancing discreetly at her clothes, the attendant adds, "We also share his belief in fashion as a path for reinvention." Maren suppresses a laugh but nods, already fond of this associate.

Cream-colored sofas are arranged around a low, gilded table. Its surface is shaped like a ginkgo leaf and topped with bouquets of white flowers. Gowns are on display on racks throughout the salon. Playful modern art mingles with stately

Louis XVI chairs upholstered in pale gray silk. The atmosphere is serene but surprisingly exhilarating to Maren. She wonders how many women enter this space and leave with a renewed vision of themselves. For the first time in ages, she actually feels a spark of excitement to see what the magicians at Dior might do with her rather plain, practical self.

A senior vendeuse, Madame Valois, greets her in French and offers her a cup of tea. They sit together, Madame Valois poised to take notes in a small black notebook. Maren notices the interaction between a vendeuse and a couture client just leaving the salon, and senses that in the world of haute couture, a certain formality is accepted. She imagines that if a close relationship develops, first names might be used—but it's clear that such familiarity is neither typical nor expected.

"Valois," she says, somewhat shyly. "That's an illustrious name in France. A name of royalty."

Madame Valois nods solemnly, studying Maren with newfound interest. This tall, somewhat gangly brunette with a pixie cut and questionable fashion sense has surprised her twice in just a few moments. First, by speaking fluent French, and now by knowing the history of her family name, a detail many of her own friends wouldn't recognize beyond its association with a region in France.

Maren laughs in spite of herself. "I'm a history buff."

"That is wonderful," says Madame Valois. "Madame Girard mentioned only that you are an artist visiting from America."

"I'm not really an artist. Well, in the traditional sense, anyway. I work in restoration," she replies. "It helps to have a good grasp of world history."

Madame Valois finds herself warming to her peculiar new client. "Tell me about the ball in Istanbul. What kind of gown do you envision?"

Maren describes a simple strapless Dior dress she once saw a celebrity wearing in a magazine, with a wide skirt and a matching jacket, and she sketches it in as much detail as she can remember.

Madame Valois pauses thoughtfully. "I know the dress. It isn't a traditional ball gown, since it isn't floor-length, but perhaps we can adapt your idea and create something with a bit more versatility for you. I see that when you travel, you prefer to travel light."

She glances at Maren's battered leather backpack, now enthroned nearby upon its own gray silk stool, and smiles. To Sabine Valois, this client carries an air of sadness, yet seems remarkably unencumbered, at least in the physical sense—not like Madame Ainsworth, whom she saw this morning. Nell, as she prefers to be called, travels with a suite of custom-made Moynat trunks and visits Dior accompanied by her valet, Henry, and a large, scruffy dog.

"Would you like to see some fabrics?"

"Oh, yes!" Maren exclaims, rising to follow Madame Valois to another room.

"This is the Atelier," Madame Valois proclaims ceremoniously. "Here, our clients view sketches, fabrics, and toiles, and collaborate with our design team."

"Toiles?"

"Yes, Mademoiselle. A toile is a cloth mock-up of a design, made in inexpensive cotton muslin. It allows us to ensure that a garment is perfect, and perfectly fitted, before we create it in textiles that are very valuable, sometimes even one of a kind. A toile lets the designer and the client visualize the garment and request any adjustments. Then our talented petites mains, our seamstresses, often deconstruct the toile and use it as a pattern for the final piece."

She is tempted by swatches of cashmere, silk velvet, and gossamer embroidered tulle, each fabric inviting her to imagine herself draped in its folds. "I can't possibly decide. May I leave that to the designer?"

"Of course, Mademoiselle Bennett. We would be delighted to create a special gown for you."

Next, the première d'atelier arrives to take her measurements. She wraps a soft measuring tape around Maren's waist, shoulders, and arms, noting every detail. Normally, the process would begin with a bespoke sketch, a toile made precisely to the client's and Creative Director's vision, and several fittings. But with time so short, they bring out a muslin toile from a vintage collection, one close in spirit to the dress Maren described. She tries it on so the seamstresses can customize the fit.

As Maren stands before the gilded mirror, pins and chalk marks appear on the fabric, shaping the gown to her form. Madame Valois smiles reassuringly. "We will begin work immediately and plan another fitting at your hotel in Istanbul before the ball."

"You'll come to Istanbul?" Maren marvels.

"Bien sûr, but of course, mademoiselle. For our amis de la maison, as you say, our friends of the house, distance is never an obstacle. We are always delighted to provide our services wherever Madame Girard, or indeed her family, may be."

Maren imagines that to be considered an ami de la maison, one must easily spend six figures each season. She turns in the mirror, a flutter of excitement rising in her chest. Even pinned into the white cotton toile, stiff and unfamiliar, she hardly recognizes herself. This is no longer just a dress fitting. She has stepped into a fairy tale and is transforming before her own eyes.

Later, Madame Valois brings champagne and a rack of selections from ready-to-wear: a single-breasted Bar jacket in black with its iconic, nipped at the waist hourglass silhouette; matching slim black pants; another pair in camel wool; several silk blouses; cashmere sweaters; a sleek pencil skirt; and black kid pumps with a low princess heel.

Nothing Madame Valois suggests feels excessive. There are no flashy extras, just clean lines and impeccable craftsmanship in every piece. To Maren's surprise, as beautiful as the clothes are, they defer to her own style and personality, highlighting her best features and making her feel more pulled together than she had imagined possible. She could live in these clothes; they feel good.

Seamstresses return with pins and chalk as she tries on each garment. The jacket fits perfectly, cinching her waist and subtly perfecting her posture. No alterations needed. Pants are marked for hemming at just the right spot to lengthen her legs. The sleeves of a coat are taken up so they brush her wrists precisely. Even the silk pajamas and robe are carefully pinned for the perfect drape.

As each piece is adjusted, she watches herself metamorphose in the mirror, astonished by what a little precise tailoring can do. How am I this exacting at work, she wonders, yet pay so little attention to how I dress? For so long, she'd considered herself an academic, believing she was above giving thought to designers or fashion. But she sees now that wearing clothes straight off the rack, without shaping them to her own body, isn't more evolved or intellectual; it simply hands the choice of what she wears to someone else.

Even her old pea coat and jeans could feel entirely hers if she altered them to her shape instead of the generic woman imagined by the manufacturer. She resolves, at the very least, to have a few things fitted when she gets home.

"I'll take these," Maren says.

Madame Valois nods, as if she senses a change in her. Confidence, perhaps. Or is it hope? "Your purchases will be delivered shortly," she says. "And now, if you like, there is one more stop."

Maren nods, curiosity piqued. They leave the peaceful couture salon, descending the staircase to the bustling main floor.

A poised beauty consultant in Dior black greets them in the cosmetics area. "Bienvenue, Mademoiselle. It would be our pleasure to offer you a touch of Dior."

Maren takes a seat on a stool as the consultant studies her face with an artist's eye. She chooses a sheer foundation that matches Maren's skin perfectly, a rosy blush, and a classic red lipstick. Maren watches shoppers drift among glass counters lined with neat rows of lipsticks, eyeshadows, and blushes in every shade. She smiles, realizing this is probably the longest she's ever lingered in a cosmetics department.

Turning her attention to the consultant again, Maren notes how to brush on color and add definition, enhancing her features and letting her natural beauty shine. She learns to warm hair balm between her palms and gently smooth her short hair until it looks chic. Very Parisian. As a finishing touch, the consultant spritzes a mist of Miss Dior above Maren's wrists.

Maren looks at her reflection and is astonished by the transformation. Her eyes are brighter, her skin luminous, her lips just the right shade of red. She grins, "Merci."

The consultant offers her a last, approving nod and sets aside a miniature bottle of Miss Dior to be wrapped with her cosmetics as a parting gift.

Madame Valois returns. "You look radiant. France suits you." There is sincerity in her words. Maren thanks both of them and stands, attentive to her posture. She is wearing one of her new blouses, a new skirt, and the feminine low-heeled pumps. She feels lithe and a little sexy now, like a graceful gazelle.

An attendant appears, gathering her satchel and purchases from the cosmetics counter and leading her outside toward the waiting car. Edwards looks up, his expression betraying a brief, but quickly masked, look of surprised approval before he takes her bags and opens her door. Maren pauses beside the gleaming Rolls-Royce to appreciate the setting sun and the activity along Avenue Montaigne.

In the car, she thinks about her father, and the woman she was before boarding a plane for Europe. She thinks of loss, uncertainty, and the sorrow that has lived in her chest for months. The grief is still there, but it no longer defines her. She realizes she is no longer merely surviving. She is beginning to live again.

Six

ICONS

P ARIS LANDMARKS PASS AS Edwards steers the sleek black
Phantom through rush-hour traffic. Maren sits silently
in the back seat. She smooths her skirt and contemplates
her new clothes. Since her arrival in Paris, every detail has
been orchestrated for her, every wish anticipated, every need
arranged. She has never experienced anything like this level
of care and comfort. In Madame Girard's refined and graceful
world, things simply happen: seamlessly, silently, without visible effort.

Maren's youth was happy, but much less grand. Her mother
is beautiful, French, and brilliant. She met Maren's father by
chance on a spring afternoon at the Sorbonne. He was an
American, tall and earnest, his notebooks crammed with ideas
and plans. He had come to Paris to study, lured in part by the
city's heritage but also by the promise of a fresh perspective.
She was browsing the university's rare books collection when
he noticed her and inquired about the text she was reading.

Their conversation began with a shared love of art and
history. It was the spark between them, though—the way his
teasing made her blush, the way she listened intently and
asked him thoughtful questions—that turned a chance meeting into a future. By summer's end, they were inseparable. He
invited her to lectures in the Latin Quarter; she introduced

him to the local culture. Together, they bridged continents and customs, weaving their lives into something new and special.

Both would go on to achieve acclaim in their fields; their successes affording Maren a childhood marked not by the affluence of Parisian aristocracy, but by comfort, education, and freedom to explore. It was a world of opportunity, shaped by the unspoken expectation that she, too, would find her own path in life. This legacy made Maren grounded but curious, independent yet connected to a lineage of love and achievement.

Maren is well-travelled, yet as she watches the city beyond the tinted glass, she's struck by the reach of Madame Girard's influence. Her wealth is not merely a comfort and convenience, but a force that, for better or worse, shapes destinies.

Maren's thoughts go to the Talisman necklace, and Madame Girard's determination to possess it. The question nags at her: why does Madame Girard want it so badly, and why has her mother searched for it for so many years?

As far as Maren knows, there are no photos of the necklace, only renderings drawn from myth and word of mouth. Sketches show a substantial collar set in gold, with rows of enormous diamonds, large emerald cabochon teardrops, and a prominent oval central stone that may be lapis lazuli, with a teardrop-shaped pendant below. If indeed the central stone is lapis, then the gemstones in the necklace match her ring. She wonders whether they are connected somehow.

The jewels in the necklace alone must be worth millions. Still, Maren has the uneasy sense that what drives Madame Girard goes beyond money. She wonders who else the necklace's promise might draw—and what unseen forces she, and possibly her father, may have set in motion by accepting the bewildering task of searching for it.

Edwards' hands are steady on the wheel; his eyes calm in the rearview mirror. He is the picture of discretion, but there's gravity to his silence; a sense that he is weighing every word before he speaks. As they approach Le Bristol, he finally says, "You will find the staff here attentive, Miss Bennett. Madame Girard has ensured that every detail is to your liking."

Maren offers a polite smile, meeting his eyes in the mirror. "She seems very... thorough."

An almost wistful smile touches Edwards' lips. "Madame Girard is a woman who believes in the importance of legacy. She does not do anything by halves."

"She trusts you with a great deal," Maren observes, watching him.

Edwards' eyes meet hers in the mirror, then away. "A lifetime's trust. There are few people she relies on, and fewer still who understand her reasons."

Maren hesitates. "And do you?"

He pulls up under the awning and puts the car in park. For a moment, he seems to consider how much to say. "Madame Girard is passionate about her pursuits. Sometimes she forgets that not everyone shares her sense of urgency. But she is loyal and generous to those who prove themselves loyal to her."

Maren nods, sensing an undercurrent she can't quite name. "Thank you, Alistair."

He steps out and opens her door, offering her his hand before passing her bags to one of the hotel porters. "If you need anything, Miss Bennett, you have only to ask. I will return in the morning to take you to the train." Their eyes meet for a moment—hers searching, his guarded. Then he inclines his head, and she steps into the hotel.

The lobby is busy at this time of day. Some travelers are checking in, while others return from an afternoon of shopping, chatting happily in half a dozen languages. Guests depart for early dinners or the theater, and some gather with friends at the bar or the cafe just off the marble lobby.

Le Bristol stands on Rue du Faubourg Saint-Honoré, just a short walk from the Élysée Palace and the city's celebrated fashion houses. During World War II, the hotel served as the residence of the American embassy and has welcomed royalty, film stars, and diplomats since opening in 1925. It was the first hotel in Paris to receive "Palace" status, a rare distinction granted only to five-star hotels with exceptional service, luxury, and cultural importance. Maren has always wanted to stay here, to see if it truly lives up to its reputation.

Maren's suite is on the fourth floor, with windows overlooking the garden courtyard, now groomed for winter. The guest manager guides her through the adjoining rooms: a dining area set for tea, a king-sized bed draped in ivory, and a large marble bathroom. French windows are dressed in the hotel's signature floral fabrics, gathered in deep folds, and caught up with thick tasseled ropes. Cream-colored walls, pale blue damask sofas, and a vase of pink roses complete the welcome.

Her bag is already waiting on a stand beside the bed. How do they manage that? Wanting to swim before dinner, she pulls her bathing suit out of her bag, changes and slips on the hotel's plush terrycloth robe before taking the elevator to the 6th floor. A sleek teak deck reminiscent of a yacht surrounds the pool. Notes of classical music waft through the space, dimmed for the evening. As Maren removes her robe, she notices she's still wearing the ring. A quick glance around confirms no one else is here. Shrugging, she places it on her folded towel before slipping into the shimmering water.

After twenty slow laps, Maren climbs out, slips the ring back on her finger, and wraps herself in her robe. The city beyond the slanted windows surrounding the pool is a tapestry of deep blue and scattered lights. Suddenly, the ring chills against her skin. She freezes. There—reflected in the glass: a man in a dark coat standing just outside the door, his gaze fixed on her. Maren spins around to see him clearly, but he's already gone.

Off and on since Venice, Maren has had a vague, disturbing sense that she's being followed. Each time the ring has grown cool, and she's felt that prickle at the back of her neck, she's dismissed it as ridiculous and melodramatic. She wonders now if there's good reason to trust her intuition. Has she been right all along to feel uneasy? Did her father's investigations in Venice reawaken a long-dormant interest in the Talisman? If so, others may want the necklace too.

Madame Girard's maid implied that there are also those who would rather the Talisman remain lost. Maren can easily imagine fortune hunters drawn by its monetary value, but the thought that others might actively attempt to keep it hidden had never crossed her mind. She wonders what motive could be powerful enough to make someone prefer the Talisman stay buried in the past? Who can she count on as a friend in this growing web, and who is a foe? Perhaps that's why her father warned her: *trust no one*.

Back in her suite, Maren turns on the shower and lets the cascade of hot water from the wide rain showerhead ease the tension from her shoulders. The scent of lavender French-milled soap rises with the steam and envelops her in warmth and calm.

She towels off and hears the evening turndown service come and go. She takes her time, smoothing her new scented body lotion over her damp skin from head to toe. Sitting on the edge of the tub, she paints her toenails red, then dries her hair and styles it in the new chic style she learned today. It's so her: simple, sleek, and not fussy.

This. This is the self-care she has always neglected. How silly I am, she thinks, brushing her teeth. I want others to care about me, but I rarely bother to care about myself. She clicks off the blow dryer, runs her fingers through her hair, and looks down, wiggling her candy-apple toes. "Why did I never think of this before now?" she says aloud. The ring warms on her finger, as if in agreement.

Maren empties the contents of her backpack and walks to the closet to hang up her things. She hadn't noticed the blue silk ribbon earlier, looped through the closet door handles and tied in a bow. Maren reaches out, mystified, and tugs one end. The bow loosens, and the ribbon slides free. She opens the closet doors with a gasp. Her Dior selections were delivered. They are hung evenly spaced, boutique-style, each sleeve and hem neatly aligned.

But here are other things too. A lot of other things: a suit in fine gray wool, two smart day dresses, a buttery-soft suede jacket, a winter parka and boots, ski leggings, a handful of silk scarves, and an assortment of lingerie, each piece carefully wrapped in black-and-white striped tissue paper. There is a pair of short, black leather boots, much finer and more feminine than her scuffed combat boots, and a pair of tall suede boots with a low heel. On the floor are several matching pieces of Louis Vuitton luggage in supple black leather.

Near the safe, a padded white leather tray displays a pair of pearl drop earrings, gold sun-shaped earrings, and a distinctive red box holding a gold Panthère de Cartier watch. Next to it lies a long rope of pearls and a folded note: *For your journey, enjoy! G.G.*

"Good heavens!" she says aloud. "And I was worried I'd underpacked." She shakes her head, laughing, surprised to realize she's beginning to take this opulent fairytale in stride.

From her own things, she selects an ankle-length slip dress in deep sapphire silk satin. It glides over her skin, and she fastens the pearls around her neck. Who is this glamorous woman? she thinks, as she adjusts her dress in the full-length mirror.

Only yesterday, she was Maren Bennett, an ordinary woman with a slightly dull life, her days measured out in the usual work, emails, texts, and errands. She'd thought of herself as relatively insignificant, perhaps even invisible, in the grand sweep of things. Today she is an explorer on a daredevil mission, in a five-star hotel suite, backed by an enigmatic patron and about to board the fabled Orient Express to Istanbul in search of a legendary necklace. All because she said yes.

Though the mysterious blue ring sparkles and flirts with her, there is no mistaking the reality of the quest she has accepted. She has no idea how to find the Talisman, scarcely even where to begin. And woven through it all is a bewitching, relentless current, as if the Talisman were a living thing, drawing her ever deeper into its dark world.

In the hotel bar, she orders a glass of Sancerre and surveys the room. At a corner table, a man sits alone: dark hair, a beautifully tailored suit, and a certain contained elegance in the way he holds himself. Their eyes meet, and a spark passes between them.

He rises and approaches, stopping just beside her. "You look as though you've just arrived from a long journey," he says, his voice low and smooth, tinged with a subtle French accent. "Or are you about to begin one?"

She smiles, wary but intrigued. "A bit of both, I suppose."

He offers his hand. "Alexander." His grip is warm, assured; his features arrestingly composed, as if he's spent a lifetime learning how to reveal nothing he doesn't intend.

She hesitates, then takes it. "Maren."

"Enchanté," he says. As their palms touch, the ring on her finger tingles, subtly at first, then more intensely. Maren's pulse quickens, unsure which is more disconcerting, the ring or the man.

He glances at the empty seat beside her. "May I join you?"

"Yes, of course," Maren replies.

They talk at first of Paris, its changeable moods, and the way it seems to reinvent itself with every season. Alexander's charm is easy and understated, the kind that lulls her like waves lapping at a shore. It's a refinement likely cultivated and passed down, unspoken, through generations for whom polished self-assurance was as natural as breathing.

He tells her with self-deprecating humor that he works in finance. "The family business, you know."

His answers remain vague, as if the details hardly matter. Still, there's a watchfulness beneath his smile, and he responds to her questions with questions of his own, almost imperceptibly steering the conversation time and again back to her. Meeting his eyes, she feels he sees straight through her. She has told him her life story, and still knows nothing about him.

From the start, being with a man like Alexander makes Maren feel intensely feminine—aware of her own softness—desired and exposed, every nerve attuned to the subtle dominance in his presence. The sensation is heady, almost dangerous, as if she's floating yet perilously close to losing herself in the undertow of his quiet command.

He gives the impression that he's entirely comfortable handling whatever comes his way. With Ethan, she'd often felt obliged to take charge, stepping in to fill the spaces he left unattended; with Alexander, there's no room, or need, for that. But she senses he wouldn't welcome anyone, least of all a lover, trying to manage him. The realization entices her, even as it leaves her slightly off balance.

Dinner follows at a corner table in the restaurant. The conversation deepens. Alexander asks about her work, her travels, and her reasons for coming to Paris. As the meal winds down,

Alexander's expression grows serious. He leans in. "You're searching for something. Something rare. Perhaps something dangerous."

She tenses, but keeps her tone light. "Aren't we all?"

He studies her in the candlelight. "The Talisman. You should be careful. People have died for less."

The words hang between them, sharp as broken glass. "You seem to know a lot about things that don't concern you," Maren says stiffly.

"On the contrary," Alexander replies softly, "they concern me very much. There are others looking for it as well. People who won't hesitate to do whatever it takes to get it. If you value your life, you'll walk away from this."

The world outside the hotel falls away, and Maren wonders if she's stepped into the opening moves of a high-stakes game of chess.

"I can't," she says. "Not anymore."

He nods, as if he expected nothing less. "Then you should know what you're up against. The Talisman is more than folklore, Maren. It's a curse. It brings power, but it also brings danger to anyone who seeks it."

For a moment, neither speaks. Then Alexander leans back, his expression softening. "But we don't have to talk about that all night," he says, lightness returning. "Paris is full of stories. Perhaps we could share a few of the better ones."

Maren relaxes slightly, grateful for the release. The conversation turns to small talk, the best restaurants in the city, the hidden jazz clubs, the way the Seine looks at dawn. The conversation flows, but beneath the surface, the tenseness of their earlier words remains.

Maren finally rises to leave, and Alexander stands as well, insisting on walking her to her suite. The corridor is empty. At her door, she searches her bag for her room key. Without a word, she hands it to him.

He unlocks the door for her, holding the heavy silver keychain between his fingers for a moment before returning it. Alexander meets her eyes, his words calm, but with an ominous edge. "Don't trust anyone, Maren."

That's exactly what her father said.

"It was a pleasure meeting you," he says. "Good luck."

For a heartbeat, neither of them moves. They simply look at each other.

Then she turns and slips inside. Maren closes the door gently behind her, the key warm in her palm from Alexander's touch. The darkness outside her window is unchanged, but nothing feels the same. She glances at the ring on her finger, emeralds glowing in the lamplight, and wonders just how much this man knows. And what he's not telling her.

SEVEN

PASSAGES

M AREN WAKES IN THE pre-dawn darkness to the clatter of porcelain and a knock at her door. She sits up, stretching in the cocoon of sheets, and reaches for the bedside lamp.

"Petit déjeuner, mademoiselle."

"Come in!"

The waiter wheels a cart draped in crisp white linen. "Bon matin, Mademoiselle Bennett," he says with a polite nod, stopping beside the small dining table, where he arranges a linen-lined basket brimming with pastries. There are small jars of jam, a silver dish of sweet butter, a pot of hot chocolate, whipped cream, hot water for tea, and coffee. The Raynaud porcelain is whimsically decorated with hand-painted birds and butterflies: goldfinches perched on slender branches, and a swallow mid-flight. The waiter sets a white rose in a vase at the center of the table.

"Coffee mademoiselle? Or tea?"

"Coffee, please," Maren says.

He pours Maren's first cup of coffee. It swirls into the cup as a painted butterfly seems to hover just above the rim. "Bon appétit," he says before withdrawing.

She crosses to the table and pours a splash of cream into her cup, watching as it swirls and blooms, forming pale clouds in the dark French Roast. The first sip is heavenly, and the warmth blossoms through her chest and anchors her in the morning. She breaks off a corner of Le Bristol's famous pain au chocolat, its golden crust shattering to reveal a heart of bittersweet chocolate.

I could get used to this, Maren thinks. One of the best gifts of travel has to be the chance to discover new habits and ways of living—and to bring a few home.

"This one is coming with me," she says out loud to no one in particular.

Her mind drifts to the night before: the shadowy bar, Alexander's sudden, magnetic presence, the way he spoke of the Talisman with such threatening certainty. She liked his confidence, but not how a single glance from him could so completely unravel her. Ugh, she thinks, it's embarrassing now—how easily she fell under the spell of his charm and good looks. She covers her eyes with her hand and shakes her head. I didn't even ask his last name. She was too captivated by his attention, and if she's honest, by the relief of finding someone who seemed to understand the quarry she's chasing.

The Talisman. The word is interesting and dangerous. Her internet searches have yielded mostly broad overviews of history and legend: talismans as objects of power—protection, healing, sometimes curse. She recalls reading about the Seal of Solomon, symbols of balance and struggle, and stories of jewels and amulets that crossed time and continents.

Several years ago, she was doing some work for the Smithsonian in Washington, DC, and was invited by the head gem specialist to see the famous 45-carat Hope Diamond up close. She was stunned to learn that when it was first mined in India in the 1600s, it may have been 112 carats or larger.

The diamond was sold to King Louis XIV, who had it re-cut, and it stayed with the French royal family until it vanished in 1792 in the ruckus of the French Revolution. It turned up in London twenty years later, having again been re-cut. It passed through the hands of King George IV, then to Henry Hope and his family, and was sold several more times before Pierre Cartier acquired it and sold it to Evalyn Walsh McLean of Virginia. According to legend, the Hope Diamond is cursed because it was supposedly stolen from the statue of a Hindu goddess, and misfortune seemed to follow its owners as the gem traveled the world. Indeed, the gem's blue-violet radiance makes it appear almost alive.

Strange how this ring, with its intricate design and luminous emeralds, warms beneath her gaze. It's as if it has always belonged to her, and finally found its way home. Beneath all the history and mysticism, this mission is deeply personal—for answers about her father's death, and about her mother, a woman whose secrets seem to multiply the closer Maren looks. What is it about the Talisman that has obsessed both Madame Girard and her mother for a lifetime? What power does it hold? And what if Alexander was right? What if someone will kill for it?

She wraps her hands around the warm cup and stands by the window looking out, pensive. Alexander's knowledge had felt like a lifeline in unfamiliar waters, but she can't afford to be dazzled again. The journey ahead will demand all of her focus. Beneath her determination there's hope: that in Istanbul, she might uncover the truth about the Talisman, and perhaps about herself.

After breakfast, she takes her time getting ready, then steps into the dressing area wrapped in a giant white towel, pausing before the open closet. She settles on a fine double-breasted gray wool suit she hadn't chosen herself. It's a perfect travel ensemble: neat but casual, comfortable, and wrinkle-free, with beautifully tailored lines. She selects ravishing new lingerie in the most delicious shade of blush pink and pulls on a black cashmere turtleneck sweater that draws attention to her heart-shaped face. She slips into the trousers and jacket, finishing the look with flat black Hermès ankle boots, size 39. Appraising her reflection, she decides on the gold sun earrings.

She looks composed: a woman being reshaped by new rituals, certainly by grief, but also by adventure. Maybe the clothes do make the woman, she thinks, crossing her fingers that she's ready for whatever comes next. In any case, she's dressed for it.

By mid-morning, Maren's luggage stands at the door, her ring glinting on her finger as she takes one last look around the suite. Downstairs, Edwards waits in the lobby. He makes polite conversation on the drive to Gare de l'Est, but his eyes are sharp, missing nothing. At the station, he helps her with her luggage. His hand rests briefly at her elbow.

"If you need anything, Miss Bennett, you have my card."

She nods, grateful. "Thank you, Edwards. For everything."

He offers a smile and turns to leave just as a new voice cuts through the general hubbub of the station.

"Going somewhere interesting, Maren?"

She turns, startled. Alexander is heading towards them. Edwards stiffens and pivots.

"Alexander! What in the world are you doing here?" Maren blurts, her surprise unguarded.

"Mr. Edwards, this is Alexander. We met last night at the bar in the hotel." She glances at Edwards, suddenly aware of how this must sound, and a flush creeps up her neck.

Alexander's gaze rests on her earrings, and then the embroidered sun on Edwards' jacket. He raises an eyebrow, but doesn't comment.

"How do you do." His tone is polite, but there's a challenge beneath the civility.

Edwards meets his gaze, unflinching. "Very well, thank you. I trust your stay at the hotel was... pleasant."

Alexander's lips curve in a faint, inscrutable smile. "You could say that. As you know, I have a house in Paris. I wasn't staying at the hotel—I just stopped by and happened to meet Miss Bennett."

Maren's head snaps up. "You know each other?"

A look passes between the two men. "We've crossed paths before," Edwards says, his voice measured.

Maren senses that there is something old and unresolved between them. Suddenly, she feels as if she's stumbled into the middle of a story that began long before she arrived. The uncertainty troubles her, but she lifts her chin, determined to hold her ground.

Alexander turns back to her, his expression softening even as his voice remains hard. "You're really going through with this?"

She nods. "I have to."

He studies her, the noise of the station fading for a moment. "Be careful, Maren." His eyes rest briefly on Edwards before returning to her. "Not everyone involved in this is what they seem." His words are casual, but the warning is clear.

She hesitates, searching his face. "Why are you here, Alexander?"

He gives a small shrug. "I only came to talk you out of going. But I can see you've decided."

She wants to ask him more, but before she can, Alexander offers a nod to Edwards and looks at her with cool detachment. "Goodbye, Maren. Mr. Edwards."

He turns and disappears into the crowd, leaving Maren with more questions than ever—and a sharp, unexpected pang as the train prepares to depart.

Edwards touches her arm. "Come, Miss Bennett. It's time."

A uniformed attendant greets Maren on the platform. "May I see your ticket?"

Maren hands it to him.

"Oh, of course. Welcome back, Ms. Bennett."

She expects to be led to a classic cabin, like the one she had from Venice to Paris. Instead, he gestures toward a different carriage. "If you'd like to come with me, you've been upgraded, Ms. Bennett. Your cabin this time is in carriage 3309. You're in the Paris Suite," he brightens. "It's one of our new Grand Suites."

Not bothering to hide her surprise, Maren follows him along the platform and up into the carriage. He unlocks the cabin and offers a brief history of the railcar, its Art déco origins, the dignitaries and celebrities who have traveled the storied tracks, and the meticulous renovations that restored its original splendor. Her previous experience on the Orient Express was lovely, but this is another world entirely.

On her trip from Venice to Paris, her compartment had a washbasin cleverly concealed behind a mirrored door, pressed monogrammed towels, and fine French toiletries, but only one lavatory per carriage, shared, down the hall. This time, the luxury of an ensuite marble bathroom greets her with a frosted Murano glass washbasin, a plush terrycloth robe and slippers, and a brass rain shower.

Her steward for this trip soon arrives to demonstrate the features of her suite, including the old-fashioned lock on the door. "They can be a bit fiddly, so be sure to close it just so." He assures her he will prepare the room for evening while she dines, or should she prefer privacy, dinner can be served in her suite. With a slight bow, he asks, "May I bring you some champagne?" and then withdraws with an enthusiastic, "Welcome aboard, Ms. Bennett."

She smiles, tempted to write thank-you notes to the mothers of all these courteous young stewards. Then she wonders what on earth Alexander's mother must be like, and at what age he became so intimidating. He spoke with that formal, upper-class French—l'accent de la bourgeoisie, her mother calls it—marked by deliberate enunciation, a neutral Parisian accent, and a complete absence of slang. His manners were flawless, too. The woman must be absolutely formidable. He might have been a fascinating man to get to know—if only he hadn't been so gruff.

Oh well, Maren thinks, c'est la vie. She's had enough man trouble for one year.

Maren takes in the suite's opulent details: walls paneled in varnished marquetry—rosewood and mahogany inlaid with intricate Art déco patterns and slender bands of mother-of-pearl. Opposite the wide window, a plush beige velvet sofa invites relaxation and conversation. Beneath the window, a polished walnut table stands between two comfortable armchairs. A mirrored partial wall separates the living area from the bedroom, where a full-size bed is dressed in snowy linens.

She runs her hand over the glossy wood, marveling at the craftsmanship and the history that lives in these rail cars. She hangs a few garments, smooths her hair in the bathroom mirror, and refreshes her lipstick. Finally, she sinks onto the sofa with a sigh.

Daniel, her suite steward, returns and expertly eases the cork from a bottle of champagne and pours it into a slender crystal flute etched with the VSOE monogram, then nestles it into a silver ice bucket on the table. "To your adventure, Ms. Bennett," he says. "If you need anything at all, here is your call button."

Maren lifts the glass, savoring the chilled effervescence as the train moves from the station. She could easily have flown to Istanbul in a matter of hours. She even texted that to Edwards earlier. But Madame Girard was adamant: she had arranged meetings for Maren with various experts at each stop along the route.

Perhaps the train is more than a gesture of indulgence; Maren thinks. Maybe Madame Girard truly believes it's the safest, most discreet way to travel between the encounters she has arranged. "You'll be contacted," her maid had said. Now, as the train glides east, she scans the itinerary and wonders who might be waiting at each city, and if they can help her discover the whereabouts of the Talisman. She plans to spend the rest of the day doing further research online and organizing her notes.

A knock at her door interrupts her thoughts. When she opens it, it's Daniel again, with a thick gray envelope on a silver tray.

Curious, she unfolds the gray cotton paper. The note is penned in an unfamiliar, slanted hand:

Welcome aboard, Miss Bennett. If you need anything, your neighbor is just next door.

Maren looks up from the note, but the steward has moved on through the doors at the end of the carriage. She steps into the corridor, flooded with light from large windows along one side. Unlike her previous cabin, in this carriage there appear to be only three suites, and hers is at the end of the carriage. She notices that the door to the next cabin is not quite closed, and the gap reveals a sliver of the room within. Maren peeks inside and stops. Alexander? He's seated by the window with a slim, worn leather book on the table in front of him. For a moment, she simply stares, stunned, certain he'd left the station.

Then her eyes drop to the book: the pattern of interlocking symbols carved into the leather on the cover stirs something in her memory. She's seen those shapes before. In her father's things. A gasp escapes before she can stop it. Alexander looks up, meeting her eyes through the narrow gap. He knows exactly what she's noticed.

EIGHT

DETOURS

T HE BOOK CAN'T POSSIBLY be her father's journal; he had always guarded it closely. Still, the resemblance is chilling.

Maren is suddenly angry. She pushes the door open, ready to confront him—demand answers, demand the truth about who he is and why he's following her.

But as she steps inside, she stops short. In a chair half-hidden by the angle of the door sits a striking woman with platinum-blonde hair, flawless skin, and the clearest blue eyes Maren has ever seen. Eyes that now coolly appraise her.

"Maren, good morning. May I introduce Simone de Villiers. She's...an old friend. Of the family." Then, looking at Simone, "Maren and I just met in Paris."

"Hi there," Simone offers. Her smile doesn't quite reach her eyes. She looks away, then reaches over and rests a hand on Alexander's arm.

Heat rises in Maren's cheeks, her words evaporating. Whatever accusation she meant to hurl dies on her lips. She mumbles a greeting and backs into the corridor, dropping the crumpled note and shutting the door with more force than she means to.

Without a backward glance, Maren heads for the bar car, desperate to escape the suddenly stifling atmosphere of her carriage. The bar is lively for this time of day, with a few people gathered around cocktail tables, chatting and laughing over mimosas and Bloody Marys. She finds a seat on a long banquette and turns to the window, fighting back tears of shock, humiliation, and anger. He's some kind of slick hustler, that's all. Edwards must have known that. How could she be so stupid as to be drawn in by such an obvious con man? Oh, Maren, she thinks. And worse, she misses her father all over again.

Maren stares out the window, blinking back tears. A man in a noticeably expensive suit slides onto the seat beside her. He's older than Alexander, with silver at his temples and a sympathetic smile.

"Tough morning?" he asks gently, offering her a monogrammed white handkerchief.

She hesitates, but takes it, grateful for the gesture. "Something like that," she manages.

He nods as if he understands perfectly. "Travel can be brutal on the heart. But you strike me as someone who bounces back." His accent is hard to place, but it's continental and polished. "I'm Lucien."

Before she can answer, the waiter appears. "What may I bring you?"

Maren is about to decline, but Lucien smiles at the waiter. "She'll have a shot of whiskey. I'll have the same."

She opens her mouth to protest, but Lucien just winks. "Trust me. It's the best cure for disappointment."

The whiskey arrives, amber and sharp. Maren takes a sip, feeling the burn and the sudden lightness in her head. Lucien thankfully keeps the conversation easy, asking nothing too personal, spinning stories to entertain her about art auctions in Vienna and wild nights in Budapest. For a moment, she almost forgets her humiliation as Lucien orders another round.

He grins as Maren knocks back her whiskey, her cheeks already flushed. "You know, I once tried to order a whiskey sour in Scotland and the bartender just handed me a glass of regret," he says.

Maren snorts, nearly choking on her drink. "That's nothing. I ordered a martini in Venice and got a lecture on vermouth ratios that lasted longer than most of my relationships."

Lucien laughs, delighted. "I hope the martini was worth it."

"It was mostly ice and existential dread," Maren deadpans, then giggles, surprising herself.

The waiter returns. Without so much as quirking an eyebrow at their empty glasses, he asks, "Another round?"

Lucien doesn't miss a beat. "We'll have two more. And if you have any snacks that pair well with questionable decisions, bring those too."

Maren grins, her mood lifting. "And maybe a glass of water, so I can pretend I'm making good choices."

Lucien raises his glass. "To questionable decisions and excellent company."

He glances at the sunlight slanting through the bar car windows and flashes Maren a sly smile. "What do you say we take a stroll? The view of the countryside from the observation car is supposed to be spectacular, and I promise not to bore you with any more stories about failed cocktails."

Maren laughs, feeling lighter and just reckless enough to agree. "Lead the way," she says, sliding off her bench.

They're just stepping into the corridor, Lucien's hand lightly at her elbow, when Alexander appears in the doorway. His gaze lands on them—on Lucien's easy charm and Maren's flushed, tipsy smile—and his expression hardens.

"Maren." Alexander says, his voice low but firm. "A word?"

Lucien's grip lingers a moment before he lets go. "Don't get lost," he says with a wink to Maren and a nod to Alexander, then disappears down the corridor.

Maren bristles, the room spinning just a little as she turns to Alexander. "Hey—he was nice. We were going to the observation car to look at...to look at something."

Alexander's jaw tightens. "You were going the wrong way," he growls.

She frowns, glancing back over her shoulder, then shrugs, a merry laugh escaping her. "Well, maybe he was going to give me a tour of the rest of the train first."

Alexander sighs, taking her hand and steadying her with an arm around her waist. "Let's get you some air."

He guides Maren down the corridor, catching her as she stumbles. She tries to glare at him, but her vision blurs and her indignation fizzles into a giggle.

"You know, Zander—I don't actually need a babysitter. Especially you," nearly tripping over the plush carpet.

"Clearly," Alexander says dryly, catching her elbow before she careens into the wall. "But I draw the line at letting you tour the luggage car with a charming stranger."

She laughs, then squints up at him. "You're just jealous—he had better hair."

He scowls, not bothering to hide his annoyance. "I have excellent hair, and for the record, if I were jealous, I wouldn't have let you out of my sight, especially with him. And he wasn't headed to the observation car, because there isn't one on this train."

She snorts but lets him unlock her suite and guide her inside. Alexander helps her out of her jacket, then hesitates at her sweater.

"Do you want help, or should I avert my eyes and let you wrestle with Dior yourself?"

Maren waves a hand, nearly losing her balance. "If you can get this thing off, you deserve a medal."

He mutters under his breath—something that sounds suspiciously like, "What I deserve is a week in Bali"—but deftly

pulls the soft cashmere turtleneck over her head, his movements brisk and unsentimental. The fabric catches at her hair,
and she laughs again, the sound echoing in the opulent suite.

She sits on the bed in her pink silk camisole and matching
tap pants while he searches the closet for a nightgown. Unsuc-
cessful, he returns to the bed, still glowering. She shoots him
a lopsided grin and flops back onto the bed, feet still on the
floor, shoes askew. "I bet you want to kiss me."

Alexander sighs as he kneels to take off her boots and lifts
her legs onto the bed. "I'd settle for you staying out of trouble."

She laughs, rolling her eyes. "Coward."

He tucks the blanket around her with exaggerated care.
"Let's call it self-preservation." She sighs as the sheets envelop
her and falls immediately asleep, snoring softly.

When Maren wakes, the room is bathed in the colors of
early evening. For a moment, she's disoriented. The gentle
sway of the train and the faint clink of ice in a glass, grounds
her in the present. Then she sees Alexander, seated in the
armchair by the window, reading in the lamp's glow. He's
wearing round tortoiseshell glasses and dressed in a cable-knit
sweater, soft, faded chinos slightly frayed at the hems, and
brown suede driving mocs. His leg is crossed, and the book
is open in his lap. In his hand, he cradles a wide crystal glass
filled with bourbon and ice. His profile, sharp yet softened by
the fading sun, is a study in contrasts. Distance and intimacy,
shadow and light.

She watches him for a long, quiet moment, wondering how
long he's been watching over her. Her heart is unexpectedly
full as she tries to decipher the storm behind his eyes. She
wonders if a woman could ever really know what he's thinking.
Something yields inside her—a recognition, a surrender. She
realizes she might be falling in love with him, and she still
doesn't even know his real name.

NINE

SILK AND SECRETS

MAREN SITS UP AND swings her legs to the floor, suddenly aware of the silk against her skin, and how little she's wearing. She glances down, then at Alexander, her eyes widening in surprise. "Did you help with this?"

Alexander looks up from his book, his expression veiled behind the glasses. He takes a slow sip of bourbon, then sets the glass aside. "You were determined to sleep in your shoes and a turtleneck. I intervened for the sake of both comfort and dignity."

She flushes, half-embarrassed, half-amused, and pulls the blanket toward her. "So you're saying I owe you a thank you?"

He closes the book, marking his place with a finger. "I'll settle for not having to explain to the steward why you passed out fully clothed shortly after boarding. Though I suppose now you're part of the legend."

Maren manages a crooked grin, pulling the blanket a little higher. "I guess I should be grateful I didn't wake up in the luggage car."

He allows the faintest hint of a smile. "That was Plan B."

She studies him for a moment, curiosity edging out embarrassment. "How long have you been sitting there?"

He glances at his watch, then back at her. "Long enough to finish most of this book and contemplate the wisdom of whiskey before noon."

She laughs, tension easing. "Next time, maybe just coffee."

He nods, his gaze softening just a fraction. "Noted."

Outside, the train glides on into twilight. Maren stands, pulling the blanket around her like a shield. "Alright, avert your eyes," she says, giving Alexander a pointed look as she walks past him to the bathroom.

She closes the door behind her and turns on the shower. The small marble-tiled space quickly fills with steam. She brushes her teeth, then steps under the hot water, feeling it clear her head and revive her. When she emerges, she wraps herself in a thick white robe. She looks at her reflection in the mirror—a little pale, a little pensive, but better than she expects. She ties the robe tighter, squares her shoulders, and steps back into the suite, ready to face whatever comes next.

Alexander looks up, noticing her wet hair and bare feet, and an involuntary smile breaks across his face for just a moment. He quickly clears his throat, glancing away as he reaches into his briefcase.

"Feeling better?" he asks, his tone carefully neutral.

Maren sits in the chair across from him, running a hand through her damp hair. "Much. I think I owe you an apology for earlier. And *maybe* a thank you."

He shrugs, still rummaging in his briefcase. "No apology necessary. The Orient Express has seen far worse."

Alexander places the black journal on the table between them and meets her eyes. "I thought you might want to see this," he says, his words measured. "It was among your father's things in Venice."

Maren holds her breath, recognizing the familiar pattern on the cover. She draws the journal closer, her fingers brushing the worn leather. "How did you get this? And more importantly, Alexander, who are you?"

Alexander stands. "Alexander Girard, at your service, mademoiselle."

Maren leaps to her feet, clutching her robe tighter as she paces the small space. "What? Girard? No. No, no, no—oh, this is catastrophic. I...oh, fabulous. Why do I feel like I want another drink?"

Alexander gently but firmly takes her by the shoulders. "Look, before you start drinking again, which, judging by earlier, doesn't seem to end well, let's take a break. Get dressed. We'll go to the dining car, get something to eat, and you can ask me anything you want."

She lets out a shaky laugh, the tension in her shoulders easing just a little. "You're not worried I'll cause a scene?"

He almost smiles. "On this train? I doubt anyone would notice."

Maren lets out her breath, her grip on the robe loosening. "Fine. But don't expect an encore of last night."

Alexander releases her shoulders. "Deal."

He opens the door. "Lock this," he says, his tone leaving no room for argument. He pauses in the doorway, meeting her eyes. "I'll see you in the dining car in an hour." With that, Alexander steps into the corridor, the door closing softly behind him. Maren stands for a moment, unsure if the sway beneath her feet is the train or the result of her earlier excesses. Her mind spins: questions, possibilities, and the memory of his touch all tangled up.

Leaning back against the door, she thinks. What does Alexander have to do with any of this? Was he sent by his mother? She presses her palms to her cheeks, willing herself to focus. Enough. Go get ready, Maren.

Maren dries and styles her hair, the scent of her favorite shampoo mingling with the soapy clean of her skin. She chooses a long gown knit of the softest black cashmere. It's a piece that feels almost casual. It has a discreet high neckline in front, but is surprising from behind, dipping daringly low to reveal the graceful line of her back. Sometimes she's secretly glad she's small-busted, because she loves going bra-less with dresses like this. She slips on satin ballerina flats, tying the silk ribbons in neat bows around her ankles.

She experiments with variations of jewelry: a bracelet, gold filigree earrings, jeweled hoops—before settling on just the pearls. She swings the strand around so it drapes down her back, understated and sexy. In the mirror, she looks over her shoulder to see the effect. "Hmm," she says aloud, "I might be getting the hang of this style thing."

Maren moves through the carriages, feeling buoyant and oddly nervous about spending the evening with the in-scrutable Alexander Girard. She hears the sounds of cutlery and crystal and is about to pull open the door to the dining car when a thought stops her cold. The journal. She left it on the table in her suite, carelessly, as if it were just another book. Oh, Maren, she thinks. Seriously. You have got to pull yourself together.

She turns, retracing her steps. The carriage appears empty, shadows stretching long in the lamplight as she unlocks the door to her cabin and steps inside. She's relieved to find everything as she left it: a small pile of jewelry on the sofa, her robe thrown over the armchair. A trace of her perfume in the air. Then her breath catches. Alexander's crystal tumbler is still on the table where he left it, bits of ice melting inside, but the journal is gone. She looks around. This is silly. It has to be here.

She checks the floor, the cushions, the drawers. Nothing. Her movements grow frantic as she hikes up the hem of her dress and kneels, running her hand along the carpet beneath the settee. The journal has vanished, as if it had never been there. Then a chill creeps up her spine. Someone has been in her room.

She straightens, clutching the back of the chair, her thoughts racing. Who else could know about the journal? She glances at the door, half-expecting to see a shadow in the corridor, her cabin suddenly feeling like a gilded cage.

Her mind reels through possibilities: Who would take an old notebook and leave the jewelry? Alexander? But that makes no sense—he gave her the journal. Why would he take it back? Then, a memory surfaces: Alexander in his suite, with the beautiful blonde—what was her name? Simone—leaning in.

Maren tells herself to relax and breathe. The sting of violation sharpens into resolve. She smooths her gown, straightens her posture, and steps into the corridor, locking her door and then checking it again.

As she turns, she spots the steward at his post, professional in his uniform, hands folded behind his back. "Good evening, Ms. Bennett."

She musters a steady voice. "Hello Daniel. Did you see anyone near my door a few minutes ago?"

The steward shakes his head politely. "I have only seen you, Ms. Bennett, but I did step away for a few moments a little earlier to get the extra towels you requested.

"Daniel, do you keep the keys to our cabins with you, or are they kept here?" nodding to his vestibule.

"The keys are always in a secure place here, Ms. Bennett. Is everything all right?"

Her pulse jumps. "Yes, thank you, Daniel, everything is fine," she says, forcing a smile. "Have a good evening."

"Thank you, Ms. Bennett. You as well."

With every stride toward the dining car, panic coils tighter in her chest. She didn't ask for towels. Someone used her name to get the steward away from his post. Someone who knew how to slip in and out unseen, and take the one thing she can't afford to lose.

On the Orient Express, to cross between carriages, passengers exit a narrow door at the end of one carriage and move into a small enclosed area with a flexible gangway that bridges the gap between cars, before opening the door to the next carriage. The passage is protected from the wind and weather, but Maren can still feel the subtle shift beneath her feet and hear the muffled rumble of the wheels on the rails below.

She steps into the vestibule of the dining car and nearly collides with Simone de Villiers. Simone is nothing short of radiant in a low-cut red gown that hugs every curve, her platinum hair swept into a glossy chignon. Long, lush lashes frame her striking ice-blue eyes; her makeup is dramatic and sensuous.

Maren forces a polite smile, but her words have a slight edge. "Excuse me, have you been around here in the past hour?"

Simone arches a perfectly shaped brow. "Why, darling," her words colored by a slight British accent, "I've been in the bar car. With Alexander, actually. He may still be there if you're looking for him."

Maren tries to keep her tone casual. "You two seem... close."

A slow, knowing smile. "We are, darling. Or, we were. It's rather sad, really. He practically confessed this evening that he's still in love with me. Never quite got over my leaving. Some men hold on to the past too long, don't you think?" She looks down at a giant oval diamond solitaire and delicately adjusts a ruby bracelet on her wrist.

Maren catches the gesture, wondering if it's meant to suggest that the ring and bracelet are gifts from him. "Is everything all right, Maren? You seem... agitated."

Maren's grip tightens, and the ring goes cold. "I'm fine. Thank you, Simone."

Simone's eyes narrow slightly, as if weighing Maren's words. Then, apparently satisfied, she floats past, expensive perfume trailing behind her.

Maren watches her go, and her heart plummets. Of course he is in love with Simone. Who wouldn't be? She looks like a movie star. Oh, for heaven's sake, why do I care who he's in love with? I barely know the man, and he's been lying, either directly or by omission, from the moment we met. More importantly, if Simone has been with Alexander this whole time, then who took the journal? And who, exactly, is playing whom on this train?

TEN

REVELATIONS

A LEXANDER STANDS WHEN MAREN approaches, and for a moment, seems to simply drink her in. He looks dashing in what is certainly a custom-made dinner jacket: black worsted wool, peaked lapels faced in black silk, and a fine, white piqué cotton shirt with a precise quarter-inch of cuff showing beyond the jacket sleeve. A black silk bow tie is, Maren thinks, the cherry on top. She feels a stab of awkwardness, acutely aware of the way he's looking at her. She also registers how easy and unselfconscious he is navigating his world of nuanced traditions and unwritten rules.

Maren knows she's dwelling too much on her recent transformation, but there's a learning curve with every new undertaking. Frankly, getting her Ph.D. was a lot easier. So much for being a cool-girl, she thinks wryly, wishing she felt half as self-assured as she appears.

She slips into her seat before he can fully pull out the chair.

"You look beautiful. I ordered the wine. I hope you like red," he says, picking up the menu.

"Alexander," Maren says, interrupting him. Her voice is low and urgent. "The journal is gone. I went back to my cabin just now to get it, and it's gone."

"What do you mean, 'gone'? Are you sure?"

"Yes, I'm sure. I checked everywhere. It was on the table. When I went back, it was... it's just... gone. Someone must have been in my room. The steward said he had stepped away for a few minutes. Someone used my name to draw him away from our carriage."

He leans in, his voice even lower. "Did anyone see you with it? Or know you had it?"

Maren shakes her head. "Only you. I passed Simone in the corridor just now, but she said she's been in the bar car. With you."

"Did you lock your door?"

"Yes, of course. Well, I mean—I think so."

"Whoever took it knew exactly what it was and where to find it." Alexander says.

"How would anyone know that? You're the only one who's read it, Alexander. I never had a chance to look at it. But maybe that was the point." She hopes he'll offer something that might convince her she's wrong about him.

She tries to sound casual and adds, "Simone also said you're still in love with her. That you never got over her leaving you. She's wearing an enormous diamond and hinted that the two of you were engaged." Even as the words leave her mouth, Maren winces. This has nothing to do with her father's journal, and she knows she's strayed into his private life.

Alexander says nothing, just a quick tightening of his jaw. He looks down and adjusts his watch.

Maren is interrupted as the waiter arrives again, filling their wineglasses with Alexander's selection. They wave off the first course and order dinner, neither really wanting it, but relieved for the distraction.

"I don't have any interest in... whatever is going on between you two. I'd just like to have the journal back. I'd also love to know why your fiancé is here on the train—and for you to let something true slip through that mask you wear."

For just a moment, Maren thinks she sees something wounded in Alexander's eyes, but when he looks back at her, his gaze is remote. Untouchable as usual.

"Simone is my former fiancée, and she is here because she's invited to the ball in Istanbul. Like half the people on this train. It's purely coincidence she ended up in our carriage. Or maybe we ended up in hers." The tension between them is broken only by the waiter's arrival with their dinner.

Alexander speaks when the waiter is gone. His words are clipped. "Can we just focus on the journal?"

"Okay." There is an edge to Maren's voice. "The only one who knows the contents of that journal besides my father is you." The ring on her finger tingles; a warning, or just nerves? "If someone wanted to steal it before I could read it, their timing was spot on."

He doesn't answer right away. Instead, he studies her. "I see," he finally says, "what is it that you want to know?"

Maren eats her dinner in silence for a few minutes, not trusting herself to say anything. Then finally, "I want to know why you had my father's journal. And why, every time I ask you a direct question, you answer with another question or a half-truth?"

He looks past her, out into the night. "I was in Venice on business. I heard a rumor about the journal, and I followed it. That's all."

"That's not 'all.'" Maren's voice is steady, but her eyes are searching. "When exactly were you in Venice?"

Alexander's reply is measured. "Recently. There was talk about your father, and what happened to him."

She frowns. "What kind of talk? I thought I received all of his personal effects from the embassy. How did they miss his journal?"

He lifts his shoulders. "I don't know, Maren. Your father was very well known. I heard a rumor it ended up in the local archives, so I went to see."

"Why?" she presses.

"Because," he looks at her levelly, "as you know, my mother has a keen interest in the work he was doing."

"So you found it in the archives?"

"Yes. As it turns out, it was suggested that a small donation to the archives would ensure the journal would not be missed."

Maren folds her arms. "A small donation," her tone edged with irony. "How very Girard of you."

Now it is his turn to say nothing, and they eat without speaking until the waiter clears their plates. "Would you like dessert?"

"No. Thank you," they say in unison, a little too emphatically.

Alexander orders coffee for them both, and the waiter disappears, looking grateful, Maren thinks.

"Why didn't you give it to your mother?"

"Because there was nothing in it that she would be interested in, primarily. And also because I don't want to get involved in all this."

She searches for cracks in his composure and finds none. "You don't want to get involved, but you made a donation to the Archives to get it out?"

He meets her gaze, patient but guarded. "I thought it was safer with me than gathering dust in some back room."

"You could have told me the moment you met me," Maren whispers. "Instead, you waited. Why?"

He exhales, shifting in his chair. "Because I wasn't sure what you'd do with it. Or who might be watching."

"Do you think someone is watching me? Because I have felt that way since Venice."

A dark look crosses Alexander's face before he quickly smooths it away. "You think you're being followed?"

"There was a man watching me in the swimming pool room at the hotel," she confesses.

"What?" Alexander's tone sharpens. "When?"

"When I went up to swim before dinner last night. Someone must have been standing there while I was swimming, but when I turned to look, he was gone," Maren says.

"Why didn't you tell me that, Maren?" Alexander's voice is grave.

"Well, because I didn't know you then. And I still don't."

Their waiter brings coffee, and both of them straighten and smile at him. Maren's fingers tighten around her cup. "Who are you thinking of? Simone? Or someone else?"

He takes a drink of coffee, then shakes his head before setting the cup down. "Simone has her own interests. Look, Maren—this train is full of people with agendas, not just Simone." He changes the subject. "Did you ever see anyone following you in Venice?"

"No. Not directly. I just felt funny sometimes," and then not letting the previous thread go, "So now you're protecting Simone?" Maren asks, though it hardly sounds like a question. She knows she's being irrational, but can't quite help herself.

"I am not going to discuss Simone with you, Maren," he says evenly, "and I'm trying to keep you from making the same mistakes your father did."

After a pause, he adds, almost as if reminding himself, "That is the only reason I am here. Will you tell me please the next time you feel you're being followed?"

To Maren, his reasons sound less like a statement for her benefit and more like something he needs to convince himself of. She ignores his question, leaning in instead. "You said you read the journal. Did you find what he was looking for?"

Alexander's jaw tenses. "I heard enough in Venice to know your father was in over his head. And that there are people who would do anything to get what he was looking for, or keep those secrets buried."

Maren's question hangs in the air. "Why did you finally give it to me?"

He sits back, the lines of his face drawn tight with fatigue and something like resignation. For a moment, he doesn't answer. Then, quietly, he says, "Because there was nothing in it, Maren."

She sits back, thrown by the flatness in his voice.

He goes on, "My mother has been chasing this 'Talisman' her whole life. And although the two of you, and apparently your entire family, want to believe in it too, there's nothing there, Maren. Nothing. Do you understand?"

The words land between them, heavy and final.

"You're wrong," she says, her eyes involuntarily filling with tears. She looks away, takes a deep breath and composes herself, her voice barely above a whisper. "You didn't know my father. You don't know what he found."

"Maybe not," his voice softening. "But I know what obsession looks like. I've seen what it does to people. It wastes lives. It changes people. It ends relationships."

She hesitates, uncertain whether this is honesty or just another mask. "Then why keep the journal at all? Why not destroy it if you think it's worthless?"

"Because I heard my mother had hired you into this mess, there was nothing in it, and I thought you should have it."

Maren narrows her eyes. "Then why are you really here?"

A muscle jumps in his cheek. "I don't know. I guess I wanted to make sure you wouldn't get hurt in all of this."

She searches his face, her fingertips resting on the table in front of her. "*Why* Alexander? You don't know me. Why would you care about me?"

For a long moment he looks at her and says nothing.

The silence stretches. Just the usual sounds around them of dining and conversation. He looks down, as if turning over words in his mind. In that instant, he seems suddenly younger, his usual confidence stripped away.

Maren watches him. She's confused now and totally off balance. Whatever conversation she thought they were having has disappeared in the dark.

He shifts his watch on his wrist again—a defensive tell she's only just learned to see.

Maren's heart tugs with empathy. She realizes that whatever he's about to say isn't just for her. It is something he's hidden even from himself.

He sighs and looks up. "Because you look like the girl in my John Singer Sargent painting."

She blinks. Her mind scrambling to keep up. He has a Sargent? That alone is enough to upend her, but it's the way he said it, as if sharing it cost him dearly.

She sinks back into her chair. "You have a John Singer Sargent?"

"Yes." His voice is quiet.

Maren is at a loss. A story has unfolded just beyond her reach. The sense of it hovers, half-formed, fragile and charged, a door opening to a room she didn't know existed. She doesn't know what to say, and Alexander offers nothing more. The ring on her finger is a cold, insistent reminder of what's been lost, and what might now, irrevocably, be at risk.

Alexander takes a last sip of coffee, then stands gracefully. He offers his arm out of habit; the gesture is smooth. They walk together down the narrow corridor, the train swaying gently beneath their feet. Maren feels the heat of his arm against her side through the fine wool of his jacket.

At her suite, she pauses, handing him her key, and looking into his eyes for some sign. "I don't want the evening to end like this," she says softly, her voice tinged with frustration. "Can we talk about it?"

Alexander unlocks her door and holds it open, but doesn't step inside. "Goodnight, Maren," he says, returning her key. "I'll see you in the morning."

She stands in the doorway, wanting to say more but unable to find the words, watching as he turns away. Instead of heading toward his own compartment, he walks toward the end of the carriage and Simone's suite. She turns away and tells herself it shouldn't matter if he is in love with Simone, or where he spends the night.

Inside, Maren closes the door behind her. The click of the latch echoes in the silence. She sinks into the chair where Alexander sat, regret and uncertainty plaguing her, as her finger traces the pattern on his glass. Even the ring is heavy and silent on her hand. For the first time since Venice, she feels truly alone.

ELEVEN

BUDAPEST

A FINE NOVEMBER MIST blurs the city when the Orient Express pulls into the station in Budapest. Maren wakes to a muted clatter of wheels and the soft knock of the steward at her door. She sits up as he announces, "Breakfast, Ms. Bennett."

She pulls on a thick cashmere robe and opens the door to find Daniel with a silver tray. Soon the table in her suite is hidden by white linen, and upon it, a pot of blessedly strong coffee, a carafe of freshly pressed orange juice, a basket of Viennese pastries, and a soft-boiled egg in a porcelain cup. The aroma of warm bread and coffee fills her suite, and she eats slowly, snug in her robe, savoring the buttery pastry and the sweet tang of apricot jam. She gazes out the window. Her only company is Budapest waking beneath a pewter sky.

She imagines Alexander next door, taking his own breakfast in solitude. Or maybe not. Last night she thought she might hear his door, but either he didn't return, or she fell asleep before he did.

Maren doesn't seek him out this morning, and he doesn't come to her. The memory of last night's conversation hangs between them, each of them retreating inside the sanctuary of their private compartments, grateful, she thinks, for the small mercy of solitude.

Just before nine, a knock on her cabin door signals it's time to leave. Maren wears a tailored navy shift dress in wool gabardine and her strand of pearls, the ring slipping reassuringly onto her finger. She pulls on a pair of tall toffee-colored suede boots with a flat heel and wraps herself in the belted camel-hair coat that had been delivered to Le Bristol. A new cashmere and silk Hermès shawl with a pretty stirrup pattern in blue and brown loops around her neck. She tucks the ends inside the collar of her coat and meets Alexander in the corridor. Her heart skips a beat when she sees him. Their greetings are courteous, and there's no sign of the Alexander from last night.

He offers his hand, always the gentleman. Maren contrasts his noble manners with his rakish reputation; if you believe the tabloids, you'd think he's a walking cautionary tale. And yet, to her, he seems as steadfast and courtly as the knights from her childhood storybooks: honorable, unflappable, prepared to shield her from whatever the day might bring. She takes his hand, letting him steady her as she descends to the platform, and wonders if his white horse is parked nearby.

The dull knot in her stomach has been constant since last night. Regret and remorse, she knows, for being so uncharacteristically sharp with him. Knight or not, though it's probably unfair, she has no intention of apologizing. She suspects he'd gladly take the smallest overture from her as permission to excuse everything on both sides and not discuss it further. She's not about to hand him that absolution.

A large black sedan awaits them at the station, its driver holding a placard bearing Madame Girard's sun crest. The drive through Budapest is somber. Even the city's usual pastel facades and flower stalls seem subdued by the season. The Danube is a ribbon of steel beneath a low, clouded sky.

Their destination is a small jewelry store near the principal shopping streets, tucked between a bookbinder and a cafe. A bell chimes on the door as they enter. The shop is not at all what Maren expected. She imagined it would be musty and cluttered, perhaps presided over by a stooped old man with a loupe. Instead, the store is sleek and modern, with blonde wood floors, soft lighting and alabaster-colored walls. The antique jewelry rests on frosted glass plinths and pedestals, making it seem to almost float in the minimalist glass cases. The proprietor, Árpád Molnár, is also much younger than Maren expects, late forties at most, she guesses. He's handsome in an underwear-model sort of way, dark brown hair constantly flopping into his eyes. The effect is undercut only slightly by the small, round, wire-framed glasses he pushes up on his nose every few minutes—a constant reminder (perhaps to himself as well as clients) that he's the expert here, not merely decorative.

One would never guess from his unassuming manner that he's known worldwide for his discerning eye and collection of century-old diamonds. His shop sells only antique jewelry spanning the Art déco, Edwardian, and Georgian eras, and even further back. He greets them with a courteous bow as Maren removes her glove and holds out her hand.

"I know this might sound odd," she says softly, "but this ring... it reacts to things. Sometimes it warms or cools; other times it tingles or vibrates. It almost feels like it's trying to communicate with me, but I can't make sense of it."

She takes off the ring and hands it to the jeweler. He examines it with professional interest. "Many people believe gemstones have properties beyond their beauty. Some say they carry energies and even have individual personalities, shaped by the earth and the wearer." He turns the ring under his jeweler's loupe, studying each stone intently.

He looks up briefly. "Lapis lazuli is the largest stone here. It has always been prized for its deep blue color. In ancient times, it was known as the stone of truth, and the Egyptians believed it offered protection against evil. Artists once ground it into ultramarine pigment, the most precious blue for centuries."

Maren nods. She knows about ultramarine blue from her restoration work.

He speaks as he examines the turquoise cabochon. "Turquoise is one of the oldest gemstones used by humans. It's associated with protection, especially for travelers. It's said to bring good fortune and healing. In Persia and among Native Americans, it was worn as a talisman to ward off misfortune and connect the wearer to the spiritual world."

He looks up, removes his headlamp, and points to the emeralds. "Emeralds are said to represent renewal and harmony. In some cultures, emeralds are believed to bring insight. It's interesting that there are only four, and stationed at the four points of the compass."

Maren glances at Alexander, but he's completely focused on Molnár, his hands clasped behind his back, expression as calm and impenetrable as ever.

How do men compartmentalize so well? Maren wonders if it's some ancient survival mechanism, hard-wired from the days when someone had to go out and club a woolly mammoth for dinner. Maybe back then, feelings in a man were a liability. If you paused to process your emotions, you'd end up as a sabertooth snack, or worse, lose your share of the mammoth to a less sentimental caveman. She suspects that deep somewhere in the male DNA, there's still a little switch labeled "Do Not Disturb: Hunting in Progress."

Maren shakes her head, a little smile tugging at one corner of her lips, and looks back at Mr. Molnár.

Finally, he touches the diamonds. "Diamonds are the hardest gemstones, and people believe they symbolize purity, strength, and clarity. They're also associated with eternal love, which is why they're so popular in engagement rings." He smiles.

He sets the ring on a thick piece of brown felt in front of them. "The arrangement is unusual. Lapis as a foundation for protection, turquoise and emeralds for guidance and growth, diamonds for strength, clarity, and love. If I had to guess, I'd say the ring was constructed this way on purpose, each stone chosen for both its meaning and its beauty. It's very rare, and very old. I would even say ancient. This ring is worth a considerable sum.

Maren leans forward. "Any idea who made it, or where it comes from?"

He shakes his head ruefully. "Not with any certainty. I'm sorry I can't be of more help," he says, looking at the ring on the felt. "But I do think you have something special here."

A shadow of disappointment crosses Maren's face, but Alexander offers her a reassuring glance. "You've given us some insight. That's more than we came in with."

Molnár says, "While you are here, if I may, I have something you might like to see."

He returns with a velvet tray. A pair of earrings rests on it: each one a turquoise oval set in gold, with a luminous cabochon emerald teardrop suspended below, and a large diamond linking the two. Like the diamonds in the ring, this one also has a flat base, a domed top, and triangular facets.

"Rose cut?" Maren asks.

The jeweler nods. "These earrings are from about the same period as your ring," he says, turning one earring over, revealing an inscription etched in delicate script. "They bear the same inscription."

"What does it say?"

"I believe it says, Nur. That means light in Arabic. And then something I can't make out. There are other words for light, but Nur is more abstract. It can have a spiritual connection. It's possible these pieces came from the same workshop. If your ring was part of a parure, these earrings could have belonged to it."

Maren reaches out, almost touching the earrings, then draws her hand back. "A parure," she repeats, the word both familiar and thrilling.

Alexander glances up. "A parure? I'm not sure I've heard that term before."

Molnár smiles, delighted to explain. "A parure is a suite of jewelry designed to be worn together. Usually crafted in the same workshop. Parures were especially fashionable in the eighteenth and nineteenth centuries among the European aristocracy."

"But also existed long before that," Maren adds.

"A parure can include any combination of matching pieces: a ring and a brooch, a necklace and earrings..." Molnár trails off.

"So, a matching ring and earrings would count as a parure?" Alexander asks.

"Yes, fewer than three pieces is sometimes called a demi-parure. A complete set might also include a necklace, perhaps a bracelet. But parures can be even more elaborate. Some of the most famous have belonged to royalty. For example, the late Queen Elizabeth II had several parures that included a tiara, necklace, earrings, a bracelet, and a brooch, intended to be worn together for formal occasions. Empress Joséphine of France was renowned for her emerald parure, and the Russian imperial family had jewelry sets with sapphires, diamonds, and pearls. The pieces may not match exactly, but each echoes the design of the others."

Alexander is thoughtful. "My mother had one of the pieces."

They both turn to him in surprise.

"It's a bracelet. I think you'd call it a cuff bracelet. I remember having seen it as a child. She never wore it. It was, or is, if she still has it—gold, with stones similar to these. Teardrop-shaped emeralds radiating around a cabochon turquoise."

"If these pieces are part of a parure, other pieces of the set may still exist as well." Molnár exclaims, fascinated now by this mystery.

"Workshops that made exquisite sets like this were renowned in their time," adds Maren. "Some say their craftsmen encoded messages in the designs, like mottos, secrets or clues to the family's fortunes."

Alexander studies the inscription, his curiosity piqued. "The inscription—could it be a clue?"

"It could," the jeweler smiles, "but collectors can spend a lifetime chasing down the pieces of a parure."

"Each piece brings them closer," Alexander says, looking at Maren.

"Each one carrying part of the story," breathes Maren, thinking of her mother. And Alexander's mother.

"Yes," Molnár replies, settling his glasses on the bridge of his nose. "Parures were a statement of wealth and taste, but also of unity and identity. To own a full parure was to possess a kind of wearable legacy."

Maren glances at Alexander again and finds him still looking at her. Her heart flutters. He is so incredibly handsome; she thinks.

For a moment, neither of them speaks. The Talisman necklace might be out there somewhere.

She slips the ring onto her finger, and as if in agreement, she feels it warm on her hand.

Alexander breaks the silence, turning to Molnár. "Are these earrings for sale?"

Molnár nods. "Yes, of course. I hesitated to buy them from the dealer because the price was so dear, and these Ottoman pieces seem to be out of fashion now. I wasn't sure anyone would be interested, but the craftsmanship was irresistible."

Alexander glances at Maren, then back at the jeweler. "Has Madame Girard seen them?"

Molnár shakes his head. "No, monsieur. I acquired them only a few days ago. A dealer from Venice. You are the first to see them in my collection."

Before Maren can object, Alexander says, "I'll take them."

She turns, startled. "You don't have to—" but then stops and blushes. Maren inwardly cringes. He never said the gift is for me.

He meets her eyes, reading her thoughts. "I want to. Consider it a gesture of good faith. And they may help lead us to the necklace."

Molnár wraps the earrings and hands the small package to Maren. The ring on her finger tingles. A reminder that their fates and the fate of these stones are now intertwined.

They thank the jeweler and step out into the cold. The wind silences any attempt at conversation. Maren slips the earrings into her pocket, suddenly wistful. They may carry secrets or old wounds, but they also provide the faintest hope that perhaps the story is not yet finished; between her and Alexander, or between her and the mysteries that have drawn her across Europe.

TWELVE

SHADOWS AND LIGHT

T HE WIND WHIPS THROUGH the canyon of buildings and cuts through Maren's coat as she and Alexander step out of Árpád Molnár's jewelry shop, buoyed by their discovery. The lapis ring on her finger responds to the earrings as if aligning itself with its twin. She doesn't question how she knows where their driver waits; she simply looks in that direction.

Their driver, a stout, professional-looking man in a dark wool coat, stands exactly where she expects. As the car pulls away, Alexander leans forward and gives instructions for the day.

"Mr. Varga, we'll be exploring this afternoon. Please collect us at six."

As an afterthought, he adds, "I'll send you a pin so you know where to pick us up. Miss Bennett and I are each staying in rooms at the Corinthia tonight. Our luggage will be delivered there this morning, and we'll return to the train tomorrow for the next leg of our journey."

Maren notes how Alexander makes it clear on her behalf, and in the most subtle way, that they are staying separately. He glances back at her, seeing the relief in her eyes, and she smiles at him.

It's such a minor thing, yet so many of the men she knows are either painfully self-conscious about what others think of them, or completely oblivious. Alexander hadn't made a show of it, hadn't sought her approval. He simply understood her concerns.

To Maren, Alexander gives the impression of knowing exactly the outcome he prefers, but seems to adjust his approach to suit the circumstances, a trait just as evident in his appearance. Even his clothing is a study in subtlety: dark colors and immaculate tailoring, chosen not to draw attention but to deflect it. She would have expected that dressing so well would make him conspicuous, yet he is so appropriate and quietly refined that, in any room, he blends in without a trace. As if invisibility were its own form of mastery.

Mr. Varga pulls over at their destination a few minutes later and opens the curbside door. Thanks and well wishes are exchanged with genteel formality, and soon the car vanishes into the midday flow of Budapest traffic.

At Café Gerbeaud, Maren and Alexander step back into the Belle Époque. Warm woods and marble-topped tables make it a cozy destination on a blustery day, and the cafe is brimming with travelers and locals alike. Silver trays pass by bearing pastries and steaming porcelain cups of coffee, and Maren's hunger catches up with her. She orders paprika-scented goulash, then a slice of Esterházy torte. Alexander opts for just Dobos cake and coffee, noting his sweet tooth.

"That, I believe, is the only weakness you have."

"Oh, you give me far too much credit," Alexander replies. "My weaknesses are legion, though unfortunately not as delicious as this one."

He asks if she enjoyed the goulash and comments on the Hungarian love of paprika. "It's such a staple in Hungarian cuisine; one would never know it isn't native."

"Yes," Maren agrees. "Chili peppers are a New World food, brought to Europe after Columbus's voyages. Ottoman traders on the Silk Road helped spread them through Turkey and into Hungary."

"If the humble chili pepper traveled the Silk Road, you can bet valuable gems and jewelry did too," Alexander says.

Maren is relieved that the tension from last night has mostly faded, replaced by the excitement of the jeweler's information. She hopes this means Alexander will help her find the Talisman. She smiles, recalling how Mr. Molnár seemed a bit let down this morning when she asked him to dispense with the box and bag and simply wrap the earrings in tissue.

"You deprived him of the ceremonial packaging moment," Alexander remarks. "You'd never get away with that at Tiffany's."

Maren laughs. "I'm sure you're right—they do love tying up those ribbons. Do you spend much time at Tiffany's, Alexander?"

He lifts his coffee cup. "Only in emergencies. The blue boxes are a bit theatrical for my taste."

"And what kind of things constitute a Tiffany's emergency?"

"The kind requiring an apology that can't be trusted to mere words. Or when someone's idea of subtlety is a five-carat diamond," he says.

Maren laughs again. "So, last resorts and grand gestures?" She makes a mental note: one day, she'll have to ask him about five-carat diamonds.

He shrugs and smiles, and they fall into conversation easily. The Alexander from last night, the one who briefly let his guard drop, is nowhere to be seen, but at least now he doesn't sidestep her questions about his family. He offers stories, each laced with the dry humor she's come to expect. Maren listens, feeling the ring's subtle influence heightening her senses.

The connection between the ring and the earrings is growing; she wonders if the Talisman parure is more than just a suite of beautiful Ottoman jewels. Perhaps it's a conduit—something ancient and powerful hiding within hundreds of years of legend.

She leans back, savoring the last bite of torte. "You said your mother has always lived in Paris? Her family is from Paris?"

Alexander stirs his coffee. "Yes. The de Sévigny, D'Orléans and Girard families have been in Paris for generations, since before the Revolution. My grandmother lived in a vast house on Rue de Grenelle. Portraits of scowling relatives everywhere. Silver so polished you could see your soul in it. When she wasn't holding intimate candlelit dinners for ninety, she hosted salons to raise money for the A.N.F."

"The A.N.F.?" Maren asks.

"The Association d'entraide de la Noblesse Française."

She arches an eyebrow. "French nobility mutual aid association? Is that a thing?"

"It is," Alexander replies. "My mother rebelled. She preferred poetry to protocol."

"And where do you fall in on that philosophy?"

Alexander signals the passing waiter for another cup of coffee for both of them, then considers Maren's question.

"I suppose I inherited a little of both. I have a healthy respect for tradition, but I've never been much good at following rules for their own sake. My mother says I'm too hard-headed for mandates, but too sentimental for outright rebellion."

He smiles. "I can appreciate a footman behind every chair and a well-set table as much as the next stuffy aristocrat, but I'd much rather talk to someone I enjoy than spend the evening counting the minutes until the hostess turns the table."

Maren recognizes the reference: at formal dinners, conversation begins with the person on your right. Then, halfway through the meal, the hostess "turns the table" by addressing the guest on her left, signaling that everyone else should do the same.

"If there's a choice between poetry and protocol," Alexander continues, "I know which one makes for a better evening."

Maren grins, recognizing those slightly roguish leanings in herself.

"My mother says she prefers to be judged for her mind, not her name. But my father always said she had a regal bearing, even when she was young and stubborn."

"My mother is French as well, but her family is different; distinguished, but artsy. Her father taught literature at the lycée, and her mother ran a gallery in Lyon. They were comfortable, but not grand. France is so different from the United States. I think my mother still feels a little out of place in the social whirl of Washington and New York."

"So, you grew up between worlds."

She nods. "Not quite fancy, not quite ordinary. My mother is pragmatic, but she has stories: about Paris, about the Sorbonne, and about a life she left behind."

"My mother says the Sorbonne is where she met the most important people in her life."

Maren's brow furrows. "It's interesting, isn't it, that our mothers were at the Sorbonne at the same time? Your mother's housekeeper—"

"Camille," Alexander interjects.

"Yes, Camille. She told me they consulted off and on about the Talisman." The ring warms against Maren's skin, as if confirming the connection. "Alexander, I hope this doesn't sound crazy, but the ring and the earrings seem to talk to each other."

"What do you mean?"

She searches for the words. "The ring has been a presence since Venice. But now, with the earrings near, I'm beginning to—" she lowers her voice. "Well, I'm seeing things."

"You think the Talisman jewels are showing you these things?"

"It's uncanny," she says. "The closer the pieces are together, the stronger they seem to become. I can't explain it, but that feels like an important characteristic of these jewels."

Maren fingers the lapis lazuli ring. "My mother only spoke of a necklace, and that's the piece your mother hired me to find. Our mothers may believe the necklace is the Talisman. But what if the actual power only happens when every piece is together?"

"Then," Alexander says, "the Talisman isn't just the necklace at all—it's the entire set together—the parure."

"Alexander, what if the parure was separated on purpose?"

He's quiet for a moment. "To keep it from growing too powerful."

She nods. "Or to prevent it from falling into the wrong hands."

Alexander leans back slightly, thinking. "My mother never talked about it. But Camille? She was cautious of the Talisman. I remember overhearing her say, probably to my mother, that the Talisman wasn't meant to belong to anyone. That it chooses, and tests who holds it."

Maren shivers. Not from the air, but from the idea settling between them.

Alexander is silent, thinking. "That would explain why Camille was so wary," he says finally. "Not of the necklace itself, but of what might happen if the pieces of the parure were ever reunited."

Maren nods. "And now we've started doing exactly that."

"If that's true..." he says slowly, "every piece we reunite helps realign whatever forces were meant to be suppressed."

She studies him. "Do you think your mother knows that?"

Alexander's jaw shifts slightly. "I'm not sure. But between us, we have three of the pieces."

He reaches over, then stops himself. Maren wonders if he'll take her hand, but he draws back, folding his fingers on the table in front of him instead. She looks intently at something across the room for a moment, so he doesn't see she's noticed. The urge to touch his hand is overwhelming. She studies his fingers and thinks they look strong and capable.

The ring pulses with her heartbeat. For a fleeting instant, she imagines those fingers brushing her cheek. Tracing the line of her jaw. The thought startles her; too intimate. Too bold. She lets her hand drop to her lap; the moment passes.

"Shall we go?" she asks. "I'd love to do some shopping."

They stroll slowly side-by-side along Andrássy Avenue, Budapest's grand boulevard, where Neoclassical mansions house fashionistas' most coveted labels. Maren pauses at Louis Vuitton, admiring a pyramid of travel trunks. Alexander points out the opera house, the old ballet school, now a hotel, and a small plaque marking the home of a composer.

At Jimmy Choo, they stop in front of a window displaying sky-high heels.

"Those would look great on you," Alexander says.

She laughs. "No way. How could I run in those? Or even walk?"

"Who says you need to be wearing them standing up?" Then, innocently, "I just mean you could be sitting. That's all."

She gives him a sidelong glance. "I know what you meant."

My goodness, Maren muses, aren't you full of surprises today, Alexander?

On the other hand, according to a People magazine left in the bar car, Alexander Girard is number 27 on the list of the world's most eligible bachelors. The article describes him as a "smoldering French lothario." I don't suppose he got that reputation being an angel, she thinks.

On Fashion Street, Maren is drawn to the Hungarian brand Nanushka's minimalist designs, admiring the sculptural silhouettes and the brand's commitment to sustainability.

"Clothing as art," she says, impressed, savoring her new exposure to fashion and aesthetics. These styles might translate beautifully into clothes for her to wear to work. She doesn't want to collect clothes, though—she'll never be interested in excess. But it's appealing to think of owning a small, thoughtfully curated wardrobe.

They go into Hermès to buy Alexander a belt, and Maren wanders off, browsing shoes. From the corner of her eye, she catches Alexander handing his business card to a sales associate, who studies it, then looks at him with interest. "One moment," she seems to say.

The next thing Maren knows, they move to a private room, where a sales associate unveils a black Kelly bag in glossy box-calf leather. The sales associate tells Maren about the history of Hermès and explains that they pride themselves on servicing the bags they sell for the life of the bag. "Our president, Mr. Dumas, told us, 'Luxury is what you can repair.'" Maren nods, appreciating an ethos that prizes longevity over disposable fashion.

The sales associate shows Maren the features of the bag—the strap, the Chevre lining, the lock and keys in their own miniature dust bag, and finally, the raincoat. Maren grins at this last flourish. That her handbag will always be prepared for the weather, while she can never remember to carry an umbrella for herself, strikes her as funny and charming. Then, the associate removes the protective coverings from the gold hardware for her, and hands her the bag.

Alexander settles the bill and makes arrangements for the box to be delivered to the train. When they step outside, dusk has settled over the street. A few shoppers remain, but most of the storefronts are dark.

"Okay," Maren jokes, "How did you do that? People don't just walk into Hermès and buy Birkins and Kellys. Even I know that."

Alexander smiles, slipping his hands into his coat pockets. "True," he says. "It helps to know the right people, and to manage their portfolios."

Maren laughs. "I thought you must be magic. Or maybe it's just your good looks."

For the first time since they met, Alexander laughs out loud. The sound surprises her as much as his relaxed posture.

"So it's not magic, it's finance?" she says.

"Maybe a little of both. But I promise I only use my powers for good."

Alexander looks down, checking his phone, and frowns. "Mr. Varga is changing a flat tire and will be a few minutes late."

A chill runs through Maren—a sudden, inexplicable premonition. "Alexander, we have to go. Something's not right." Even as she speaks, two men emerge from the shadows.

"Excuse me, Madame," the first says, stepping in front of Alexander and blocking his path. "We're shopping today, and you have just what we're looking for."

Alexander keeps his voice steady, trying not to escalate the situation. "Leave her alone." He slips off his watch and holds it out, his movements slow and deliberate. His gaze is fixed on the man's hands. "Here—take this. It's worth a great deal. I can give you cash as well. Just let her go. No police. We walk away and forget this happened."

"Just a small thing first," the second man replies, grabbing Maren's wrist with an iron grip. She tries to turn and pull away, pain shooting up her arm, but he twists the ring from her finger with brutal efficiency. The moment narrows to her pounding heart, the ring, and Alexander's voice somewhere behind her. It all happens in a blur. It feels like slow motion, but it's only five violent seconds, and the men vanish into the alley.

"Are you hurt? Maren! Are you okay?" Alexander grips her upper arms.

"Yes. No! Alexander—the ring. They have it." Her voice trembles. "Oh, I'm so sorry. It's all they wanted. They didn't take my purse or even your watch. Why?"

"Because they were already well paid." Alexander says grimly, "This wasn't a random mugging. Come on, Maren—we need to go."

A pedestrian had flagged down a police officer, who arrived at a run seconds too late. Alexander steps forward, speaking to him in English and then German, just as Mr. Varga screeches to a stop at the curb with the sedan.

Mr. Varga jumps out of the car, moving with surprising speed for such a large man. He places one hand gently on Maren's elbow, the other around her shoulders, and guides her into the car. Alexander slides in a moment later, pulling the door shut.

"We're in. Go, Thomas."

"Where to, sir?"

"The hotel. And please wait while I check us in."

Thomas Varga is beside himself, apologizing over and over. Alexander stops him. "It's okay, Thomas. It wasn't your fault, and no one's hurt. Thank you for getting to us. You must have seen my pin."

Mr. Varga nods, worry etched across his face.

They pull up at the beautiful Corinthia and are soon shown to adjoining suites. Maren stands in the middle of her room, bereft, still wearing her coat, uncertain what to do next. The despair and regret of losing the ring leave her shell-shocked. The ring had become a part of her, and losing it was a physical blow. She tries to think of what she could have done differently, if she could have prevented it. Then she's angry. How dare they? Who were they, and how did they know about the ring?

Then Maren remembers—the earrings. Her hand flies to her pocket, and she feels the earrings, still there, wrapped in their little bundle of tissue paper. Relief surges through her entire body. She is so glad she didn't take the large suede box and the jeweler's lovely, but well-known violet and gold bag. How did I know to do that? Then, suddenly, icy dread grips her. "Alexander, Mr. Molnár! Is he in danger?"

Alexander's voice comes from the doorway. "I called to warn him as I was checking us in. His shop was broken into. He said the place had been turned upside down, but nothing was taken."

Maren's heart sinks. "Oh no. Is he all right?"

"He wasn't in the shop. He and his wife are heading out of town now. I saw to that. But if anyone knows about the earrings... they may come looking for us."

"'Knows about the earrings?' How could anyone possibly know?"

"I don't know. What I do know is that we're not safe here. Don't unpack. I'll speak to the manager and arrange security. Lock your door."

Alexander opens the door from the adjoining room half an hour later. His shirt is torn, and there is blood on his lip.

"Alexander! What happened?"

He doesn't answer. Instead, he scoops up his briefcase and grabs his blazer. His calmness makes her pulse spike all the more.

"I'll explain in the car. Come with me, Maren. Leave the luggage."

She barely has time to snatch up her coat before he's through the door again. They take the stairwell at a near run, her heart pounding to keep up with his pace. Minutes later, they're in the car.

"I was talking to security when we spotted one of them waiting for the elevator," Alexander says. "He may be big, but he's not very smart. We beat him up the stairs and were waiting when the doors opened."

Maren stares at him. "What happened to you?"

"There was a little scuffle getting him into handcuffs."

"A little scuffle? Alexander, look at you!"

He winces, pressing a handkerchief to his lip, and manages a grin—at least, as much as the cut will allow. "You should see the other guy."

Maren closes her eyes, equal parts exasperated and re-lieved.

"They've got him in custody," Alexander continues, as if he's discussing a business meeting. "And they're picking up his partner. The manager called Gresham and got us in."

As he talks, he pulls on the blazer, smooths down his hair, then winces again and dabs at his face with the handkerchief.

Maren watches him, amazed. If it weren't for the large bruise forming on his left cheek, you'd never guess he'd just been in a fight for his life. He looks like a man getting ready for dinner, not someone who tackled a criminal in a hotel hallway.

Alexander gives a few more instructions to Mr. Varga and steers Maren through the revolving doors of the Four Seasons Gresham Palace. The guest manager on duty is waiting for them in the lobby.

"Good evening, Mr. Girard, Mrs. Girard. I'll show you to your room if you'd like to come with me."

Maren trails behind them through the lobby, looking up at the magnificent glass atrium ceiling and the enormous chandeliers sparkling overhead, and thinks, under different circumstances, this would be a marvelous place to stay.

The manager ushers them into a suite that looks like a watercolor painting in soft gray and lavender, with French vanilla walls. There is a fire burning in a marble fireplace, a selection of gourmet canapes arranged on a platter, and a bottle of wine breathing on a silver coaster.

"Courtesy of the Four Seasons, sir," the manager says with a smile. "Please let us know if there is anything you need."

The peaceful luxury is almost surreal after the chaos of the evening. There is a living area, a study, a powder room, but only one bedroom.

"I'm sorry, Maren," Alexander says when they are alone. "They're fully booked. It's all they had left. I'm afraid you won't have much privacy tonight."

Maren looks at him gratefully. "It's okay, Alexander. Thank you."

"I'll sleep on the sofa in the study," he says. "Oh, and here. I have something for you. He had this with him." He opens his palm. Resting there is her lapis ring.

THIRTEEN

THRESHOLDS

T HE BUTLER ASSIGNED TO their suite has come and gone. The rooms are prepared for the evening: the bed turned down; a small lavender sachet left neatly on each pillow. Soft jazz filters through hidden speakers—sultry and relaxing. The lights are dimmed. A tidy white mat has been placed on each side of the bed—assuming, Maren suspects, that they are husband and wife.

All Maren can think about is a hot bath and sinking into that glorious bed.

A porter has just delivered the bags Mr. Varga retrieved from the Corinthia. Alexander is making calls and periodically holding ice on his face as he stands at the console desk just behind the sofa, his sleeves pushed up, his voice low.

He watches her with concern as she robotically shrugs off her coat and pulls off her boots, tired eyes and disheveled hair. She's moving on muscle memory now. She doesn't even look at him as she crosses to the closet and hangs things up one by one, as if that small habit might restore some order inside her.

Behind her, he cradles the phone between his good cheek and shoulder. As he listens, he opens a drawer in the desk, rummaging for a pad of paper and pouring wine into a stemmed glass.

She takes the wineglass from his hand, her fingers brushing his. Then, on impulse, she leans in. Alexander shifts the phone away from his ear, thinking she's about to say something. Instead, she presses a kiss to his right cheek, the un-bruised one. A quick, light moment of gratitude.

Before she can see his reaction, Maren turns and walks toward the bathroom, glass in hand. The door closes softly behind her.

She flips on the exhaust fan for a bit of white noise, and dials up the music when she locates the small chrome knob that controls the volume. She has no desire to relive the attack, not even remotely, as Alexander speaks with people at the train, the police department, a detective, his public relations office, his assistant, and his secretary.

In the decadent marble bathroom, she turns on the tub faucet, pours in a generous handful of lavender bath salts, and lets the tranquil scent and soft jazz wrap around her like a warm hug. She slowly peels off her clothes and hangs them on the various hooks placed thoughtfully around the room. I need more hooks in my bathroom at home; she thinks offhandedly. Such a simple grace note, not having to search for a place to hang things up.

While she's waiting for the tub to fill, she cleanses her face, then smooths and pats the serums and creams into her skin the way the makeup artist showed her. She used to just brush her teeth and rinse her face before going to bed. Now she looks forward to this little nightly ritual of pampering.

As steam rises from the tub, she drops a folded towel onto the small table nearby and steps in. As soon as she feels the hot water on her feet and legs, she sighs. She didn't realize how cold her feet had been all day.

She thinks about Alexander and his cold feet, and wonders if meeting with the jeweler had been a turning point for him. But then there's still Simone, whom she can't quite disregard.

Maren tries to picture Alexander and Simone together: yes, they must have been quite a power couple. A perfect match in looks and style. Was he as devastated by their breakup as Simone claimed?

He gave her extraordinary gifts today, yet until now, he has really offered almost nothing in the way of overt affection. No overtures. Not even a flirtatious remark until this afternoon. And yet, there was that moment between them with the painting. What had that meant? Most of the time, Alexander frowns at her. But every so often, she catches a look from him—fleeting, but almost ravenous—that leaves her reeling. Maren can't shake the feeling of being pulled taut, then slack, as if caught in some invisible tug-of-war.

She lets out a long, helpless sigh. Their magnetic connection from the moment they met has been impossible to ignore. Surely, she can't be the only one who feels it. Can she?

But compared to the goddess Simone, she thinks, what on earth could he possibly see in me? It's not that I have low self-esteem, per se. I like myself just fine. I mean, I enjoy my own company. She smiles. I'm just surprised that anyone else would too.

Maren assesses herself the way she'd appraise a painting, aiming for objectivity. She's definitely not beautiful, she decides. Smart, though. (Professors still remember her for catching errors in their answer keys.) Easy-going about most things—though lately she's started to speak up about her preferences. She's funny, honest, and loves animals. A loyal friend, though not really the type to show up with homemade soup when you're sick.

I have good knees—that's something—observing them as they poke up out of the water. But she isn't convinced that knees are any sort of man-magnet. I don't understand it; she shrugs and gives up the inventory unfinished.

"Ahhh," she sighs, sliding down until the warm water covers her shoulders. And on the seventh day, God made bathtubs and rested. Thank heaven.

The lapis ring rests on the marble near the sink. As she looks over at it, she feels a mix of relief and reverence. Losing it had felt like a part of her was missing; having it back is like reuniting with an old friend. Did the ring warn her? Maybe. She can't tell. Its 'messages,' if that's even what they are, come in flashes, dreams, and visions, mostly just out of reach. She wishes she could understand it more clearly; wishes it could speak to her in sentences.

But maybe that's not how this works. Maybe it wants her to pay more attention to her intuition. What if the ring is less a guide and more a mirror, reflecting the wearer's instincts back to her? If so, Maren thinks, the ring must be just as frustrated with her, because she constantly overrides her own feelings.

She takes a sip of wine and thinks about the suite of jewels. Mr. Molnár said their parure might have a ring, earrings, bracelet, and a necklace; possibly a tiara. Do the thieves know the parure gains power as the pieces are rejoined? If a sultan commissioned the original set, at one time the parure must have been complete. Anyone aware of the legend would know that—yet, like the Hope Diamond, the pieces may have been re-cut or reimagined across the centuries, transformed by many owners and changing fortunes.

Her mind shifts to Paris, and the mysterious cuff bracelet Alexander's mother keeps hidden. Is she in danger? How did she come to possess it? Why didn't she tell me? Why, of all things, did Madame Girard hire her to track down the necklace and nothing more? Maren finishes her wine, feeling overwhelmed again. The answer will have to wait until tomorrow.

A few minutes later, scrubbed, fresh-faced and wrapped in a plush robe, Maren emerges to find Alexander just ending a call. He never takes his eyes off her as she crosses to the bed and sits on the edge. He walks toward her, concern in the lines of his face. Before he can say anything, she looks up at him and, for no apparent reason, bursts into tears.

Alexander crosses the space between them in a stride, and gently pulls her to her feet, wrapping his arms around her. She presses her face against his chest, the scent of clean wool and his warm spiced cologne grounding her again.

"I'm so sorry," she manages, her voice muffled. "I don't know what's wrong with me."

He holds her tighter. "You're fine. I'd be worried if today didn't get to you. We had quite a day."

She gives a little laugh and pulls back just enough to look at him. "I got your sweater all wet."

He brushes a tear from her cheek with his thumb. "I'll survive."

For a moment, he simply looks at her, then traces the line of her jaw, cradling her face in his hands. His touch is gentle and familiar, and Maren feels a jolt of recognition. The fleeting thought she had in the cafe was actually a premonition. He couldn't possibly know, but this moment feels like destiny.

For a moment, she thinks he might kiss her. But Alexander takes her hand instead, lets one of his drop to her waist, and guides her in a slow dance to a song playing softly in the suite, Someone to Watch Over Me.

His touch is firm but not possessive. Even here, his self-control is clear: he keeps a respectful distance, allowing her to lean in if she chooses. The song is the same one she sang in the bar car on the Orient Express to Paris. Was that a premonition too?

Her world, and maybe his too, is centered on the rhythm of their bodies and the heat where they press together. "Why a dance, Alexander?" she whispers, her cheek against his shoulder. "Why not just say something supportive?"

"Sometimes words get in the way."

He holds her closer. "This... this is how I know we're still okay, even when everything else is chaos."

"I feel safe," she murmurs. And she does. He feels warm, solid, and real.

"That's all I wanted," he says softly, "to give you a moment where you feel safe. Even if it's only the length of a song."

She looks up at him. "You always seem so unfazed. Like nothing rattles you."

He brushes a strand of hair from her cheek. "That's not true," he says. "You do."

At that admission, from this complex man who has rarely even smiled at her until today, tears well up again; but all she does is smile into his chest.

"You're such a girl," he says.

She laughs. When the song ends, he takes her hand and brushes her fingers with his lips. The gesture is restrained, but so intimate it takes Maren's breath away. He leads her back to the bed and sits her gently on the edge. For a moment he does nothing, and Maren watches him, attuned to every nuance of his body language.

He seems to weigh something, caught between desire and discipline. His breath is slow and measured, as if he is willing himself to remain calm. He runs a restless hand through his hair. His eyes, dark and full of things unsaid, play over her face. He finally tears his gaze away and tenses his shoulders as if bracing against an invisible pull.

When he reaches the double doors, he closes them behind him. The click of the latch sounds final, but she senses the effort it took for him to walk away and choose the sofa and solitude over the warmth of her bed.

The next morning, Maren pulls on her robe and joins Alexander in the other room.

He is sitting at the table wearing jeans and a turtleneck, already showered and shaved, and reading the newspaper in his tortoiseshell glasses.

"Good morning," he says, rising. "How did you sleep?" His tone is polite and...almost jovial.

"Wonderfully. I didn't even hear you walk past to the shower," Maren replies, doing her best to keep her voice as breezy as his. "How were the accommodations in the study?"

"Perfectly adequate," he says, and gestures toward the coffee. "Would you like a cup?"

She nods. "Thank you. Yes."

He pours her coffee, careful in his movements. Not too close, not distant either. A choreography that feels, suddenly, like a new formality between them.

He sits down and opens the paper again.

What is it about a handsome man in glasses? Maren muses, watching him tilt his head toward the business section as if nothing has changed between them.

She steals a glance through her lashes, watching him over the rim of her coffee cup, searching for any trace of the man from last night—the warmth, the soft music, those protective arms, the way he nearly... But he's gone. Disappeared in the bright morning light.

Well, of course, she thinks.

This is Alexander Girard: international jet-setter, smoldering French lothario, or whatever it is they call him. Seductive in the dark, cool in the daylight. He's done this scene before, no doubt, probably several times a week. She almost rolls her eyes. Classic. Breakfast silence. Clean exit. If no one gets too close, no one gets hurt.

She tries to settle into the rhythm of the morning, but the disappointment is sharper than she expected. Reflexive and unfair, maybe, but there all the same. Maren rises, picking up her coffee more briskly than necessary and sloshing it over the side, with a clatter of cup and saucer. She tells herself that for Alexander last night was about adrenaline and exhaustion. Nothing more.

At the sound, Alexander looks at her over the paper.

"We should plan to leave by ten if that's all right. Less fuss at the station if we get there a little early."

His voice is polite. Measured. Last night never happened. Exactly as she feared.

"Sure," Maren says. "Alexander, have you thought more about who hired those men? It seems so... targeted. Do you think it could have been Simone?"

He shakes his head. "I doubt it." Then, folding the paper as he stands, he says, "She doesn't operate that way."

Maren turns to go, finding it hard to keep the edge out of her voice. "You're awfully sure of her," she says over her shoulder, and heads for the bedroom without waiting for a reply.

She showers and does her hair and makeup. Looking in the mirror, she thinks her new skincare regime is having a lovely effect on her skin. She has always had a peaches-and-cream complexion like her father, but now it feels smooth and looks so even-toned that she doesn't need foundation. She skips eyeshadow as well and applies a coat of black mascara. A swipe of red lipstick brings out her green eyes, and she smiles at herself with approval.

She decides on a pair of camel pants, an ivory silk blouse, that soft brown suede jacket cinched at the waist, and a pair of matching suede loafers. She puts on what she now calls the Girard sun earrings, and then finally the lapis ring. For a moment she hesitates about the ring, remembering how much trouble it has brought. Then, meeting her own gaze in the mirror, she thinks defiantly, if someone wants it, come and get it.

A steely resolve settles beneath her newfound polish. I may be more pulled together these days, she thinks with the little lift of her chin inherited from her mother, but I am no cream puff. I am an intelligent, capable, independent woman. I will no longer be just a bystander in someone else's drama.

Maren takes her bags to the door and turns from the hall mirror just as Alexander pulls on his own brown suede jacket, with buttery leather very similar to hers. For a second, their reflections stand side by side with their matching jackets.

Maren smiles and quirks an eyebrow. "Coordinated travel ensembles. Is this the next phase of our partnership?"

Alexander glances at their reflection, amused. "Apparently, we both have excellent taste. Or we both shop at Dior."

Maren pretends to inspect his jacket with expert seriousness. "Good suede. Paris?"

"Milan." His grin softens the look of the bruise on his cheek. Then, meeting her gaze again in the mirror, he adds, "I've never noticed before, but we have the same eyes."

She studies him. They are cool grayish-green, just like her own. "I suppose we do. That bruise really brings out the color of yours."

Alexander laughs, the genuine sound that Maren loves. "We're both wearing the evidence of this adventure a little too well," he says, gently lifting her hand to reveal the faint purple mark on her wrist.

"Let's try not to acquire any more souvenirs in Bucharest," she replies, reaching for her bag. In their reflection, matching jackets, matching eyes, she glimpses the beginning of something interesting.

Mr. Vargas drives them to the station, overseeing the transfer of their bags before bidding them farewell. As Maren and Alexander step up into their carriage, Simone appears in a form-fitting pale blue dress, her lush blonde mane cascading down her back. She's about to descend the steps, phone pressed to her ear. She offers a half-smile, waiting for them to pass, her eyes lingering on the sun earrings in Maren's ears. In that instant, Simone's demeanor is like a tranquil lake icing over in midwinter. She turns away, but not before fixing Maren with a look that lets her feel the freeze.

Maren unlocks her suite, dropping her new bag onto the sofa. As she slips off her jacket and turns to hang it up, she sees something unexpected: a scuffed, black leather-bound journal tucked behind one of the sofa pillows. For a moment, she stands unmoving. This was not here before. She's certain she checked every corner of this room. Or, she thinks she did, wondering if she's losing her mind.

How did this get here? Did anyone know she would find it? Did Alexander? She forces the thought away.

She perches on the edge of the sofa, journal in hand; the now-familiar sensation from the ring quickening her heartbeat. Intuitively, she closes her eyes, fingertips hovering just above the leather cover, as if proximity might summon the feeling or memory closer. There is something here. A presence, possibly a warning. It's just out of reach. She sees her father's face, then notices he is holding out something in his hand.

Before she can grasp it, the vision shifts: the train is barreling through the night, malevolent shadows racing past the windows; Simone leans over Maren's shoulder, lips nearly brushing her ear, a message poised on the edge of her whisper.

Maren holds her breath, but the vision changes, replaced now by a river of mosaic tiles on the floor at Saint Mark's, the pattern leading her to...where?

Then, she is alone with Alexander, her hands sliding over his chest as she slowly unbuttons his shirt, the air charged with longing and something more mysterious, more necessary.

Her eyes snap open as a gasp escapes her; her pulse hammers in her ears, and the world lurches. Nausea rises, sudden and overwhelming. She stands, the journal thudding to the floor, and rushes to the bathroom sink. Bent over the glass basin, she has the raw certainty that the answers she needs, about her father, the Talisman, and the complex web drawing all of them together are entangled somewhere in these images, almost within reach, if only she can withstand the storm.

FOURTEEN

WAITING HEART

MAREN PICKS UP THE black journal and steps next door to let Alexander know she found it. He's on the phone, one hand holding a glass of club soda with lime. He glances up at her and raises the glass in a wordless question, does she want one? She shakes her head and, without interrupting, scribbles a quick note on the notepad on the table: I'll be in the dining car. Without missing a beat, he leans over to read it, nods, and gives her a thumbs-up.

Maren pushes open the polished door to the bar carriage on her way to the dining car, and hears a lilting sound on the roof: rain. Streaks of slate and silver race across the windows in wind-driven patterns, but inside, the carriage is warm and bright. A few passengers relax along the perimeter, chatting with companions, some reading or doing a crossword puzzle.

Lucien sits in a blue velvet chair by the window, his bone structure chiseled from a Renaissance painting. His brown hair is swept smoothly back, save for a rebellious curl at the nape, and it frames a face more striking than conventionally handsome: high cheekbones, a sardonic mouth, and pale hazel eyes.

He sips a cappuccino and leafs through a copy of Le Monde. When he glances up, Maren gives him a small wave. He gestures to the empty seat across the table and stands. Tall and lean, with a straight, almost regal posture, he is as graceful and composed as a jungle cat.

"Well, hello. If it isn't Miss Bennett, the intrepid historian." His voice is deep and languid, but distinctly enunciated. "Won't you have a seat?"

"Historian?" says Maren, looking up at him. Does he know she's looking for the Talisman? She sits and orders a glass of orange juice with club soda.

"No whiskey this morning?" he asks, folding his paper.

Maren laughs, "Not before noon today. Unless you know something I don't about how this day is going to go. I can always reconsider."

"Ah... rain, gloom. What's not to like?" He smiles, his humor coiled with intent. "Secrets have a way of revealing themselves on days like this."

Maren doesn't take the bait. "That may be true. But I seem to recall from English Lit. that rain is also famously an omen of disaster."

"Ah, but disaster, Miss Bennett, is the best guarantee against boredom. I expect you get far less of both than you deserve."

Maren grins at him. "You seem unusually well-informed for a man who claims to be just passing through. Should I be flattered or concerned?"

His grin is slow and mischievous. "Why not both? It keeps the conversation lively. Tell me, what are you reading? Hemingway?"

"It's just an old journal that belonged to my father before he died, and I recently found it. It's useless, really."

"Never judge a book by its cover, Miss Bennett. Most people spend their lives overlooking what's staring them in the face."

Maren is thrown by the remark. "Is it safe to assume you aren't interested in publishing lost family memoirs, Lucien?"

He smiles. "Safe enough. I only collect things that want to be found. Sometimes things are better left hidden." He takes another sip of his cappuccino. "Not every quest is about possession, you know. There's an article right here in the paper about organizing. The writer says one can enjoy beautiful things without bringing them home."

She studies him, wary but amused. He apparently knows something. She decides to take a risk. "So, you want me *not* to find the Talisman?"

Lucien chuckles. "Want is too strong a word, Miss Bennett. My employers are chiefly concerned about protecting it."

"Your employers." Maren echoes, thinking. "And you?" Maren has the distinct impression that Lucien isn't all that concerned about doing what his employers want.

He shrugs almost dismissively. "Me? I don't really believe in all this magical nonsense. But I have a job to do. Someone must keep food on the table and the wolf from the door."

"I'm getting the feeling that perhaps *you* are the wolf at the door." Maren says dryly.

He leans in, voice suddenly silky. "I only bite when necessary, Miss Bennett." Then, with a rakish two-finger salute, he stands. "Bon appétit. Enjoy your lunch. And Maren—beware of pretty things—sometimes they bite for no good reason at all."

As she heads for the dining car, she thinks about his words and truly can't decide whether Lucien is her adversary... or the most elusive ally she'll ever have.

She is in the blue dining car today and hopes Alexander will know where to find her. One of these meals, she'll have to try ordering in her suite, but today, the steady rhythm of rain on the carriage roof, the pleasant conversations and laughter of diners, and the contagious enthusiasm of the waiters, makes it a cheerful place to be. The headwaiter is about to show Maren to a table, when she sees Simone de Villiers seated

alone at a table already set for two—each place with diminutive salt and pepper grinders nestled in their own miniature
silver trays, and a folded napkin angled toward the empty
brocade armchair. Maren sighs; it's now or never.

Simone glances up. "Maren! Darling, please join me. The
chef is doing something special with trout today—and it would
be a shame to let superb wine and better company go to
waste."

Maren takes the seat, placing the journal on the chair to
her right. As she sits down, she notices a black Hermès bag on
the chair next to Simone. The exact bag Alexander bought her
in Budapest. Simone runs a manicured hand along the satiny
leather.

"Do you like it? Alexander bought it for me last year in Milan when he bought this," she says, holding out the hand with
that enormous diamond. Five carats from Tiffany's? Maren
wonders.

"Such a thoughtful gesture." Simone purrs.

"Yes, it certainly was," Maren says thoughtfully.

Maren can't get over how beautiful Simone is. I'm a
woman, she thinks, and even I do a double take. It's hard not
to stare at her. She has those wide, high, model cheekbones,
with the hollow beneath that ordinary mortals can only hope
to emulate with makeup contouring. Her ice-blue eyes are
almost too wide-set, yet this quirk somehow enhances her
ethereal, sylph-like allure. She has full, bee-stung lips that
Maren tries not to imagine Alexander kissing. All this, and a
bewitching, almost hypnotic quality. It makes perfect sense
that he is still in love with her. Gosh—I'm surprised I'm not,
Maren thinks wryly. I might as well forget Alexander right now
if this is the level of my competition.

Simone leans in conspiratorially, lowering her voice as if
they are sharing private confidences. "So, how did you two

meet? When I first bumped into Alexander, he didn't mention you."

Maren schools her features into an unbothered smile. "I don't know why he would have," Maren says. "I hardly know him, actually. We're just friends thrown together by circumstance." She adds.

"Honestly, he was a great catch... I suppose I should rethink letting him slip away." Her tone is relaxed and confident, as if Alexander is still very much hers whenever she reaches for him. She speaks of him like a cat toying with a mouse, knowing she can have him any time she wants, but wanting to play with him first. She seems to enjoy the drama of the chase.

Conversation is light over lunch, which Simone barely touches. She talks about shopping in Budapest and asks about Maren's purchases.

"Did you buy anything, darling? Budapest is a marvelous place to buy enormous gems and antique jewelry. There are dealers there who specialize in it. Some have pieces that date all the way back to the Ottoman Empire. Can you imagine?"

"No," Maren says, "I didn't buy a thing for myself, but Alexander had some fortunate finds."

"Oh, do tell. He's terribly lucky."

"I imagine he is. I wouldn't know," Maren replies, and Simone laughs, not probing further. Satisfied, perhaps, that she's achieved what she intended, she stands, gathering her bag. Maren and this conversation are already old news.

"Try the mousse, darling. It's spectacular," Simone says. With that, she's gone.

Maren adds cream to her coffee and replays Simone's casual reveal: so, Alexander buys jewelry and expensive purses for his girlfriends. Does that make Maren a girlfriend now? Why is it, she wonders, that women always want to label the relationship but expect the man to define it for them?

Everyone is right about the mousse. It is so good that she savors every decadent dark chocolate bite. Speaking of gems, Maren remembers a rare gem of advice that her mother gave her once. She didn't quite understand it then, but she does now. "Never underestimate your power as a woman," her mother had said, "but that power is in receiving, not pursuing."

Alexander's gifts so far would likely thrill her mother. "Don't waste your time trying to decode a man's feelings," she said. "Your strength is not in mind-reading, pleasing, or managing. That's just control by another name. Make yourself happy. Let your joy be your compass. Your father married me because I was a magnet. I chose him. I decided we would be married, but he chose the timing." She had said, "Remember this, dear, never obsess over what he wants. Ask yourself what you want. That's where the magic hides. Happiness isn't a prize you chase; it's a gift you carry. That's what draws love in."

Maren smiles, half-hopeful, and finishes the last bite of the mousse, scooping every last bit out of the parfait glass. The ring pulses on her finger. She is getting closer to finding the Talisman; she can feel it.

When she leaves the dining car, the carriages she passes through are empty. Outside the train, the rain is still falling, heavier now. Maren enters their carriage thinking she'll ask Daniel for a pot of tea, but he isn't at his post. As she makes her way toward her cabin, she hears tense voices coming from Simone's suite, and slows a little.

She hears Simone's voice. "You owe me, Alexander, unless you want your little girlfriend to know what happened in Venice..." her voice trails off. "I'd be happy to tell her for you if you like."

"Maren is not my girlfriend, Simone, so you can relax."

"You're lying," she says. "I know you." Then lets out a laugh. "Or maybe you're exactly as calculating as I've always known you are."

A pause.

"You don't know me," Alexander replies.

"I know she's an art specialist." Then, "Maybe you and your mother are just using her to find the necklace. The way you used me."

Then Alexander's voice again, lower. Maren strains to hear.

"And she doesn't know me either. We met only a few days ago."

Maren's heart plummets.

"And—"his voice soft and deep. "I don't owe you anything more either, Simone. We were engaged for six months. You kept a ring worth nearly a half-million dollars, and the apartment in Milan—worth twice that. Anyone, including a court of law," he added, "would say I've been more than generous. Let's call it even."

Simone's voice again. "No, Alexander. We won't be even until you've lost something that truly matters to you, starting with the necklace that you and your mother love so dearly—much more than you loved me—then we might be square."

She hears nothing until Alexander responds, "I heard you're marrying a Habsburg. You can't need the money."

She steps closer, her voice calm but cutting. "You're right, I don't care about the money. But as you know, I heard you and your mother talking. I know what the necklace means to her. And I know what she means to you." She continues, "More than anything, I want you both to feel what I did: the devastation and the public humiliation when you threw me away. It was all over the tabloids. You were the one who wanted to get married in the first place, not me. Yet everyone blamed me for the split, and it was my name dragged through the mud. The Girards came out of this smelling like roses, and our friends have been gossiping about me ever since. But not you. You moved up five places on the eligible bachelor list. I swear, Alexander, you may never have faced consequences for anything you've done, but you will for this."

From the corridor, Maren can't hear Alexander's response.

Then Simone's voice again. "I will find out the truth, Alexander. And I will get the necklace. Whatever it takes."

A pause, then Simone, almost playful: "Now come here, darling. For old time's sake. Let's not let this get between us."

Maren shivers at the threat, slips quietly down the corridor, and lets herself into her suite. So, Simone is after the necklace too, just as Lucien warned. But it sounds like the necklace is the only piece Simone knows about. What happened in Venice? Maybe it's connected to the archives and her father's journal. For all Maren knows, Alexander could have been the one who took the journal from her cabin and then quietly gave it back.

Lunch and the rocking lull of the train lure Maren to the bed. I'll just lie down for a moment, she thinks, watching the rain sheeting down the glass. Before long, she is asleep with vivid, fitful dreams. She sees herself at a ball in a sapphire-blue dress. Dancers are swirling and spinning around her as she stands in the center of the floor searching for someone or something? Maren wakes to a ping and fumbles for her phone, the screen casting a glow on her face, now the only light in her dark cabin. It's a text from Alexander.

"Sorry I missed lunch. Calls ran late. Can I make it up to you with a nightcap? Come by my cabin whenever you like. A."

Maren answers Alexander's nightcap invitation with a lightness she hasn't felt in days. She chooses a glamorous short silk pajama set with a subtle pattern. Then she drapes her soft cashmere robe across her shoulders, feeling pretty and completely herself.

When she knocks, Alexander opens the door in faded jeans and a striped dress shirt, untucked, the sleeves rolled to his forearms. He grins, more relaxed than usual, his eyes crinkling at the corners. "You look..." He hesitates, gaze sweeping her with genuine admiration. "Comfortable. That's a good look for you."

She laughs as she steps inside, giving an exaggerated twirl of the robe. "It's called 'luxury train chic,' obviously. And aren't you the rebel wearing jeans on the Orient Express. I thought that was verboten."

"I promise not to leave my cabin, officer."

They settle side by side on the sofa, shoulders nearly touching. Alexander flips through a menu of old movies, then looks to her for approval. "Casablanca, Charade... or... ah, this one's à propos: How to Steal a Million."

"Surprise me. Just no spoilers," Maren threatens, aiming a playful finger at him. "Obviously, I thrive on suspense," she says and laughs.

Daniel, the best steward ever, delivers a large bowl of popcorn, which makes arcs through the air when Alexander can't resist leaning over to whisper, "Watch this, Peter O'Toole's about to—" Maren promptly chucks a handful at him, laughing as he protests in mock outrage.

Maren lets herself simply be: curled in comfort, caught up in the movie's fun and the warmth of Alexander's presence. She likes this version of him: the unguarded smile, the way he stretches out, one arm draped over the back of the sofa, looking at her as if she's the best scene in the movie.

Maren feels friendly warmth in Alexander's private glances. She teases him for being invested in the happy ending, but her own heart beats a little faster every time he smiles in her direction.

By the time the credits roll, there's popcorn everywhere and the space between them has lessened. It's just friendship, Maren thinks. An ordinary evening among pals. At the door, they exchange plans for the morning.

"Well then, goodnight," she says, and opens the door. Alexander closes it. His hand over hers on the handle. With his other hand, he reaches out, tips her chin up, and kisses her softly. Maren doesn't lean in, but doesn't pull away either. She lets him end it, then smiles at him and says, "Thanks."

"For the kiss or the popcorn?" Alexander asks.

"All of it," Maren says, meaning it.

Fifteen

BUCHAREST

T HE TRAIN ARRIVED AT the Gara de Nord station in the middle of the night. The rain in Hungary had turned to snow, falling heavier the farther east they traveled, until it wrapped Bucharest in an early, ghostly winter. Maren wakes to a window covered in frost. She presses her palm against the cold glass. This is not the vibrant capital city she imagined; this is a city slumbering beneath a frozen blanket.

A short while later, she drinks a cup of hot tea with milk, nibbles a piece of toast, and paws through her wardrobe, wondering what to wear. She selects a heavy black turtleneck, gray wool flannel trousers, and silver Bogner snow boots. After lacing them up, she stands—then glances outside and sits back down, tucking her trousers neatly into her socks and boots.

A moment before Alexander knocks, Maren opens her door and smiles, partly at the timing, partly because, once again, they're dressed alike. He's in a black parka, though, belted at the waist, while hers is bright metallic silver.

"You didn't get the memo about the coat?" she teases.

Alexander gives her a brief, assessing once-over, amusement flickering in his eyes. "Sorry, I left my spacesuit at home this trip."

Snow dusts the narrow station platforms almost as soon as they're swept. A short walk from the train, their driver waits beside a hulking black SUV, snowflakes swirling over the roof and melting on the hood. He takes their luggage with a nod and stows it in the back. They slide inside, the heated air pushing out the sharp winter chill. Alexander hands the driver an address, neatly penned on Orient Express writing paper.

Maren settles into the seat and pulls off her gloves, feeling warmth return to her fingertips. She watches him pass the slip of paper forward, unexpectedly soothed by the formality of Alexander's gestures. He never rushes. Never fumbles. His smallest movements seem intentional, not rote. He's dignified; partly upbringing, certainly, but also born of self-respect. His courtesy and poise anchor her.

In a world that so easily lapses into the jangled energy of hurry and noise, Alexander's restraint feels almost radical. She thinks of home, where the cult of busyness reigns. Overcommitment is a badge of honor; time is rationed, conversations clipped; pleasantries are perfunctory, if people bother with them at all. Emails and texts are trimmed for efficiency. She thinks of all the little ways she makes her own life more difficult for herself: rushing around, forgetting things, dropping things, digging through her purse like a crazed squirrel. How many times a week does she lose her car keys or her phone? She smiles to herself when she thinks about the time she swore she'd lost her sunglasses and they were sitting on top of her head. She is very particular about her work. Indeed, everyone knows her for it. Why couldn't I apply the same focus to the rest of my life? Maren thinks.

Something loosens inside her. She hadn't even realized how tightly she'd been holding herself. She lets go of the script in her head, stops imagining what should happen next. There's a luxury in relaxing into someone else's certainty. She breathes deeper, her shoulders lower.

It's more than comfort. There's a subtle thrill in watching Alexander approach life the way he does. She wonders what it would feel like to exist at his pace, and to trust that circumstances will yield to you, not the other way around. She imagines a life with more mental space, every moment given its due; her phone less insistent, her thoughts less frazzled.

She thinks about how she could carry that sense of composure inside her, as he does, and let the world, for once, adjust to her needs. And somewhere in that imagining, she realizes it isn't only peace she wants; it's him. The way calm lives in him. For a moment, she wonders if it has always been this: Alexander's graceful way of moving through the world that has been calling her from the start.

The SUV creeps through the city, heater blasting. Alexander leans forward, trading an easy joke with the driver about the weather. Maren traces circles in the condensation on her window, her pulse stilling, her mind growing quiet; everything inside her inclining slightly, almost involuntarily, toward him.

"It's like being inside a snow globe," she says. "Or Dr. Zhivago."

Outside, statues hunch beneath powdery shrouds. Heavy iron gates turn to delicate lace, and rooftops vanish into a pearl-colored sky. The car turns off the main street into a long, empty alley, where the wind has sculpted the snow into drifts piled against abandoned storefronts. Even the graffiti is softened by clinging snow, emerging through the storm like faded murals in an ancient, lost city.

The silence presses against the glass, and Maren shivers, not entirely from the cold.

Alexander shifts. "We're meeting an art and antiquities dealer my mother knows," he says. "Florian Dascălu." The SUV pulls to a stop outside a shuttered gallery. Maren raises an eyebrow. Alexander pauses with his hand on the door. "Stay warm, I can manage from here," he tells the driver. The man nods, grateful. Alexander steps out into the snow and shrugs back at Maren, mouth quirking. "Apparently, this is it."

A little bell over the gallery door announces their arrival with a tired jangle. The dealer barely looks up as Alexander and Maren enter, a wiry man perched on a creaking wooden stool, lips pursed tight around a thin, hand-rolled cigarette. Smoke curls around his head in lazy ribbons. "Gallery" is stretching it, Maren notes, as she looks around the dim, brick-lined space that is a warren of stacked wooden crates and shipping containers. She can hear the whir of a small space heater and see her breath in the frigid air. Maren notices patches of ornate gold frames peeking from under dust covers, their edges chipped. Whatever lies beneath is almost certainly of dubious origin and, she suspects, worth a fortune.

Alexander steps forward. "Mr. Dascălu?" He is polite but alert. "I'm Alexander Girard, and this is Maren."

"If you're looking for your partner, you just missed her," Descălu says, tapping ash into a porcelain saucer.

"Our partner?" Alexander asks, puzzled.

"Yeah. The ice princess." The dealer says with a half-smirk. "She said she was with you."

Maren glances at Alexander. "She's not our partner."

The dealer leans back, folding his arms, sizing both of them up. "Meh. Didn't tell her much. She had a vibe. Like she already decided what to do with the goods before she even saw them." He takes another long pull from his cigarette. "I've been at this a long time. You get a feel for people."

His sweater is moth-eaten but somehow genteel, like the man himself, a once refined relic of a vanishing era. He gestures to a pair of battered chairs. "So. What is it you want to know?"

"We are hoping someone can start from the beginning," Maren says. "We're trying to trace the history of a 16th-century Ottoman parure. At first, we thought we were only seeking a necklace. Called Roxelana. Crafted for Sultan Suleiman's favorite wife around 1530. Now, it appears the necklace is only one piece of a set, a parure. The necklace and the rest of the jewels apparently became separated during the fall of the Ottoman Empire. In the 1920s, similar jewelry resurfaced in Venice, then disappeared again. We hope you can fill in the story."

The dealer's eyes fix on the curling smoke. "People always want stories," he says, "but they never ask why the stories were hidden in the first place." He leans forward, voice low.

"This isn't a fairy tale. The set was in Paris in 1939 and was split up on purpose. People were afraid of it, but they were more afraid of the Nazis getting a hold of it. The jewels of the Talisman parure have passed through the hands of scholars, thieves, and royalty alike for hundreds of years, but the most important hands are those of the Sorbonne Society."

"The Sorbonne Society," Maren repeats. "You mean the Sorbonne in Paris?"

He inclines his head, tapping ashes from his cigarette into the chipped dish. "Yes. A group formed loosely after the First World War. Aristocrats, professors, women and men who'd survived enough to know exactly what power can do in the wrong hands. Power like the Talisman had, rumored to change fate, reveal truth, and show the future—always draws hunters."

Alexander asks, curious, "And the Society survived the Second World War?"

"Survived?" Dascălu's laugh is short and humorless. The lines around his eyes barely move. "Parts did. The rest—gone. Some kept faith. Some sold faith for a night's shelter, a new passport. That's how war does it." His gaze settles on Maren, appraising her character. "What's left?" He flicks his fingers, sending another spiral of smoke upward. "Bits of knowledge, secrets passed down through families. Remembered in letters by people with enough scars to know better than to chase legends for glory."

He stubs out the cigarette, hand steady, a twitch of irony in the set of his mouth. Chin dipped, he looks at her from under his brows, slow and deliberate. "You come here wearing your mother's stubbornness, asking questions that carry more weight than you realize."

"You know my mother?" Maren asks, surprised.

"Anyone who has any interest in the Talisman legend knows your mother." Then nodding toward Alexander, "and his. You want answers—fine. There's someone else you need to see: Professor Antonescu. Ask the right questions, she'll tell you things even your mothers may not know. But be careful," he says, looking directly at Alexander. "Sometimes when you chase the truth, it circles back on you."

He jots an address and phone number on a scrap of paper, tears it off, and hands it to Maren. "It's supposed to snow for another day. If you get out there, tell her Dascălu sent you."

He nods toward the door, signaling that the conversation is over. At least for now.

Outside, two more inches of snow have fallen. They climb into the warm SUV, the wipers sweeping in a steady rhythm, pushing slushy ridges of ice to the base of the windshield. Alexander leans forward, conferring quietly with the driver while Maren unlocks her phone out of habit, expecting the usual flood of emails and texts; someone always needing an answer. The screen is as empty as the frozen street outside; not a single new message. Her well-connected life is completely cut off in this otherworldly place, suspended in another kind of winter.

She looks up to see the driver studying the address Alexander has handed him. After a long pause, he shakes his head slowly. Alexander shifts to look at Maren. "The driver doesn't think he can get out there without getting stuck. He says it's too dangerous under the current conditions." Maren lets the information sink in. So close. She's about to ask what they should do next, when a sleigh appears around the corner, two bay horses tossing snow from their manes as they pass, pale clouds pluming in the air around their nostrils.

Alexander's eyes light up. "I have an idea," he says, leaning forward again. "Follow that sleigh."

The driver hesitates only a moment before pulling out into the street with a grin, trailing after the disappearing runners. They catch up at the next intersection, where Alexander rolls down his window and negotiates in German with the sleigh's driver. Maren watches a roll of cash change hands.

A moment later, they're out of the car. The sleigh driver offers Maren a gloved hand, helping her aboard, and tucks thick wool blankets snugly around their laps.

Then they're off—gliding through snowbound streets to the steady snort and breathing of the horses. Harness bells jingle, keeping time with the muffled clop of hooves and the hiss of runners slicing over freshly fallen snow.

Maren's disappointment dissolves, replaced by pure delight. She glances at Alexander beside her. Without speaking, he wraps his arm around her shoulders and scoots her closer to the warmth of his side, drawing her knees beneath the blanket until they're pressed against his. She can't help but wonder what other impossible marvels he's capable of.

They travel through the snowy countryside for nearly twenty minutes, passing occasional white-roofed houses and snug barns, fields and forests unfolding in silvery silence. The landscape lies still and untouched beneath the low winter sky. Eventually, the sleigh turns down a narrow lane, trees arching overhead in a tunnel of soft green and white. At the far end sits a small cottage, tucked deep among a grove of firs, its steep roof softened by a thick layer of snow. Windows glow, and wood smoke swirls from the chimney, lavender in the light of dusk.

Maren leans forward slightly and sighs. Has Florian Dascălu ever seen this place? Maybe it's a fairytale after all.

SIXTEEN

COTTAGE IN THE SNOW

A LEXANDER STEPS DOWN FROM the sleigh, boots sinking into powdery drifts as he crosses to a periwinkle-blue door tucked beneath snow-laden eaves. Before he can lift a hand to knock, the door swings open.

The professor stands framed in the doorway, short and sturdy, fastening the last buttons of her coat. She'd probably been on her way out to shovel, Maren thinks. She clasps Alexander's hand, then glances past him with a smile, waving to Maren and motioning her in from the cold.

Just your standard storybook cottage. Maren smiles to herself as she takes in the scene. A fire burns low in the large, central stone fireplace, its glow falling over a faded olive-green sofa flanked at right angles by two paisley-patterned English roll-arm chairs on brass casters. There is a low, rustic coffee table between them, the surface lost beneath towers of books. One precarious stack is crowned with a basket of mismatched, home-grown apples.

Beyond the chairs, a small, bright kitchen centers on a butcher-block island almost too big for the space. By the window, a single coffee cup sits atop a round table draped in red-and-white checks. The air is rich with wood smoke and pine, and the sweet promise of something delicious baking in the oven. Open shelves hold old blue-and-white china, a nest of copper pots, and an assortment of well-loved pitchers and bowls, without a trace of dust anywhere. Despite its diminutive size, Maren can easily imagine living here. This is a house made for friends and laughter, a place no one ever seems in a hurry to leave.

Alexander takes Maren's coat, and as she turns, the woman steps forward, offering her hand. "I'm Maria Antonescu; please call me Maria."

Maren shakes her hand, introducing herself, then looks down and notices a small gray dog seated patiently nearby, watching with unblinking attention. "Hello there," she says. His floppy brown ears lift and twitch at the sound.

Turning to the professor, she smiles. "His eyes are so solemn and wise."

"That's Béla," Maria replies affectionately. "He knows a warm heart when he finds one."

Soon Maren is settled on the sofa with a steaming porcelain mug of the most delicious hot chocolate she's ever tasted. It is deep and rich, luxuriously thick, but not overly sweet, with hints of coffee and vanilla, crowned with a dollop of whipped cream. So, she muses, this is the cocoa they serve in fairytales. Béla is curled against her thigh and sighs as she idly ruffles his fur.

Maria joins Alexander, and together they clear a path from the door to the lane. Minutes later, she comes back inside and sinks into a chair by the fire with Maren. From somewhere beyond the walls, Maren hears the clean, ringing crack of an axe. Then the door opens again and Alexander steps in, cheeks flushed from the cold, with an armful of freshly split logs, trailed by the honeyed scent of linden wood.

He lowers the load beside the hearth and kneels to add a log to the fire, coaxing the embers until the flames leap. Straightening, he stands with his back to the blaze, rubbing his hands briskly, the orange light sharpening the hard planes of his face. Maren exhales, silently chiding herself for feeling a little light-headed when she looks at him.

In her armchair, Maria watches them both, teacup paused halfway to her lips, with the kind of contemplative curiosity that makes Maren wonder how much she's already guessed. "So," she says in her accented English, "you have questions for an old history professor?"

"Yes," Maren says, "and thank you for seeing us on such short notice. I had hoped you might know something about the Sorbonne Society and a talisman necklace."

Maria grows thoughtful. "Talismans, memories. They travel too, just as you have."

Maren smiles, her hand absently stroking Béla's soft fur.

"My mother," Maria begins, "Elisabeta Cantacuzino, left Bucharest for Paris in 1937, carrying with her all the advantages and burdens of old Romanian nobility. At the Sorbonne, she became known not just for her intellect but for the company she kept, because among her closest friends were Mathilde de Sévigny and Annette de Beaumont, daughters of old French families."

The wind rattles softly at the window, and Maren exchanges a glance with Alexander.

"Mathilde was my great-grandmother." Alexander says, riveted.

The professor nods. "Yes, your great-grandmothers. The girls were inseparable for a time. I think there was something urgent about those friendships then, not just youth or ambition, but the shared sense that the world they knew was ending. They wanted to understand how power worked—how it could be misused, or loosed upon the vulnerable, to every-one's detriment."

She pauses, and for a moment her eyes seem far away. "It was in those café-lit years that Elisabeta was introduced to the Sorbonne Society. It had been formed after World War I, but lived mostly in hearsay and speculation, drawing students and scholars intent on safeguarding precious art and artifacts. Clandestinely if necessary. Then, another war loomed. Paris changed."

Alexander moves from his place in front of the fire to the sofa, taking a seat beside Maren. He leans forward, forearms resting on his knees, hands loosely clasped.

The professor folds her hands in her lap. "Your mothers will know more than I do about your great-grandmothers," she admits. "My mother volunteered in the decorative arts department at the Louvre. It seems two young French women, students at the Sorbonne, also volunteered there just before the occupation began."

She glances between Maren and Alexander.

Alexander's brow furrows. "You think—?"

Maria's answer is simple, but charged. "My mother never shared specifics, but there are letters suggesting that, beyond friendship, she and your great-grandmothers worked closely together at the museum."

"The secrets they shared, I think, forever sealed the bond forged in those years. The legend of the Talisman jewels wound through all their lives, shaping their futures and form-ing their legacies. It has touched our families, yours and mine, for generations."

Maren feels the layers of history opening up, not just as pages from a textbook, but as a living inheritance; a network of choices and ties running straight from Elisabeta, Mathilde, and Annette, to herself and Alexander.

"In 1939, just before the occupation, the Society hid arti-facts and art," says Maria. "They helped others, objects and people, quietly leave France. I'm sure you've heard the stories about the curators at the Louvre, how they spirited away masterpieces into safekeeping before the city fell. It's rumored the Talisman parure was among them."

Maren glances at Alexander, reading the same astonish-ment and gravity mirrored on his face, recognizing perhaps that this story is bigger, older, more tangled than either of them imagined. Their families linked for generations by the depth of this saga, still rippling through time.

The professor continues, "Then, around 1941, as the city struggled under occupation, Elisabeta escaped back to Roma-nia with help from her friends."

Maren rises to heat water for tea, enjoying the small do-mestic gesture. The professor calls to her in the kitchen. "There's a plate of sandwiches in the refrigerator, and cookies on the counter, Maren. Bring those over too."

She returns with the teapot, plates, and napkins on a tray, offering it first to Maria, then to Alexander. As she sits down again, their shoulders brush. He glances at her and angles him-self so the contact remains. Not crowding, just near enough that she feels the deliberate choice of it. She tucks her legs beneath herself, and he makes no move to shift away, his arm radiating a warmth to match the fire. He looks perfectly content, despite a lifetime in far grander rooms, Maren thinks, and she can't help but feel they'd be at ease anywhere, so long as they were together.

"In Romania, Elisabetta and her wide circle of friends became a bridge between resistance movements from across Central and Eastern Europe. From clues in the coded letters between the girls and local stories, I think she may have brought the necklace back with her from France and helped it get from Romania to Venice or Istanbul."

"The girls were asked to risk more than anyone outside the walls of the Louvre could imagine, on dangerous work entrusted only to a chosen few."

"Because of their family names?" Maren asks.

"Yes, in part. I believe they were expected to do the right thing. And they did. Somehow, those three brave young women managed to protect the ancient Talisman parure, which is not only exquisite and irreplaceable, but said to be powerful as well," the Professor replies.

The professor gazes into the fire. "I think there were many things my mother did not dare say directly. But she preserved letters and coded messages. That informal archive became part of our family's private history, passed down from mother to daughter."

"Okay, but can we back up a little?" Alexander looks between Maren and Maria. "How did an Ottoman parure end up in Venice in 1920, and then how did it get to France in the first place?"

"Well," Maren lets the history run through her mind. "The Ottoman Empire existed for six hundred years. It was one of the largest and most powerful empires on earth. At its height, it spanned two million square miles."

Alexander says, "Remarkable, isn't it? It included western Asia, southeastern Europe, northern Africa, and the Caucasus."

"Yes," Maren says, smiling at him. "Cracks had already begun, but World War I shattered what remained of the Empire. The upheaval meant shifting borders and collapsing fortunes."

"It makes sense that Anatolia, now Turkey, of course, was thrown into chaos. You're saying that in the mayhem, priceless artifacts that had belonged to sultans or old families were sold or traded?" Alexander asks.

Maria nods, settling deeper into her chair. "That's correct." She hesitates, then adds, "But a terrible legend also runs through this history. They say the empire's last days were partly brought about when a scheming courtier kidnapped the princess who owned the Talisman parure. To gain power, he forced her to reveal the names and secrets of his rivals. He raised an army and crushed or jailed anyone who might stop him. The court turned against itself. Alliances broke; innocents perished. Destroyed by guilt, the princess leapt from the palace cliffs into the Bosphorus. Some say she placed a curse on the parure. In the madness, the jewels were hidden beneath the palace but later found by treasure hunters during the scavenging that followed the empire's collapse."

Maren meets Alexander's eyes and sees in them the dawning certainty that what brought them here, across countries and generations, isn't only a legend but the unfinished work of their own family's history.

"After 1918," Maria continues, "Western archaeologists, collectors, and fortune-seekers flocked to Anatolia, eager to scour Ottoman ruins. If the stories are true, the necklace was discovered on the body of a treasure hunter lost in the interior. Two years later, it surfaced at an auction in Venice, along with other pieces of the parure."

"Of course," Maren offers. "Venetian auction houses were always a crossroads for displaced treasures."

Alexander leans in, intrigued. "And the Louvre acquired the parure?"

"Yes," Maria says, "the parure was at the Louvre. At least until 1939. But the jewels never entered the public galleries and were removed from records."

"Why?" asks Maren, mesmerized.

Maria's voice lowers. "The stories say they were displayed briefly after arriving and caused such distress, the museum never showed them publicly again. A woman collapsed, overcome by a vision that foretold her husband's death. Rumors spread: the public wanted the parure destroyed; others wanted it sold. Instead, the jewels were sealed away in a special vault, lost to public memory. The Sorbonne Society intervened when it became critical to move valuable artifacts out of France."

Alexander says, "I have heard that the director of the French National Museums, Jacques Jaujard, orchestrated the evacuation of the Louvre's art collection in 1939. But I was under the impression that this evacuation was meticulously planned. That each piece was cataloged and assigned a destination away from Paris."

"That is true," the professor replies, "but the pieces of the parure were not included in the documents, and the jewelry slipped into shadow. I believe that is, in fact, how it survived. Adolf Hitler was very serious about finding anything that he believed would give him a military advantage."

"How many pieces escaped France? And where did the jewels all go?" Maren asks.

Maria exhales softly and gives a small shrug. "If my mother knew, she never said."

"My mother has spent her life searching for the necklace in particular," Alexander says. "She never told us there were other pieces. But when Maren and I found a pair of earrings in a Budapest jewelry store that matched Maren's ring, I recognized the design immediately. The earrings and the ring match a bracelet my mother has kept hidden for years."

Maria looks intrigued.

Maren brushes her fingers over her ring, nodding slowly. "And then there is this ring. It feels like a current. And when I'm wearing it and the earrings, I feel... energy. And clarity. As if something inside me is lit up."

Maria studies her for a long moment, then says simply, "Wait here."

She disappears down the hallway. When she returns, she carries a gold locket on a braided gold chain, along with a tiny gold key tied to a pink silk ribbon. A starburst is cut out of the head of the key, but it's the only detail in an otherwise unremarkable design.

"This locket was my mother's," she says, holding it out. "And the key was among her belongings when she died. She wore it as a charm on another gold chain. It is so small, I tied the ribbon around it so it wouldn't get lost."

Maren takes the locket reverently. It's solid in her palm, the front worked in a sunburst. The rays are deeply chased into the gold, flaring outward from a central stone: a vivid turquoise, bright as a summer sky. Maren's ring grows warm on her finger.

The edges of the locket are worn smooth; with faint nicks where it has been turned in someone's fingers again and again. The back is plain save for a shallow dent, as if it once pressed against something hard in a pocket or bag. Crafted with the same care as the face, the hinge is almost invisible.

Maren opens it. Inside is a small photograph: three young women, shoulder to shoulder, in front of the Louvre.

"The one on the right is my mother," Maria says. "The other two... I believe they are your great-grandmothers."

Maren holds it out to Alexander. He studies it, looking for a moment as though he's on the verge of speaking, then only nods, filing something away behind his eyes.

Alexander leans closer. "And the key? How is that connected?"

"Remove the photograph," Maria instructs.

Maren opens the tiny glass cover of the photo and lifts the picture free. Beneath it, etched in script, are the words: La clef est la lumière. She turns the locket toward Alexander.

"The key is the light?" he translates and looks at the professor.

Maria lifts one shoulder. "It could be a password. Or a metaphor. I can't say for certain."

"It's beautiful," Maren says, meaning not only the crafts-manship but the almost-tangible sense of devotion it carries, a connection passed from mother to daughter.

"It's yours now," the professor says with a smile. "My work here is done. And you may need it for the rest of your search."

"There's something I haven't mentioned," Maren says, "something Lucien told me." She turns to Maria. "He's a man we met on the train, who is also trying to find the parure. He is working for a Turkish brotherhood that supposedly wants to protect it."

Maria's eyes sharpen. "I know the group you're talking about. They call themselves the Sevket Society. Most just call them the Turkish Brotherhood. They've existed in one form or another for hundreds of years. They were originally a circle of antiquaries during the Ottoman era, dedicated to preserv-ing certain artifacts they believed held power or significance. Their methods haven't always been gentle, and their motives are... complicated. Protection, sometimes. Other times, con-trol."

She stands. "And now it's late. We'll talk more in the morn-ing. There's only one bedroom, I'm afraid, but the sofa is comfortable enough. I'll bring you blankets."

She vanishes for a moment, then returns with an armful of blankets and plump, linen-covered goose down pillows. "Good night, my dears," she says, retreating down the hall and shutting her door. The cottage falls silent, except for the crackle of the fire and the muted rush of wind as it rattles the eaves.

Alexander eyes the sofa. "You take the sofa."

"And you'll freeze on the floor?" Maren cuts in. "Not hap-pening."

"All right," Alexander says, "we'll call it an agreement be-tween nations. You hold that end of the sofa; I'll hold this one. Any border disputes will be resolved through... mutual negotiation."

Maren smiles. "Peace talks?"

"Exactly," he says, "and if that fails, we may have to consider... joint occupation."

She laughs.

In the little bathroom, Maren brushes her teeth and changes into a pair of gray sweatpants from college, soft from years of wear and washing. She pulls on her old Harvard sweatshirt with a satisfied sigh; it's the one she usually sleeps in, a sign the day is over and she can let go. Not wanting to misplace her strand of pearls, she leaves it on, tucking it safely beneath the sweatshirt. Later, she and Alexander are stretched out at opposite ends of the sofa, a wool blanket lying loosely across them both.

"See. It's all about diplomacy," Alexander says, lacing his hands behind his head.

Maren looks at him across the length of the sofa, thinking about the wild chase she's dragged them on, all because she has questions she can't let go. And yet, he isn't irritated. If Alexander disagrees, he says so, but he has never once demanded she see the world his way, or wished aloud that she were different. He is unfailingly kind to her, yet never waits for her permission to act on his convictions. Sometimes it seems that he just enjoys being in her company.

"Alexander," she asks, half-teasing, "aren't you ever... overwhelmed?"

He meets her eyes. "By you? No, I like the view from wherever you are. Even when you are running us in circles."

Her mouth curves. "Well, that's generous."

"If I didn't want to be here, I wouldn't be." His voice is matter-of-fact. "My mother asked you to find the Talisman for a reason, and I can see she chose well. Like her, you aren't afraid of the world. Both of you think big thoughts, and you keep growing."

You know that saying that people never really change? It's a cliché for a reason. Most people form opinions early on, then spend the rest of their lives carefully avoiding anything that might challenge their ideas. They cling to dogma and comfort, not knowledge. They think it makes them safe.

But you are fearless. You're willing to explore and be changed. That alone makes you more intelligent and beautiful than you realize."

He completely surprises her, and it must show on her face, she thinks.

"I like that I don't scare you," she says softly. The confession is more vulnerable than she intended.

"Not even close." He looks at her thoughtfully, as if he's just learned something more about her.

"I like you. All of you."

She smiles at him, suddenly a little shy.

Alexander's voice drops. "Come here, Maren."

Before she can think of a reason not to, she slides toward him. His arms open; her head settles against his chest, and he adjusts the blanket around them. Outside, a branch scrapes the glass; inside, there is only the solid beat of his heart beneath her cheek.

She tilts her face toward him, her palm resting over his ribs. "Is this part of the diplomatic protocol?"

"Let's call it... an alliance."

Her lips hover near his collar. She tells herself she's only adjusting, but the rasp of stubble and the warmth of his skin pull her closer. She places a soft kiss where his neck and shoulder meet. He inhales sharply. "Maren..." Almost rough. It's a warning, or an invitation.

Before she can decide, she lifts her face to his. His hand slips behind her neck, drawing her into a kiss that deepens quickly.

"You're terrible at international boundaries," he says when they finally break apart.

"Only with friendly countries," she replies, smiling drowsily and kissing the dimple on his chin. She folds herself into the curve of his arm and closes her eyes, listening to the slowing rhythm of two hearts, so close she can't tell which is hers.

Long after the fire fades to ash, the warmth between them remains: a mix of promise, longing, and comfort. For tonight at least, the borders have vanished entirely.

SEVENTEEN

LIKE NIGHT AND DAY

MAREN WAKES TO THE rhythmic crack of splitting wood in an otherwise still morning. Each strike is sharp, followed by a single dull bump as the axe finishes its course through the log. She unwinds her legs from the blanket, sits up on the sofa, stretches, and smiles, remembering last night.

In the kitchen, Professor Antonescu moves between the counter, stove, and table, setting out plates and cutlery. Then she brings a crock of butter, a platter of crisp bacon, a golden-topped quiche, and a pan of cinnamon rolls still warm from the oven.

Maren stands, wearing the gray sweatpants and sweatshirt she slept in, and not quite awake yet. She glimpses Alexander through the window. His coat collar is turned up, breath white in the cold, the axe swinging in clean, precise arcs. She's always been impressed by anyone who can split wood, having tried it herself and learned how much harder it is than it looks: the heft of the axe, the wide swing that uses its weight to bite through the log, and the precision needed to hit dead center.

The path to the lane has been shoveled clear; another is cut through the snow leading to an outbuilding that looks as if it once housed horses. Alexander carries a load of wood to the barn, then stacks more by the front door.

From the kitchen, Maria offers, "Coffee?"

"Oh, yes. Thank you."

"How did you sleep?" Maria asks. "And please help yourself to everything."

"Thank you. Better than well," Maren says, warmth creeping into her cheeks. She takes a sip of coffee and adds a teaspoon of sugar from the bowl on the island, her gaze drifting to the window as she smiles at the memory of Alexander's arms. "It helps to wake up somewhere with a beautiful view. And good company."

She drops into a chair at the table, crossing one leg over the other. Reaching down to scratch Béla under the chin, she can't help thinking she probably looks a lot like him this morning, hair sticking up in every direction. "This really is a lovely house," she says. "Have you always lived here?"

"Thank you, it's my favorite place on earth. And no," Maria replies, settling into the seat across from her and serving herself a slice of quiche. "I spent most of my life teaching at the university in Bucharest. This place," she gestures toward the frosted window and the woods beyond, "is what came after. Close enough to the city for old friends and archives, far enough that the seasons belong to me now."

"Is Mr. Dascălu an old friend? Yesterday he told us to be sure and give you his regards. I can tell he's fond of you," Maren says as she takes a cinnamon roll from the pan.

The professor smiles, almost to herself. "We've known each other for a long time. Our parents were close friends, and we attended school together as children. We were always... very good friends. Then I went to the university, and he moved away to work in Vienna as an apprentice at one of the big auction houses. He's been all over the world, and has only recently come back to Romania for good. He was always sure of himself. Very charming, and like his father, devastatingly handsome." A soft laugh escapes her.

Outside, Alexander stacks the last of the wood by the door. Satisfied, he gathers a small armful and steps inside. A swirl of cold air follows him, snow dusting his shoulders, his cheeks flushed from the work.

"Good morning," Maren says, looking up at him.

He nods and smiles, looking at her just a moment longer than casual, then hangs his coat and accepts the coffee Maria offers. Taking the seat beside her, he wraps his hands around the mug.

Maria watches their exchange, passing him the quiche and bacon. "Florian never had much patience for bureaucracy," she goes on. "Eventually, he began working on his own. Less paperwork, more profit. He's a rogue, but a good man when it matters. He probably got that from his father as well. You may have heard of him—Xavier Dascălu."

"Oh my gosh," Maren exclaims. "He's *that* Dascălu? I knew the name sounded familiar; I just couldn't place it. Of course. Now it makes sense."

Alexander looks puzzled and helps himself to a cinnamon roll. "Should I know him?"

Maren laughs. "No, but I should have. Florian's father was Xavier Dascălu. He was possibly the most talented art forger of the century. Maybe in history. And indirectly, a thorn in my side."

Alexander looks up, curious. "Why is that?"

"Because I come across his work every year."

"That often?" Alexander says, incredulous.

"I'm sure she does," Maria interjects. "Experts estimate that as much as twenty percent, perhaps even more, of the artworks in major museums are mis-attributed or outright forgeries. Xavier was a master at making the impossible pass muster. Even now, no one is sure how many of his pieces are still hanging."

Maren laughs. "And fooling the experts."

Alexander seems intrigued.

"And yes, I have heard he was apparently quite dashing." Maren adds.

Maria says, "What made Xavier peerless is that he could work in nearly any medium. That's likely why Maren finds his forgeries everywhere in her restoration work. Most forgers pick a niche, like oil paintings or sculpture, but Xavier had no such limits. Whatever the craft, he could match the technique precisely. I must say, he did beautiful work."

People assumed his range of skills resulted from arrogance, but knowing Florian's personality, I've always believed it was Xavier's high standards and precision. He had an attention to detail that makes a forger almost impossible to uncover. Florian is just the same. In Romanian, we say: 'Mărul nu cade departe de rădăcină.' The apple does not fall far from the root."

Maren grins. "In English, it's 'the apple doesn't fall far from the tree.'"

Alexander adds, smiling, "And in French: 'Les chiens ne font pas des chats.'"

"Dogs don't make cats?" Maren laughs. "I've never heard that one. Every language must have its own version."

The professor nods. "Florian's father was a remarkable person, and Florian shares more than a little of that. In some ways, he has the same passion. Florian has a knack for finding rare things and keeping them safe. He genuinely cares who ends up with them. That's rare in his business."

A silence settles, companionable, before Maria's gaze drops to Maren's hand as she reaches for another roll. "May I see your ring?"

"Of course." Maren slips off the lapis ring and places it into the professor's palm.

The professor tilts it to the light. "Ah, just as I thought last night."

Maren leans in. "Thought what?"

The professor meets her eyes. "Most assume artifacts like this are born of power: ambition, conquest, acquisition. But the truly remarkable pieces? They are often created from something else entirely." She pauses, studying Maren and Alexander for a moment, then says softly: "Love."

"Love?" Alexander asks.

She nods. "The sultan who commissioned this suite of jewels, couldn't shield his wife from betrayal or the dangers of court, but he could give her this, a talisman, to reveal hidden threats, help her make decisions, and in moments of need, show her exactly what she needed to see. It is said that when the entire parure is united, the wearer gains both protection and foresight."

Alexander rises to refill their coffee cups, the rich, dark aroma curling into the warm kitchen air. "That may explain why so many have tried to seize control of it."

Maria nods, reaching for a large blue-and-white cream pitcher, its crazed glaze betraying its age, and pours a ribbon of cream into her cup. "During the Second World War, the Nazis were obsessed with ancient artifacts, especially ones rumored to have some sort of power. They believed the Talisman could grant visions of military plans and betrayals before they happened."

She looks at Maren. "These are the historical accounts and myths that draw the ambitious to hunt for it, and compel those with foresight to keep it out of reach. And from what you've described, perhaps you've sensed some of its power as well."

Alexander adds, "Árpád Molnár, the jeweler in Budapest, told us he believes that every detail, from the choice of stones to the way they're set, was intended for more than beauty. He is convinced it was designed with purpose."

Maria traces the small engraving on the ring with her finger. "'Nur.' Light. Perhaps each piece of the parure is engraved with that word."

Maren nods. "Mr. Molnár said the same thing."

"I have to believe," the professor goes on, "there's a reason. I suspect it's the idea of Nur that's the true power at the heart of the parure—not darkness, not ambition. Light. Love that lasts forever. Love that illuminates. Sometimes even protects."

Alexander leans back in his chair. "These jewels have survived for a long time despite the odds. Now we know of at least three pieces that are intact."

Maren nods with understanding. "Love makes the parure resilient—just as love makes us resilient. Love isn't always safe, but it holds things together, even after suffering or loss. It sounds as if people have tried to claim the parure for their own purposes, but in the end, its strength comes from devotion, not conquest. I hope that's a power that neither time nor danger can erase."

The professor sets the ring gently on the table. "The presence and spirit of the woman who wears these jewels is not insignificant. She becomes the meeting point of love and light. Remember this, dear, when the pieces come together, what matters is not who owns them, but who is worthy."

"Do you really believe love makes things last?" Maren asks, looking up.

Maria's eyes soften. "Yes. What love creates seems to resist ruin. Even when we fail or make mistakes, love endures where all else falls away. Love prevails in the end. But you must be cautious in seeking these jewels, Maren. There is danger because not everyone pursues them out of love."

The table falls silent; the three of them lost in thought. After a moment, Maren rises reluctantly and heads to the tiny bathroom to shower and dress. She dries her hair and pulls on a soft, pale gray cashmere sweater, her charcoal gray wool trousers from yesterday, and thick wool socks. She tucks her pant legs inside them, anticipating her snow boots. When she returns to the kitchen, Alexander excuses himself. By the time Maren has tidied her things and helped clear the table, he reappears, freshly dressed, and together they bundle into coats and gloves, preparing to step out into the cold.

When the sleigh arrives, the professor walks them out, her hand-knitted scarf wrapped tightly at her neck, Béla trotting at her side.

She takes Maren's gloved hands in hers. "You'll find what you're looking for, Maren, I can feel it. What you're seeking is waiting for you, and in its way, it's seeking you too. But be prepared," she cautions gravely, "there may be a steep price to pay."

As the sleigh pulls away down the lane, Maren looks back at the little cottage and waves.

After a moment, Alexander says, "Do you suppose they were in love, Florian and Maria?"

Maren smiles at him. "If they weren't then, I have a feeling they will be soon."

Eighteen

LUCIEN

M AREN AND ALEXANDER BOARD the train at noon as the staff
readies the carriages for departure. Alexander men-
tions needing to make a few calls to his office and arranges
to meet Maren later for dinner. As they speak in the corridor
outside their cabins, Simone steps out of her suite. She glances
their way, gives Alexander a sly smile, then turns and disappears into the next carriage.

Maren glances at Alexander just in time to see deep concern in his eyes. She says nothing, but silently wishes Simone
hadn't cast a shadow over their cheery morning.

Back in her cabin, a hot shower thaws her frozen toes and
fingers. Maren turns on classical music, rings Daniel for a cup
of tea and a sandwich, and settles onto the sofa. She traces the
symbols on the cover of her father's journal with a fingertip,
then opens to a blank page, intent on capturing everything
they've learned while the day's details are still fresh in her
mind.

A few minutes later, the train manager knocks on her door
to inform her they'll be staying in Bucharest another night
for repairs. Departure for Istanbul is set for noon tomorrow.
Despite the delay, he assures her they're still on schedule, as
one of the planned border stops has been eliminated.

As a token of gratitude for her patience, he presents her with a gift: a large, sapphire-blue silk shawl bordered with long fringes that call to mind the glamour of a 1920s flapper's dress.

Maren runs the heavy silk through her fingers, playing with the fringe before draping the shawl over an arm of the sofa. She settles at the table by the window, opens the journal, and stares into space as she picks up one of the artisan-style potato chips from her plate. She takes a bite, then pauses to study it: crisp, salty, unexpectedly delicious.

Normally, Maren is immune to the siren call of junk food, except for really good chocolate, which she eats almost every day with a sense of ceremony. She doesn't fuss about her diet, and she's never wanted to own a scale. When Ethan broke off their engagement, she suspects she may have gained a few more curves, but her body has carried her farther than she ever expected, with very little complaint. She can only be grateful for it, and appreciate it, whatever size it wants to be.

She pops another chip into her mouth, then glances at the soft gray sweater and tailored wool trousers she chose this morning. Lately, she has been enjoying finer fabrics, low on logos but heavy on comfort. A little daily luxury she had never prioritized before.

Her mother's words come back to her, always half-wicked, half-wise: "French women don't waste time hiding what isn't perfect. We draw attention to what we like, and ignore the rest—et voilà."

Maren remembers her mother standing in front of the mirror, twisting her wild hair into a neat chignon, then adding a silk scarf, sometimes Hermès, almost always vintage, and always tied with flair. "A silk scarf draws the eye, distracts from a tired face, and adds color when the sky is gray. Keep one tucked in your bag so it's always available; ready to brighten a moment or rescue a look. You can tie it around your head like Audrey Hepburn, knot it simply at your neck, loop it as a belt, or, if circumstances demand, improvise an arm sling as Grace Kelly once did. Scarves are little miracles, chérie."

After any heartbreak, her mother would set out a platter of cheese, pour two glasses of red wine, and declare, "No man is worth more than half a baguette and the good brie. We eat, we listen to old chansons, and tomorrow we buy red lipstick and sexy new lingerie." If Maren ever tried to fret about calories or skip dessert, her mother would only wave her off with that musical laugh of hers. "Life is too short for guilt at the table, Maren. We eat real food slowly, savor every bite, and always leave room for chocolate."

Her mother believes in buying one high-quality bag and carrying it for an eternity, the transformative magic of a truly comfortable pair of shoes, crisp white men's shirts from Charvet, old cashmere sweaters, and sleek black pencil skirts. More often than not, she dresses in a uniform of neutral basics: elegant, effortless, and timeless.

Maren's thoughts shift to their meeting with Professor Antonescu. It raised two important questions, and as far as she can tell, there's only one person on this train both clever and well-connected enough to know the answers. Whether he'll actually share them is another matter entirely.

She takes a deep breath, lets it out in a sigh, sets the journal aside, and goes in search of Lucien.

She finds Lucien in a deserted dining car, a glass of wine at his elbow and a newspaper in hand. When he sees her, he rises automatically—a small, almost anachronistic gesture that hints at impeccable manners beneath the cynicism. Everything about him is formal, precise, and just a bit theatrical. He pulls out the chair opposite his for Maren and waves for her to sit.

"I can't believe I'm asking this, because I'm still not convinced you aren't working against me. But... I need your help, Lucien."

Lucien sets his paper aside with an elegant flick, as if discarding an unworthy line in a play, and gives her his full attention, amused.

"Let me tell you something, Miss Bennett. I've been a lot of places—had what most would call an interesting life. Some say I've done questionable things, things that don't fit their neat, fictional version of how the world works. But if there's one thing I know, it's this: in the end, the people who help you are the only ones who matter."

Maren looks at him and says slowly, "What's that supposed to mean?"

Lucien waves a hand, signaling the philosophical detour. "Think about your life. By the way, would you like a glass of wine?"

"Yes, please. I have a feeling that will help," Maren says, with a rueful grin.

Lucien turns in his chair and nods to the waiter. "Would you be so kind as to bring a wine glass for Miss Bennett?" The waiter pours from the bottle on the table and sets the glass down in front of her. "Thank you," Lucien says, and continues.

"The people who stepped in—offered you a hand, opened a door—those are the ones who shaped your direction. Everyone else? Irrelevant. Background noise. Stage dressing."

"Oh, I'm sure your sentimental little heart has been bruised now and then," he leans in "when someone didn't return a favor, or didn't connect you to the right person, didn't give you the job, didn't share the thing they knew. Maybe they even felt important for withholding it. And you thought, 'I needed that help.' You let it sting."

Maren replies thoughtfully, "Well, yes. Actually, that's true."

"You were lying to yourself," Lucien states flatly, sitting back with satisfaction.

Maren takes a sip of her wine, mulling this over. "But plenty of people haven't helped me. Some even go out of their way to make things worse. I swear, some feel good making me feel bad."

Lucien's mouth quirks, the barest suggestion of a smile. "Those people are packing peanuts, Miss Bennett."

Maren blinks, then laughs. "Packing peanuts? You mean those little foam thingies inside shipping boxes?" She shakes her head, grinning. "That's... kind of bleak."

Lucien tips his head, mock-thoughtful. "Is it? I call it scale. Maybe you're wildly popular, Miss Bennett, and everyone who's ever helped you could fill Wembley Stadium. Good for you. The rest? Filler."

He gestures, as if wiping invisible crumbs from a table. "There are eight billion people in the world. There will always be more who don't help you than do. Unless someone takes positive action in your life, or, to put it pragmatically, unless you allow them to exist for you, they're invisible."

Maren frowns, intrigued despite herself. "What about the people who actively try to stop me?" She looks at him pointedly. "Like, for example, you?"

Lucien folds his hands in his lap. "People like me, who get in your way are no different from those who don't help at all. If a tree falls across the road, do you simply give up? Of course not; you'll find a way around. And sometimes, the detour reveals better paths than the one you thought you wanted."

Maren thinks about this, and then, "When have you ever not gotten what you want in life, Lucien?"

He arches an eyebrow, faintly amused. "Hasn't happened yet, Miss Bennett. Perhaps that's because I never mistake a fallen branch for a dead end."

Maren admits, "I wanted to get married once. He called it off."

Lucien fixes her with a steady look and that signature half-smile. "Did you really want to marry him?"

She considers. "I thought I did. Not now, I suppose," thinking of Alexander.

"Well then," Lucien says, "he did you a favor didn't he?"

Maren nods, understanding dawning. "So in a nutshell, or a peanut shell, according to you, everything that happens, or doesn't happen, benefits me somehow?"

Lucien waves a hand in a small, dismissive arc. "If it helps you to embrace the philosophical, Miss Bennett, yes. That's correct."

He gives her a sardonic, self-satisfied smile. "Packing peanuts. Remember that. Just there to fill the box so you can get to what actually matters. Ignore them, work around them, but don't let them stop you."

"Even you." Maren says.

"Even me." He leans in, voice low, "Now, what is it you really want to know, Miss Bennett?"

Maren meets his gaze. "I want to know who else knows there are more pieces in the parure, and who understands that the pieces increase in power when they are put together."

Lucien swirls the wine in his glass, amused and shrewd. "You're asking the right questions at last. Most seek the jewels for their monetary value. Only a handful know what the full parure can do when assembled, or that there are more pieces than just the necklace. Myself, several old men in the Turkish Brotherhood, most of them more cautious than clever, and just now, you and Alexander. If you're wise, you'll keep that knowledge as close as the necklace itself."

"What about Simone? Does she know?" Maren asks.

He gives a sharp, dismissive laugh. "Simone? She wants the necklace, but only because she wants revenge, and she thinks denying the necklace to Alexander would be a coup. The finer points of its history would bore her inside of five minutes. Nevertheless," he says, a little smile lifting one corner of his lips, "you'll want to avoid her if possible, Miss Bennett. I don't believe she wishes you well."

Maren takes that in, her voice tightening. "If you know what it can do, if you know the risk, why not keep it out of everyone's hands?"

"That, Miss Bennett, is precisely my job. But the world is... slippery. Should you manage to find a way to secure the pieces—truly secure them, beyond the reach of anyone who would abuse their power—well, let's say I would not stand in your way."

Maren studies Lucien. "Then who tried to steal the ring and earrings in Budapest? Was it one of the Brotherhood or Simone?"

"Neither," Lucien says, almost lightly. "That was me."

Maren is momentarily speechless. "You? And did you take my father's journal too?"

Lucien merely shrugs.

She narrows her eyes at him. "You could have just asked."

"Where's the fun in that, Miss Bennett?" Lucien leans back, unruffled. "Besides, you handled it better than most. Which is why we're having this conversation now." Lucien waves the idea away. "Nonsense. It all worked out, didn't it?"

"If you know I have the ring and the earrings, why don't you just take them?"

Lucien arches an eyebrow. "How do you know I won't? I've been tasked with securing all the pieces of the parure. And believe me, I intend to do it, one way or another."

She lets out a breath, steadying herself. "You keep saying 'secure.' But for whom? Would you really turn something this dangerous over to the Turkish Brotherhood?"

He glances away and scowls. "If you want the honest answer, I'm not entirely certain they're the best destination for it. But I have a job to do. That means recovering the entire parure, and keeping it out of the wrong hands."

Maren softens her voice. "What do I have to do, Lucien, so that no one gets hurt over this?"

He considers her, the faintest trace of regret in his eyes. "You'll have to dodge every ne'er-do-well who wants to take it from you," he says, cocking his head as if that's an impossible task, "and do what I'm trying to do: safely secure all the pieces. Every single one." He tilts his head and raises an eyebrow. "And of course, make sure they never fall into anyone's hands, including mine, that will sell them or use them nefariously. That's a tall order, Miss Bennett. Most people who have tried have gotten lost along the way, or... worse."

She looks away, tension running through her shoulders, wondering about her father. "And if I can't?"

Lucien smiles, "Then I'll do my job. But I'll admit, there are times when a little misdirection is useful. Not everything that glitters is quite what it seems. Think carefully about that, Miss Bennett. You might even find that much in this unfolding story is not what it seems."

"What does that mean?"

"That Miss Bennett is for you to figure out." His words are sharpened by the trace of threat in his eyes, and something darker. "Surely you don't expect me to throw you the game now, do you?"

Her phone buzzes. "Pardon me," she says, glancing down. It's a message from Alexander, inviting her to his cabin for dinner.

"Thank you, Lucien. I think."

He stands. "Always a pleasure, Miss Bennett."

In her cabin, Maren runs her fingers through her hair and changes into jeans. No makeup. No shoes. She pads over in her socks and knocks on Alexander's door.

He opens it.

Dinner is already set out on the small table: two plates, silver cutlery, and champagne. She grins at the contrast and looks at Alexander. His usual armor seems a little less in place.

"I ordered for us," he says. "Do you like hamburgers?"

"Love them."

"And fries?"

"Of course."

They sit and eat, feet brushing beneath the table. Everything tastes better than it should, hot and familiar, like calm after an exhausting storm.

Maren recounts her conversation with Lucien, laughter bubbling up as she speaks. "You know, he's honestly kind of wise," she says, then thinks of his parting line. "Even if he is opaque. And scary. But the terms are clear: we have to find all the pieces of the Talisman and... somehow... make sure they're safe. I just have no idea how to do that yet. Any ideas?"

Alexander sets down his water glass. "I'll give it some thought."

She dips a French fry in his ketchup and says, "I think I need to go to Venice. Something about Saint Mark's Basillica has been nudging me ever since this started. Maybe there's a connection, and I might be able to find a clue there that no one's mentioned so far."

"While I'm in Istanbul?" Alexander asks.

"Yes," Maren says. "I think so, don't you? You could check with your sources there before the ball."

"You really want me to let you go alone?" he asks, sitting back in his chair.

"I really don't want to go by myself," she replies sincerely. "But after talking to Lucien, I feel like we're running out of time."

He nods slowly, thoughtfully.

"Good," she grins.

"Good?"

"Because I already made a reservation for tomorrow." Maren says.

He raises an eyebrow, but says nothing. They chat and joke as they finish eating; the easy intimacy of the past few days, and their shared purpose, Maren thinks, are bringing them closer. She feels happy. Hopeful.

But then Alexander looks at her and hesitates, a familiar guardedness returning to his eyes.

"Okay, which version is the real you?" she asks softly. "Sometimes it feels like the curtain's parted, then suddenly it closes again. You have to help me understand that, Alexander. I don't know how to cross this distance."

Alexander doesn't speak for a second. And when he does, his voice is lower.

"There are decisions I've made. Things I've done, Maren. Things I need to make right before..." And he stops.

"Before what? Before...me?" she asks softly.

He glances down, adjusting his watch—a gesture she recognizes now. She nods, half to herself. "Well, yes," he admits.

"What have I done to you, Alexander? What could you possibly have done to me? What is it you need to make right?"

He says nothing more, and she knows the subject is closed.

A few minutes later, she stands, and he walks her to the door. He cups her face in his hands, tracing her lower lip with his thumb before leaning in to kiss her.

Back in her cabin, Maren tries to read a book but finds herself restless and on edge. If only he would let her in, she thinks, they might figure this out together. What does he believe he's done to her?

She sets the novel aside and undresses, catching her reflection in the lamplight. Bare skin, the length of her legs. She wraps the new silk shawl under her arms, letting the fringe brush and swirl against her hips. Barefoot, on instinct, she slips into the corridor and tries Alexander's door. Unlocked, just as she knew it would be.

His cabin is dark except for the blur of lights occasionally streaming past the window. Alexander stands with his back to the door, gazing out at the endless black countryside, his silhouette in shadow as he slowly works at the buttons on his cuffs. At the soft click of the door, he turns.

The train rocks gently under her feet, and she moves across the room toward him. The silence between them is heavy with every touch, every word they've withheld, and all that could be.

She steps close. Close enough to feel the heat of his body, to see the raw desire in his eyes. She unties the silk scarf and lets it fall to the floor. Slowly, deliberately, she unbuttons his shirt, her palms gliding over the warmth of his chest. His arms close around her, drawing her in, and her fingers lace behind his neck, his hair cool and soft against her skin. The entire world is this moment. The dark, quiet room, his breath warm against her cheek as he lowers his mouth to hers. She rises on tiptoe, pressing kisses to his cheek, along the line of his jaw and the curve of his throat, breathing him in, memorizing the way he smells and the feel of his skin beneath her lips.

He answers her—utterly, fiercely. One arm locks around her waist; the other finds the small of her back, anchoring her against him. His mouth claims hers again—wild, hungry—pulling her into that place where all the ache of sleepless nights finally breaks free. Her body is alive with longing and a rush of something that feels dangerously close to fear.

For a breathless, unmoored instant, he opens to her completely.

Then, slowly, so gradually she barely senses the shift, his kiss changes. Softer now. His hands stay on her but no longer draw her in. His lips slow, his breath ragged, and he presses a gentle kiss to her temple, eyes closed. A low groan escapes him.

She wants to beg him not to stop, but the words won't come.

"Maren," he whispers. "I can't do this. With you." His fingers trail down her cheek, and she feels the loss like a door closing just as she's about to cross the threshold.

"You can't do this with me?" Her voice breaks on the last word.

Maren steps back, repelled by the intense loss, letting her arms fall to her sides. She meets his eyes just once, then looks away. When she turns and leaves, she doesn't look back.

In her own dark compartment, Maren feels the injustice of it keenly. She knows he wants her, feels it in his touch, sees it in his eyes. And yet, something always holds him back. Why?

A bitter thought flares: will he ever let her in, or is she destined to remain on the outside, begging for scraps of the self he offers so freely to other women? She craves to be chosen, to be trusted, to finally, finally crack the shell of this maddening, beautiful man.

She lies awake, angry at him for pulling away, angrier still at herself for wanting him anyway. Knowing with cold certainty that she may never get all the way through.

There's nothing wrong with you, he'd said as she left. I just need some time to figure things out.

Fine, Maren thinks. Take all the time you need, Alexander.

The train is silent in the early morning. She doesn't write a note; anything she could say would feel like a footnote, too much, or not enough.

Mist hangs pale outside the windows, softening the edges of everything. She walks the corridor alone, each step muted by the carpet, coat buttoned to the chin. She carries only one bag, leaving the rest behind. Her old backpack, the one that's traveled everywhere with her, is a familiar, grounding weight in her hand. She feels different now, though: surer of herself. Whatever comes next, she knows she's no longer the woman who first boarded this train in Paris.

She doesn't glance at his door. Doesn't trust herself to.

Maybe he's still asleep, shirt half-buttoned, dark hair tousled on his pillow. Maybe he'll wake soon and expect to see her. Maybe he won't expect anything, and her absence will mean very little to him at all. He'll probably frown when Daniel tells him she left. Rub the back of his neck. Dress slowly. Say nothing.

She imagines him pausing at her door, just for a moment. She imagines him not.

There had been a moment the night before, at the dinner table, when she'd been sure he was about to say something important, something real, but it passed and didn't come back. She's done waiting for the next almost.

She steps off the train. The wind is sharp, the station still half-asleep. Outside, a single cab idles at the curb. She climbs in without hesitation.

She doesn't look back.

NINETEEN

RETURN TO SAINT MARK'S

THE LIT DOMES OF Saint Mark's Basilica loom against a black slice of Venetian sky. Maren watches the last of the evening tours spill out of the illuminated portico, their voices shivering through the square before fading into the dark. She adjusts the lanyard around her neck as she walks toward the staff entrance, making sure her pass from the Procuratia di San Marco, with her name and photograph stamped in official ink, rests squarely over her coat. She picked it up that morning, after the approval arrived from the Smithsonian's Department of Medieval Art. The fax listed her as a registered researcher assigned to document pigment conditions in mosaics in the north transept. It was arcane but plausible, just official enough to keep questions to a minimum.

She'd contacted the Smithsonian the day before, mentioned she was in Venice, and offered—if they were interested—to document the current condition and color integrity of the thirteenth-century Cosmati mosaics in the north transept at Saint Mark's. Free of charge, of course. If that suited, could they please fax her credentials to the Basilica office?

A text reply from Jillian Marchand, Head of Medieval Manuscripts and Decorative Arts at the Smithsonian, arrived almost immediately—warm, enthusiastic, and grateful. Maren has collaborated with her department for years, most recently assisting in the restoration of the Adoration of St. Joan of Arc, a highlight of the medieval collection. The project drew praise from the American Art Journal and, even more unusually, earned coverage in The Washington Post and The New York Times. Jillian had laughed at the time, telling Maren, "We take those moments when we can. Medieval art rarely makes headlines unless knights start jousting in the sculpture garden."

And now, here Maren is, doing her best to look confident, professional, and just bored enough to suggest she does this sort of thing every day.

"Buonasera, signorina. You have a pass?" The guard on duty glances at the badge at her neck.

"Hello," Maren greets him, her tone friendly but businesslike. "I'm Maren Bennett, with the Smithsonian. I understand I'm to show you this pass from the Procuratia di San Marco to receive my badge?"

She offers the laminated permit. The guard studies it, then turns to a clipboard hanging on the wall and runs a finger down the list of names. Finding hers, he bends to find a plastic sleeve of badges in the desk, rifling through until he draws one out. Holding it up, he compares the photo to her face, then glances back to the image on the permit to be sure.

"You're with the Smithsonian? Visiting?"

Maren replies, "It's a working trip. I'm documenting pigment conditions on the Cosmati mosaics in the north transept." She taps the spine of the notebook under her arm.

He nods, reaching for a badge. "The barcode will open only the doors for which you've been approved. You are cleared for one hour. At,"—he checks his watch—"ten o'clock, you return to this door. You will exit here and only here." His tone is matter-of-fact, but exacting.

He explains the rest: "Your time and photograph will be recorded on this camera. Look here... good. When the light turns green, scan your badge at this reader." He points to the panel. "Once scanned at the end of your session, the badge will void—no reentry. Make sure you have all you came for before you leave."

A beep signals approval. He passes her the badge and gestures toward the interior door. Maren scans in; the latch releases with a metallic click. She steps through, the heavy door closing behind her, solid and ominous. A reminder that tonight, some doors will only open once.

Maren moves toward the river of mosaics on the floor, the winding path of inlaid tiles drawing her deeper into the still nave. The silence of the Basilica stretches around her, vast and watchful.

She follows the marble river to the place it vanishes at the base of a smooth stone wall. Just above eye level, the winged lion waits in its carved circle, its gaze fixed and eternal.

She studies it as she did weeks ago. Then she'd thought it only ornamentation, symbolic at best. But now the ring is on her hand, and there's a steady, insistent awareness pulsing through it.

"Yes, but what? What am I missing?"

She steps closer and raises her hand, in slow, reverent arcs tracing the carved circle that encloses the lion. The stone is cold beneath her fingertips. Her eyes close. I need guidance. If ever there was a moment... she draws a breath, and then... clarity, not spoken but simply known.

She hears Professor Antonescu's voice in her mind:

The lion is a guardian. The circle is eternity, the unbroken bond, the sacred convergence.

"Okay," she whispers. "But what now? What are you trying to tell me? I don't understand."

She looks down, frustrated. You've got to hurry, Maren, she thinks, searching the floor for something—anything—until the answer suddenly surfaces: her father's journal. *Never judge a book by its cover,* Lucien had said. Carved into the cover is a vesica piscis—two intersecting circles. She needs to find a vesica piscis. Thank you, thank you, Lucien, she breathes. If he were here, she would hug him, she thinks. Then almost laughs at the thought of the look on his face.

She circles the base of the wall, eyes combing mosaic and shadow. On the far side, worn by centuries, she finds it: two faint interlocking circles with a starburst radiating from their heart. Love and light.

Of course, she thinks. Love and light fused. Not just touching but holding, illuminating, protecting. The rightness of it settles deep in her chest, answering in an instant every question that has haunted her: why the Talisman endures, why people have risked everything to keep it whole. The Talisman's true power is activated at the intersection of these two forces. It isn't simply about possessing the artifact; it's about bringing into harmony the qualities it symbolizes.

Would anyone else see something remarkable in the symbol? Or would they only see a trick of geometry, nothing more? Set into the floor just above the symbol is a dull bronze square. A shape made precisely for her ring.

She bends, takes off the ring and presses the lapis into the cutout. Warmth blooms through her fingers. Nur: light, love, the promise her father was never able to say aloud. Somewhere nearby, stone grinds and air shifts.

Straightening, she scans the alcove, searching for the source. Her gaze lifts to the saints, Matthew and Mark, still serene at their post. This time, the angle of their gaze draws her attention; she pivots, circling the wall again.

There it is: a narrow vertical seam in the wall beneath the winged lion, the outline so fine she might have missed it entirely if not for the faint change in the air and the dry scent of dust and disturbed history.

She pushes. The stone gives. She pushes again, and the stone moves backward, creating a crevice barely wider than her arm. Maren steels herself and slips her hand slowly into the dark slit. Rough stone scrapes her skin, growing colder the deeper she reaches. Just when she's certain she can go no farther, her fingertips brush fabric, something wedged tight in the recess.

She curls her hand around it, prying, twisting until it comes free.

It's a pouch. Pulse racing, she cradles it to her chest, hurrying back around the column to the bronze recess to retrieve her ring. As she slips it free, the scraping sound comes again, stone sliding shut behind her. The seam underneath the lion is gone again, as if the hidden space had never existed.

Holding her breath, Maren loosens the drawstrings and eases the necklace into the light. The air in the Basilica seems to contract around it. "Wow," she whispers.

The pendant is a large oval of lapis lazuli, midnight blue and dusted with tiny gold flecks like a private constellation, its surface framed in a halo of plump rose-cut diamonds that give off a soft, candlelit shimmer. From the lower edge, generous teardrop emerald cabochons, lush and green as wet leaves, descend in a fringe, each one anchored by more diamonds that ripple upward in an endless loop around the neck. Beneath the lapis, at the very tip, a single drop of vivid turquoise swings gently, catching the faint Basilica light like a final, impossible note of color.

She turns the necklace over, her fingertips gliding over the mellowed yellow gold, tracing its curves and joins. The metal is cool and heavy; and she loses track of time in its ancient presence.

A jolt of apprehension, a flash unbidden, of the guard's approach, as if she's already seen it before. Heart beating hard, she hooks the necklace around her throat, tucking the gemstones beneath her shirt. The empty pouch disappears into the deep pocket of her coat.

She rounds the column just as the guard's silhouette emerges from the dim, his edges haloed by the faint gold light spilling from the nave.

"I'm sorry, your time is up. Did you get what you came for?" His voice is gruff, although not unkind. A man bound by rules, not malice.

Maren makes herself smile. "Yes, thank you," she says, "everything I needed."

She lifts her notebook, her usual shield. "Can I just leave this badge with you?"

He nods, extending his hand for her staff pass. Maren places it in his palm, holding his gaze, making sure her composure never cracks, even as the necklace presses its cold secret against her collarbone.

He walks her down the corridor, waits while the camera flashes her exit, then presses the release. "Have a good evening, signorina."

"You too," she replies, stepping outside as the door snicks shut behind her. The night is colder now, the smell of salt water in the breeze.

She pulls her coat tight and crosses Saint Mark's Square, half-blind with adrenaline and the rush of victory. She keeps moving, weaving past the darkened alleys that fringe the piazza.

Suddenly, a hard hand clamps across the back of Maren's neck, and she's shoved face-first into the side of a brick building. Air is knocked out of her lungs with the impact.

"Give me the necklace, Maren. Don't be an idiot," Simone hisses at her ear—the voice too close, and horribly familiar.

Maren's mind flashes: the vision on the train, replaying now in sawtooth detail. She holds a knife in one hand, inches from Maren's face, and unhooks the necklace with the other.

Simone looks over her shoulder and swears under her breath. Maren twists just enough to see Alexander rounding the corner, breaking into a run.

"Let her go, Simone. You got what you came for," he says, his voice dangerously calm.

Simone lets go, but doesn't lower the knife, so neither Maren nor Alexander dare move.

"Thank you both. Now, just one more thing." She fixes her eyes on Alexander, though her words are for Maren: "He used you, darling. That's what he does. He used your expertise to get the Talisman because he couldn't get it on his own. He planned it all, and you fell for it. The only thing he hadn't planned on was my finding out the truth and getting this stupid necklace. If you're thinking I'll sell, think again; the rich playboy would just buy it for his mother. Oh, and Maren," she adds, her expression scathing, "ask pretty boy what happened in Venice."

Then, glaring icily at Alexander, she says, "And now, darling. We are even." Her laugh rings out, and she spins, disappearing into the darkness.

The square is deserted. A gauzy haze bends time and warps the glow of streetlights, softening the edges of the palazzi and concealing the details of a thousand years. Bone-deep damp rises from the lagoon, creeping steadily inland, phantoms gliding over cobblestones and bridges, crawling up steps, coiling around windows and doors.

Maren stands motionless in the mist. Breathing hard. Her shoulders slump, and she sighs. "What happened in Venice, Alexander? I want the truth. All of it."

"I was there," he says softly. "The night your father died."

She can barely form the words. "You were... in Venice?"

"Yes."

She searches his face. "Tell me how he died. Who killed him?"

With a quiet sigh, Alexander answers, "No one killed your father. He had a heart attack. Collapsed underground. There was gas or residue in the tunnel, something toxic. He was working alone, as always."

"How do you know that? Why were you in Venice?" Maren asks, struggling to process it all.

"I worked with your father. I should have realized he was in over his head, but I thought I was helping by putting him in touch with people who could give him access to the places and information he needed. We arranged to meet that night. He didn't wait. By the time I found him, it was too late."

Her hands tremble. "Why? Why were you working with my father? How did you even know him?"

"I didn't," Alexander says simply. "I tried to stay out of all this business with the Talisman. But he contacted my mother, said he'd made a breakthrough, told her you were busy and didn't want to pull you away. I happened to be in Venice on business, so she asked me to reach out and see if there was anything I could do."

"So you were the last person he talked to?" Maren's voice is small in the fog.

"Yes."

"Why didn't you tell me? Why didn't the police tell me you were there?"

Alexander's answer is quiet, unflinching. "Because I left."

Pain swells beneath her anger. "You left him? In the tunnel. Alone?" Maren says in disbelief.

He holds her gaze, voice steady. "I spoke to him before he died. After that... he was gone."

Her voice shakes. "You left him there. Alone."

He doesn't look away. "It's what he wanted, Maren. He realized that something was terribly wrong. He told me to go." Alexander's voice is soft, and sadness shadows his eyes. "His last words were about you, and the ring he'd found. I think he realized too late that the air down there was dangerous. He said if I stayed, I'd die too. If anyone else found out, they'd just take the ring. He wanted you to have it. He believed it would keep you safe."

Maren covers her mouth, fighting back tears and disbelief. "So that was you that night outside St. Mark's. You gave me the ring."

"Yes," he says.

"Who else knows this?"

Alexander's jaw tightens, but he doesn't answer. The silence says enough.

"Let me guess. Simone was with you in Venice," Maren says, struggling to catch her breath.

Alexander shakes his head, calm but weary. "I ended things with Simone before that night at Saint Mark's."

He meets her eyes. "When I gave you the ring, she had already left."

Maren's voice trembles. "Why? Why would you do that?"

He hesitates, the hurt slipping through his self-control. "I loved her. But after she overheard a conversation between my mother and me about the Talisman, something changed. We both did, I suppose. She grew obsessed. Ruthless. I didn't recognize her anymore." He searches for the right words, then finally: "And then..."

She wipes tears from her cheeks, her voice breaking. "What? And then what, Alexander?"

He barely whispers it, but his eyes never leave hers. "There was you."

"Me? You didn't even know me," Maren says.

Alexander's gaze shifts toward the far edge of the square. "When your father texted you to come to Venice, we were in a cafe. That one, right over there." He nods slightly in the direction, and she can see the conflict on his face—pain, regret, something like wonder.

"He showed me a photo of you," Alexander says softly. "You were the girl in my painting."

Maren's anger falters.

He meets her eyes. There's no anger, only truth. "When I saw you at Saint Mark's... you looked so lost. I couldn't forget it. I felt responsible for you, whether I wanted to or not. I never expected any of this."

His gaze is steady, but softer. "It wasn't by design. It wasn't a plan. It just happened."

He shakes his head, gentle, but honest. "Maren, I was never a sure thing. I was on the train because I felt a duty to your father—and yes, because of that portrait. But I wanted nothing to do with the Talisman. It ended things with Simone. It killed your father. It created secrets between my parents that never healed. I decided to take you as far as Istanbul, and then disappear from your life. I meant to walk away from all of it—the Talisman, the history, Simone, even my family if necessary. Even you. I was finished."

Maren cuts him off, closing her eyes. Pain and grief knot inside her. "You should have told me. You let me wonder about everything—build stories in my head..."

She looks up at him, demanding. "How did Simone know I was coming here?"

Alexander doesn't hesitate. "Daniel told me you'd left early for Venice. He asked if I was leaving too. Simone overheard. She followed you. I knew she'd do anything to get the necklace."

Maren's voice chills, anger flaring. "Of course. That's how it's always been. Someone watching, someone lying. Alexander, do you realize I was the only one who didn't know the truth? You knew. My father knew. Your mother knew. Camille, Edwards, Simone, probably even my own mother—all of you, and no one told me. Oh my gosh. Dascălu..." she adds, "How could I be so stupid? That's why Dascălu looked at you like that—why he said what he did in Bucharest."

She shakes her head, incredulous. "I was the only one in the dark. On purpose. Why?"

Alexander doesn't answer. He just stands there, listening.

"You kept deciding which truths I could survive. That wasn't yours to decide, Alexander."

"I know what decisions are mine, Maren. I'm well aware."

The hardness in his tone catches her off guard. A firm boundary where there's usually only restraint. Maren draws back, suddenly unsure. She feels the sting of pushing him too far, her own anger dissolving into a knot of doubt and discomfort. She almost reaches for an apology, but pride stops her. Instead, she looks away, composing herself in the silence that follows, left painfully aware of the unfathomable space between them.

Alexander's voice softens. "I was going to give you your father's journal when you boarded the train—tell you everything that happened. But when Simone showed up, I knew I couldn't. If she realized how I felt about you—"

A hollow laugh escapes Maren. "How you felt about me? How could Simone have known? I don't even know your feelings. But you've always seemed to know mine." She presses her lips into a line.

"I was ridiculously obvious. I suppose I never made things difficult for you."

Alexander's reply is gentle, with the barest trace of a smile. "You never hid your heart, Maren. But that doesn't make you foolish."

A wave of conflicted indignation and shame sweeps through her. She wants to be angry, but finds she's almost... almost... grateful.

He meets her gaze. "If Simone had known you loved me, I was afraid you'd be in danger."

She turns away, her voice thin and worn. "If you did have feelings for me, you spent a lot of time convincing me it was all in my head." Even as she says it, she knows it's not the whole truth.

"I didn't do that to you, Maren," Alexander says quietly. "I never pretended not to care. I just didn't give you what you expected when you expected it."

She shivers. The mist has soaked them both—clothes heavy, hair dripping, cold biting straight through. And still, neither of them leaves. They just stand there, saying what needs to be said. Not shouting, not falling apart; just enduring. Close enough to see each other's breath in the fog.

Maren knows she could walk away at any moment. But she stays, and so does he. There's nothing dramatic about it. Just two people, battered and exhausted, refusing to quit—because somewhere beneath everything, they still care enough to hold their ground.

For the first time tonight, she feels the faintest trace of hope, acute but fleeting like warmth in a bitter wind. But it's not enough. She closes her eyes, then opens them again. Now there's only the sharp edge of self-preservation.

"I don't want to hear any more." Her words are quiet but final. "The necklace is gone. There's no point in going to

Istanbul. I'm going to Paris. I'll tell your mother I failed. If I were ever meant to succeed."

Alexander doesn't move. When he finally speaks, his voice is steady. "I'm sorry, Maren. I would never hurt you intentionally."

She nods, feeling that's true, which only makes it cut deeper.

Her voice is barely above a whisper. "But you did hurt me. And I let you. I'm as disappointed in myself as I am in you."

The truth hangs heavy between them. Part of her still wants to turn back. She sees hurt in his eyes, too, but she knows if she stays now, she'll lose herself.

So Maren turns and walks away.

And Alexander, still, silent beneath the empty stars—lets her go.

TWENTY

MOTHERS AND DAUGHTERS

Paris is gray and cool, dusk settling early as the streetlights flicker on along the empty avenue in front of Madame Girard's house. Maren steps out of the taxi into air that smells of rain and cold stone, the damp seeping through her coat at the seams. She's barely slept since leaving Venice. Losing the Talisman necklace and Alexander's confession are open wounds she can't bear to touch, as if even the lightest brush would make her ignite, lose her mind, or vanish into a grief she'll never escape.

She walks through the familiar pedestrian gate. It's the same courtyard she remembers: the same scent of rosemary thick in the air, the same bubbling of water from an unseen fountain, the same tall oak door. Everything unchanged except for the woman retracing these steps.

All the beautiful clothes Madame Girard gave her, the silks and soft cashmere, tokens and experiences meant to soften her rough edges, have all been left behind in that narrow train compartment in Bucharest. She wonders what will become of those clothes, and of the woman she was when she wore them.

Her hand hovers over the sun-shaped door knocker, and she sees her reflection in the polished brass. It's only then that she notices the sun earrings still in her ears. An unconscious tether to all she's gained and lost. And to Alexander Girard.

She is wearing the old boots, faded jeans, and black peacoat she wore the first time she knocked on this door, but how different she is today from when she first stood on this step. Much of her old life is scattered across Europe now, and something within her has been remade. She's become someone she never expected, and no one is more surprised than she is.

This time, she doesn't hesitate. She knocks.

Camille answers almost at once, steps forward, and gently cups Maren's face in both hands, then simply says, "Come with me."

Today, instead of steering her toward the cool blue reception room, Camille leads her through a side corridor and into the library. Stepping inside is like entering a peaceful cathedral, this one dedicated to knowledge. The air smells of beeswax, paper, and old leather bindings, some of Maren's most loved scents.

The garden beyond the windows is awash in the deep blue-black of twilight. Soft lighting from the courtyard's fountains and landscape features spills across gravel and flagstone, casting a romantic evening glow and blurring the boundary between indoors and out. Inside the library, floor to ceiling windows are draped in blush-colored damask trimmed with subtle gray and blush eyelash fringe; the curtains drawn back with platinum silk tiebacks.

So often, libraries are dark and masculine. But here, shelves of lustrous walnut rise twenty feet or more and are surrounded by walls painted a soft French gray that lift the room toward a coffered ceiling sprinkled with starry constellations. A slender balcony encircles the space, reachable by a fine wrought-iron spiral staircase.

Pools of lamplight fall across long antique tables, reminding her of the tables at Harvard, their surfaces marred from centuries of use. On the shelves lining the room are book spines in faded reds, blues, and browns, some stamped with gold leaf now dulled to brass. Glass-fronted cases hold, Maren guesses, the collection's rarities. Centered on the room, a fire burns in a rose marble fireplace as tall as she is.

Camille squeezes her hand once. "Let me take your coat, and please sit by the fire. You must be freezing. Madame will join you soon."

Maren sinks, hollow and drained, into a beige leather armchair with her father's journal in her lap. She runs her thumb along the binding and misses him. She wishes desperately that she could ask for his advice.

Madame Girard enters through a narrow door at the far end of the room. Maren stands as she approaches. Regal, like the room, Geneviève-Hélène Girard's every gesture has intention: the way she walks, smooths her wool skirt, extends a hand. Her oval face is framed by smooth dark hair swept into a French twist; a swanlike neck and high cheekbones lend her a sculptural elegance. There's no hurry, no wasted movement, only stately poise.

Maren sees so much of Alexander in his mother that the pain of it is almost more than she can bear. She misses him. She wishes she could just sink into his arms and let everything else fade away. But woven into the regret and longing are legitimate anger and disappointment.

"Maren," Madame Girard says, her feminine voice touched with that beautiful Parisian accent. "Thank you for coming." She kisses Maren on each cheek.

Maren only nods, not trusting herself to speak.

"Please, ma chère, sit down," Madame Girard says. "You have walked a difficult road. You come not at the end, but at the hardest middle, when what matters most often seems lost."

"It isn't the middle, and I appreciate your kindness, but it doesn't just seem lost. It is lost," Maren says. "The Talisman is gone. I failed the one thing you asked me to do. And now, you're at tremendous risk. Someone I met on the train—a man working for a Turkish Brotherhood—made it clear that if I couldn't gather every piece of the parure and safeguard it, he would take what's left. You and the Talisman jewels are more vulnerable now than when you hired me. I thought I could do it. I overestimated myself and underestimated everyone else."

She opens her satchel and removes the parure earrings: turquoise ovals in warm gold, each linked to a luminous emerald teardrop by a single, large rose-cut diamond, still wrapped in the crumpled lavender tissue from Budapest. She sets them on the table. "Alexander bought these from Mr. Molnár. They were very expensive."

He bought them for me, she thinks, but doesn't say.

She could apologize. She knows she's not blameless. But what stands between them is trust. She trusted him, but he didn't trust her enough to share what everyone else knew about her father's death. Including his ex-fiancée. However private he is with the world is up to him, but Maren wants to share his life, not orbit it. Had he shared what he knew about Simone, Maren knows she could have been prepared, and she would still have the Talisman.

Her fingers falter as she slips the square lapis ring from her hand and places it with the earrings on the polished wood. This loss feels physical. "Alexander told me you have the bracelet," she says. Then she adds the envelope with Madame Girard's uncashed check.

Madame Girard's eyes rest on the pieces; first the emerald earrings, then the lapis ring. Her expression is unchanged, only recognition. "There is something I want you to see," she says. "But first, let's speak as women who have each carried burdens passed down from our mothers and grandmothers."

Before Maren can answer, she hears a familiar footstep and turns. Her mother stands in the wide doorway, travel-worn but beautiful as ever. "Maman?"

"Bonsoir, ma chère Geneviève. Je suis ravie de te voir." Her mother crosses the room, greets Madame Girard with a kiss on each cheek, then draws Maren into a hug and steps back to look at her.

"I'm so glad to see you too, my friend," Madame Girard says. "I'm happy you could come. I hope your flight was pleasant. It's been such a long time. We have so much to talk about."

"Maman, why are you here?" Maren asks.

"I needed to be here, my dear. I heard what happened. There are things you deserve to know about your grandmothers, about the war, and about why we all did what we did."

Camille brings a tray with tea, hot cocoa, and a plate of sandwiches and sets it on a tea table in front of the fire.

"How did you hear?" Maren begins, then stops herself. Of course. Alexander spoke to his mother, and word traveled from there.

As they sit down, Maren's throat tightens. She has more to return. She fumbles in her bag again, fingers closing around the last objects she's carried back with her, the final responsibilities.

She places them on the table before Madame Girard and her mother: her father's journal, the gold locket, and beside it, the tiny Ottoman key Professor Antonescu gave her. A key that, before Venice, had seemed full of promise. She pushes them forward, eyes lowered.

"These are yours," Maren says. "Dad's journal," she says to her mother. Then to them both, "The locket Professor Antonescu gave me in Bucharest. And she gave me this key... I thought it might matter. It doesn't."

She doesn't know what she had expected, but Madame Girard remains composed, just like Alexander, never letting on how she really feels. Her mother rests a hand lightly on Maren's arm.

Her mother's voice is somber. "The Sorbonne Society was formed after World War I to move art and artifacts out of reach of those who see in them only money or power. The Talisman parure crossed continents because of the courage of many people with vision and heart."

Madame Girard picks up the thread. "The Louvre acquired at least four pieces of the parure in the early 1920s and stored them in a vault in the Galerie d'Apollon. As I'm sure you know, it's the gallery designed by Louis XIV to hold the French Crown Jewels. The parure was not exhibited, and very few people even knew it was there. There was a ledger in the vault with a single entry: La clef est la lumière."

"The key is the light," Maren says. "It's written in the locket."

"Yes. Your great-grandmother and Alexander's both volunteered in this gallery and pledged to protect these pieces, and others."

Madame Girard stands and picks up a square suede box from where it rests on the mantel. She opens it and hands it to Maren. Inside is a wide gold cuff bracelet. It is set with a halo of teardrop-shaped emeralds surrounding a central cabochon turquoise. There are tiny diamond stars scattered randomly all around the bracelet. The turquoise seems to drink in the light; the emeralds hold it, deep and green; the diamonds return it in bright pinpoints.

"This," Madame Girard says, "has been in our family vault since the war. Ever since your great-grandmother and Alexander's agreed it would be safest there."

Maren looks up, then to her mother, who meets her eyes. "The bracelet was supposed to leave France before the Nazi advance," her mother says. "The Sorbonne Society entrusted it to a brave courier, but he never made it. He was found near Chartres, hiding in a barn, gravely ill."

Madame Girard nods. "It was Elisabeta Cantacuzino, Professor Antonescu's mother, who found him. She was with the Resistance then. She'd studied in Paris at the Sorbonne with Annette de Beaumont and Mathilde de Sévigny, your great-grandmother and Alexander's."

"Yes," Maren acknowledges, "that's what Professor Antonescu told us."

Madame Girard goes on, "The courier gave the bracelet to Elisabeta, knowing his time was short."

"She brought it back to Paris," her mother continues, "and went straight to Annette and Mathilde. They knew Annette's family name, though respected, could be questioned. But the de Sévigny title carried weight, even under occupation."

"So, they hid it," Madame Girard finishes, "in the family vault, where neither the authorities nor those who might covet it ever found it."

She looks at the three pieces, then at Maren. "It wasn't hoarded. It was guarded. For the day someone might carry it forward again."

Maren stares at the bracelet, the earrings, the lapis ring.

Her mother adds, "Three friends. Three families. One promise."

Maren looks at her mother, then at Madame Girard, both faces touched by sorrow and pride.

All this history: bravery, sacrifice, commitment, washes over Maren like a tide she can't outrun. Every example of heroism sharpens her sense of failure: she's the one who lost the Talisman forever. In this room full of courage and steadfastness, her own shortcomings are raw and inconsolable. This is who I am, she tells herself: the end of a promise. The one who couldn't finish what all those women began.

Maren hesitates, then looks directly at Madame Girard. "Can I ask why you never told me you had the bracelet? When you hired me, I thought I was searching for only the necklace. But you knew there were more pieces. Both of you," she looks at her mother, "and you had one of them. Why keep that from me?"

Madame Girard glances at Maren's mother before answering. "You have every right to ask," she says.

Her mother continues, "We thought we were protecting you, as well as the necklace."

Madame Girard adds, "I believed the fewer people who knew, the safer everyone would be. I take responsibility for that."

Her mother nods. "We didn't think it would help you find the necklace. And the truth is, we still feel an obligation to protect what we can. The bracelet was hidden successfully for nearly a century. We wanted to keep the complete story and you safe as well. Also, Maren, we didn't know the earrings existed either. Had you and Alexander not found them in Budapest, they might have been lost forever."

"Alexander remembered seeing the bracelet—that's how he knew to buy the earrings in Budapest," Maren says quietly.

"We owe you and Alexander an apology," says Madame Girard.

"I am sorry we kept that from you," her mother says softly. "Even your father didn't know all of it."

"What did he know?" Maren says, looking from one of them to the other, trying to keep the edge out of her voice.

Her mother replies, "He knew Geneviève and I were school friends from the Sorbonne, and that she and I had taken up the hobby years ago of searching for the Talisman necklace." She adds sadly, "I regret not sharing the story with him now. He would have found it interesting. And it may have helped him."

Madame Girard interjects, "I heard a tip from a friend who knows of my interest in Ottoman-era jewelry. I called your father to see if he would like to go to Venice for several weeks to do some research for me—to see what he might turn up."

"He was working for you?" Maren says, stunned.

"Yes," her mother says, looking at her friend. "The last Geneviève or I heard about the project," her mother continues, "was that he had a breakthrough and wanted some help to make connections with archivists in Venice and Istanbul. He seemed excited, but he didn't want to talk about it on the phone. He thought about asking you," she says, "because you speak Italian, but decided not to bother you with it."

"Alexander was there for business, and also speaks Italian," Madame Girard fills in, "so I asked him to see if he could help with connections."

Madame Girard gives a small, grim smile. "After your father died, Alexander was clearly... upset... about your father's death, and the end of his relationship with Simone, and... other things... I think he had grown fond of your father, Maren, in the few days he knew him."

Maren wipes away a tear, thinking about Alexander sharing time with her father before he died.

"Why so much secrecy?" Maren asks.

"I didn't know how you were feeling, or if looking for the Talisman would be something you'd be interested in, considering your father's death," Madame Girard says.

"And you didn't want the Girard name associated with it. You thought I might be angry and speak to the authorities or the press."

"Yes," Madame Girard says honestly.

"Alexander told me he wanted nothing to do with the Talisman. And I think, by then, any of us, really. So I sent Edwards to the train in Venice, to accompany you to Paris."

Maren slowly nods.

"Alexander did not tell us that your father had discovered the ring or that he had given it to you. If I had known, I don't think I would have hired you," Madame Girard says thoughtfully.

"Why?" Maren asks. If Madame Girard had not hired her, none of this would have happened. She wouldn't have failed. She wouldn't have lost the Talisman—it would still be safe in its hiding place. But then again, she thinks, I would never have met Alexander.

Her mother responds, "Geneviève and I have searched for the necklace for so long, and investigated so many rumors over the years with no luck, we really didn't expect this time would be any different. But I should have known your father would uncover something important. He was very talented. As you are. We should have known..." Her voice trails off.

"Mr. Edwards saw my ring on the train," Maren says numbly.

"He did, and he mentioned that to me, but I had only ever seen the bracelet. None of us knew how many pieces of the parure still exist, or what they look like." She shrugs.

"I texted Alexander the evening you arrived in Paris to tell him I had hired you. I knew something was wrong because he called me back immediately. He told me he had given you the ring your father found in Venice. Alexander felt strongly that I was putting your life in danger sending you after the necklace."

"So he came to the hotel to talk me out of going," Maren says. Then she asks, "Alexander said Dad was in over his head. What did he mean by that?"

Madame Girard replies, "He thought there were people following your father in Venice. That the results of his investigations stirred several groups into motion interested in the necklace."

"Maren," Madame Girard says, "do you realize you and Alexander are among the very few who've ever been in the presence of so many pieces of the parure at one time? You had the ring, the earrings, and..." she hesitates, "the necklace—if only briefly—all together."

"Yes. I was so close," Maren says, "and now I have lost everything."

Including Alexander.

She thinks of that moment just two days ago, when Alexander, soft-spoken and steady, might have chosen her if she'd let him. But she hadn't. Couldn't. Now there is nothing left but disappointment and danger. No necklace, no Alexander.

"We can talk more tomorrow, when you've had some sleep," Madame Girard says gently.

Maren swallows a surge of emotion—hurt, anger, incredulity. "I'm sorry, but I can't talk about this anymore. I'm glad I got to see you both, but I've done what I came to do. I don't belong here."

"Camille will take you upstairs and show you your room. I understand you're leaving, and I won't stand in your way," Madame Girard replies. "But for tonight, ma chère, just rest. Edwards will take you to the airport tomorrow."

Maren nods silently. Kisses them both and follows Camille slowly upstairs, where a hot bath awaits.

A new set of pajamas, with a matching robe and slippers, is set out for her on a terrycloth-covered chaise lounge by the tub. She sinks into the hot water, the scent of roses, lilacs, and tuberose rising with the steam; a fragrance she will forever associate with Alexander's mother. She dries off, brushes her teeth on autopilot, puts on the pajamas, and climbs into bed. Turning off the light, she pulls the covers up to her chin and closes her eyes, wishing for sleep to come quickly, and for once, it does.

TWENTY-ONE

RUE DE GRENELLE

M AREN SITS IN ONE of a pair of gilded bergère chairs drawn up before a floor-to-ceiling Palladian window, a small table between them. Another identical pair stands sentry before the twin arched window, so that four low, elegant chairs seem to frame the view of the garden like a series of painted vignettes. The room is unabashedly feminine: rose-and-white striped wallpaper, an Aubusson-style carpet scattered with rosebuds and ribbons, and, opposite the windows, a canopy bed veiled in pale blue silk. The room must be on the library side; beyond the glass, she recognizes the same clipped boxwoods and gravel paths she'd seen last evening through the French doors.

An hour ago, a maid brought her a Limoges coffee pot sprinkled with tiny rosebuds on a silver tray, filled with rich French roast coffee, along with a basket of croissants and a small bouquet. She'd always written this kind of abundance off as simple wealth, but sitting here she can see something else threaded through it, an insistence on savoring details and rituals instead of rushing past them to the next distraction. How much of her own life had she numbed with background noise—emails, television, social feeds? Alexander and Madame Girard move through the world in a much more deliberate way and, in the process, seem to wring every drop of taste and texture from the present moment.

Rest, a hot shower, fresh clothes, and blissful cups of strong coffee have restored some of her energy. She'd been surprised, glancing at the bedside clock, to see that she'd slept for ten hours. If only pain and nausea didn't threaten to pull her under whenever she thought of Alexander or the lost Talisman. She wonders how long it will take to be free of that.

There is a knock at the door. She turns in her chair. "Come in." She rises quickly as Madame Girard opens the door.

"Bonjour, Maren," she says in her delightful voice. She moves with the same serenity Maren noticed yesterday, but this morning she seems softer and more relaxed. Almost maternal. She crosses the room and kisses the air above Maren's cheeks.

"May I?" she asks, standing by the other chair.

"Of course, please," says Maren. "Madame Girard, thank you for allowing me to stay last night. I can't believe how long I slept. That bed is divine."

Madame Girard smiles. "Isn't it, though? I stayed in a hotel in Cap Ferrat last year, and the bed was so wonderful I ordered new mattresses for every room here. Mine is just the same. I sleep beautifully, but now I am only enticed out of it in the morning by the thought of coffee. And please call me Geneviève, since we're friends, oui?"

"Before you go," she says gently, "I'd like to speak, just the two of us."

Maren nods. Hoping it will not be about Alexander.

"You must be hoping this won't be about Alexander," Geneviève begins with a smile. "I will be very frank with you. When he told me he had decided to see you through to Istanbul on the train, I thought the two of you could only frustrate each other. You move like weather, intuitive and emotional, and so quick to doubt yourself.

She lets this sink in. "Alexander cannot do that. His world is interior—a deep, unshakable well. He performs nothing outwardly, not even certainty. It's something he simply inhabits. When he's sure of his path, he moves through a storm as though he stands inside a bubble, untouched by anyone else's turbulence."

Maren flinches, guilt rising. Geneviève offers only a small, wry smile.

"That is not to say he is cold or unfeeling. If he is slow to speak, or silent when you want communication, it is not from neglect. He believes love means bearing burdens, not sharing them. He endures."

Maren looks away. "I was never sure where I stood with him. I felt like I was too much of everything."

Geneviève shakes her head. "He was waiting for you to decide if you needed rescuing, or if you would stand your ground. He is good at waiting. It is his greatest strength, and sometimes, I know, also his flaw."

She leans forward, voice lower. "Do you know what Alexander admires? Passion. You question yourself always, not because you are weak, but because you are curious and searching for what is true and real. I believe that is what made him change his mind about the Talisman. And you."

Maren presses her palm to her chest as the hurt returns.

"You are restless," Geneviève says softly. "You look ahead, anticipating every possible storm. Doubt is your constant companion; it makes you ask hard questions of yourself and of those you love. And you are intelligent enough, and brave enough, to hear the answers. Most people are not."

A gentle pause.

"But that does not make you 'too much,' Maren. It makes you a valiant human. Somehow, I know in your heart you believe ultimately you can handle whatever happens. So you will risk being hurt. And while Alexander might never match your movement, he is much the same. He carries a kind of faith in himself, a steadiness, that you could lean on if you let yourself."

Maren wants to believe it, but the memory of her angry words in Venice and the finality of their parting, makes it hard to reach for hope.

"If you are angry," Geneviève says kindly, "be angry. At the world, at your mother and me, even at Alexander. But don't mistake his silence for indifference. He's always held himself apart. Not just from you. That stillness is how he copes. He's learned that composure can protect his privacy. In many ways, his flawless manners are self-defense. His formality with people gives him space and time to think and do things in his own way. He does nothing for show. He lives by his own steady compass."

Geneviève says, "You are movement, Maren. He is stillness. That isn't a failing. Those differences are balance, not opposition. You move; he anchors. You question; he steadies. And that allows the two of you to meet not in perfection, but in a kind of earned acceptance."

Tears well up in Maren's eyes, and she looks away.

Geneviève sees this and says gently, "He will not chase you, and he will not fight with you. That is not his way. But I promise you, he has never doubted that you were enough."

"What has he said to you?" Maren asks.

"Very little, as you can imagine," Geneviève laughs softly, "but I am intuitive, and he and I are a lot alike. And," she smiles, "I have known him a long time."

Maren blinks at the window; the light is almost too bright. "I'm just... not sure I know how to be with someone who doesn't need me."

"You are both stronger than you think, and stronger together. He needs your questions as much as you need his answers."

"He actually scares me a little," Maren smiles in spite of herself. "And I am afraid to cross the distance."

Geneviève's smile is knowing. "Men like Alexander scare everyone a little. So do not cross the distance to him, Maren, just receive. Let him do the work. Let yourself be loved. Let yourself be chosen. Stand still. Just for once—and see what comes to you."

Maren nods, but she still doesn't quite believe. She rises, thanks Geneviève, and turns to prepare for her departure, her doubts and hope still tangled in a knot.

Geneviève studies her for a long moment at the door, then says quietly, "If you feel you should go, then you should. But before you do, there is something I would like you to see on the way. Since you are a history lover, perhaps for your work. Edwards will drive you and then take you to Paris-Le Bourget Airport. There is a private plane waiting there to take you home when you are ready."

It isn't an order, or even a request, Maren thinks, but something in between. A kind offering, perhaps, if Maren can accept it.

The Rolls-Royce glides through an arched stone gateway and onto a sweeping, tree-lined drive. At the end is an enormous house. A palace in all but name—cream limestone, tall French windows in perfect rows, wrought-iron balconies curving like black ribbons, a mansard roof crowned with ornate cresting. The central portico rises on fluted columns, its carved pediment alive with mythic figures. She half-expects to see footmen in livery spilling down the steps.

"What is this place, Edwards? Is this a museum?" She asks.

The car rolls to a stop before wide marble steps. Edwards opens her door and smiles. "It's a historic house called Le Cœur Fidèle, commissioned in the early 18th century. Have a look around, Miss Bennett. It's a beautiful place. The gardens in the back are especially nice. Enjoy; there's no rush. I'll take you to the airport when you're ready."

Her boots crunch on pale gravel. Up close, the scale is more overwhelming. Each doorway soaring twice her height, brass fittings gleaming like they were polished for a royal visit. The butler who answers the sun-shaped brass knocker is tall, silver-haired, immaculate. "Miss Bennett," he says smoothly. "You are expected. Please explore. There is a call button in every room should you require anything at all." He leads her into a magnificent marble hall and disappears through double doors on the right. The butler's footsteps fade, and Maren is left alone in the vast, vaulted space.

In the center, a grand staircase sweeps upward in a perfect arc. Above, a domed skylight floods the space with milk-white winter light.

She turns slowly, her eyes scanning upward. The ceiling is so high it makes her feel dizzy, thirty feet at least, with pale plaster moldings edged in gold. Enormous chandeliers hang like constellations, dripping with cut crystal. Portraits in gilded frames gaze down with cool detachment. She laughs. The hall alone is larger than her apartment building.

She walks through the double doors on the left and follows a long, columned corridor that seems built to impress foreign dignitaries, its niches holding marble and bronze sculptures. There are busts and torsos, animals and bird figures. Light pours through windows that rise nearly two stories, their glass panes cradled in wrought-iron muntins, draped in silk as pale as dawn. Every so often, a door opens onto a room that makes her gasp at its beauty. The hall continues and passes through a sunlit conservatory where full-size orange, lemon, and lime trees stand in large paneled pale green planters, scenting the air faintly of citrus and earth. It ends at what seems to be a study or library.

She steps through and stops.

The study is vast, paneled in dark walnut. Floor-to-ceiling shelves march in perfect lines, broken by soaring windows dressed in billowing green silk draperies. The scent is wonderfully comforting: leather, wood smoke, and the faint smell of something like tobacco and spice. A private gentlemen's club from another age. Built-in ladders rise toward the topmost shelves, where books have probably slumbered for centuries. The fireplace is a work of art in black marble veined with white, its mantel wide enough to serve as a dining table.

The sheer scale of it all is overwhelming. She's never moved through splendor like this. And yet it feels alive, not staged. Slowly, her shame at arriving in battered boots, in her ancient peacoat, fades in the exuberance of the space.

And above the mantel hangs a canvas she knows instantly is a John Singer Sargent. Even before she registers its details, she feels it on a level that makes her pulse skip: the composition, the brushwork, the unmistakable fluid precision.

Then the impact lands. The subject is a young woman in tan breeches and tall black boots. She wears a ruffled white blouse, open at the neck. It looks as if she has just returned from riding, and perhaps has removed her vest and jacket. Her gloves are held in one hand at her waist; the other hand rests on a carved chair back. She stands tall and poised; her gaze is direct. She looks exactly like Maren. It's not just a resemblance. It's as if Maren's own face has been thrown backward in time.

For a moment, her legs feel unstable. The fire snaps faintly in the grate; and all around her, the house simply carries on, as it has for hundreds of years. She stands amid all that grandeur, not knowing if she's about to fall into the painting or flee from it.

She sees herself in the lines of the woman's neck. In the sure set of her shoulders. There's a romance to her, an elegance Maren has never claimed, a kind of beauty that is not loud but inevitable. Maren just stands and stares at... well, herself. She wonders if all the things she thought she wasn't—beautiful, poised, timeless—might have been hers all along, in ways she's never dared to believe.

She's still studying the painted version of herself when the faintest sound disrupts the quiet.

She turns.

Alexander is standing just inside the room, with the light at his back, his face unreadable but entirely focused on her.

Before she can think, she says, "Why did they send you over here?"

"They didn't." He steps in, closing the doors behind him. "This is my house."

Twenty-Two

ALEXANDER

"THIS IS YOUR HOUSE?" Maren asks. Oh, great, she thinks.

After what she'd said to him that night, as they stood wet and freezing in Saint Mark's Square, and then walked away from him, Maren can imagine how he must feel, finding her here now, uninvited, in his private study. He's had time to think since Venice, after all.

Alexander simply nods. "It was my grandmother's."

Of course, Maren thinks, the house on Rue de Grenelle. Heat rushes to her face; she wishes she could disappear into the woodwork. With his unfailing courtesy, Alexander is far too much of a gentleman to ask her to leave. *He won't chase you*, his mother had said. *Or fight with you. It's not his way.* Is it unreasonable, Maren wonders, to wish she could simply sink into the floor?

Meanwhile, Alexander remains perfectly still.

"I'm so sorry, Alexander. I didn't know. I should have, though. I didn't mean to intrude. Your mother just said there was a place I ought to see before I leave. I was walking through. It's a beautiful house. And I came into this room. It must be your study."

He nods again. "Are you leaving?" he asks.

"Well, I... I don't know," she admits, the uncertainty plain in her voice. She finds herself rooted to the spot, every thought swirling, but Alexander's steady presence keeps the room from spinning. Geneviève's words echo in her mind. *Stand still—just for* once, *and see what comes to you.* So she does.

Then, just as Geneviève promised he would, Alexander crosses the distance between them.

"It is good to see you here," he says.

The painting above the mantel is larger than Maren had imagined. The portrait itself is life-size, and with its sweeping foreground and background, the canvas must be almost nine feet tall and over five feet wide. "Apparently," she says, glancing up, "I've been here for quite some time."

Alexander follows her gaze.

The woman in the painting is a barely contained whirlwind. It is as if she has only paused momentarily for the artist, and even then, only because someone insisted. There is energy in Sargent's brushstrokes, as if he had to paint quickly in order to capture her likeness before she set off again. She is Maren.

Suddenly, so much about Alexander makes sense. He is the calm at the eye of every storm, the axis around which everything turns. She wonders if the woman in the painting had an Alexander in her life too. Maren imagines she must have, because she looks happy; as if she's home. "Alexander..." she says, her voice barely more than a whisper.

He turns and gently presses a finger to her lips. "I have loved you my whole life."

She looks at him, unmoving.

"I just didn't know how to find you," he says.

Exhaling, she looks at the painting, eyes filling with tears. He lifts both hands to her face and draws her close, wrapping his arms around her. They stand like that for a long time, his cheek against her hair, her eyes closed, head resting on his chest, arms encircling his waist. They both hold on, and let go of a lifetime of searching.

She peers up at his face. "I got your shirt wet again."

"I know," he says. "You're such a girl."

Then Maren remembers, wiping her tears with the back of her hand. "Alexander, Edwards is waiting outside to drive me to the airport."

"I saw him when I pulled into the drive," Alexander says. "I told him you wouldn't need to go to the airport today."

She steps back just enough to meet his eyes, teasing. "You're awfully sure of yourself. What if I'd insisted?"

He grins. "Then I would have put you in the dungeon. That's what we aristocrats do."

She half-believes him after seeing this house. "You have a dungeon?"

He laughs. "No. But it would come in handy once in a while."

He takes her hand and leads her to the sofa in front of the fire. They sit.

"I want to apologize, Maren," he says.

This time, it's her turn to press her fingers to his lips. She smiles. "Thank you for that. And please do not change anything about you. Not one single thing." She leans in and kisses him, her hand replaced by her lips, softly at first. He draws her closer, her arms winding around his neck.

His hands slide into her hair, deepening the kiss. She shivers at the sensation; how his strength and self-control, once so intimidating to her, now feel like the safest things she's ever known. His lips trace her jaw, then her neck, sending a rush of heat that sets her skin alight.

In one effortless movement, he shifts her beneath him, pressing her into the soft cushions. Maren is suddenly aware of every detail: the crackle of the fire, the steady weight of his body—real, sheltering, overwhelming.

"You are overdressed," he says, his voice edged with a roughness she's never heard before. He moves to lie beside her, his fingers deft at the buttons of her shirt.

A laugh bubbles up. "I was hoping you'd do something about that."

She watches him as he helps her out of her clothes, each movement deliberate, as if he's unwrapping something precious and fragile. In that moment, she knows that, like the woman in the painting, she is home too—in herself, her life, this room, with him. The cool air brushes her skin, quickly replaced by the warmth of his hands as they trace her side, her stomach, her thighs. His touch is slow, almost reverent in its care.

A low, half sigh, half groan escapes him as he sheds the last of his own clothes. His body covers hers, and she wraps herself around him, feeling the deep rightness of it, no distance now, nothing held back. For a moment, they pause, searching each other's faces in the soft firelight, before drawing closer, finding shelter in each other.

Much later, in the fading light of this chilly November afternoon, they sit together on the sofa in Alexander's study. Dinner has been brought in on a tray with a bottle of wine. Maren draws her knees beneath her as he refills her glass.

"You are so much like your mother, Alexander. Although she's delightful—much less frightening than I imagined she might be."

He laughs. "She can be terrifying if she thinks it necessary. You must have charmed her."

Maren smiles. "Speaking of French mothers, I learned quite a lot about the Talisman from them yesterday, and I saw your mother's bracelet. Alexander, there's something I've been thinking about since then. Inside the bracelet, the word Nur is engraved."

"Yes," Alexander replies, moving around the room, switching on lights. "It's written inside the band of the ring, and on the back of the earrings too. If Mr. Molnar is right, every piece in the parure bears that hallmark."

"Well... the thing is," Maren says, "the necklace I found at Saint Mark's—it didn't."

"Didn't what?" Alexander pauses, giving her his full attention.

"Have it. It didn't have the engraving on the back."

"Did you get a good look at it?" he asks.

"Yes," Maren says softly. "I did. It was beautiful, flawless, actually. But there was no engraving."

He stands at his desk, brow furrowed, silent for a moment.

"Alexander...," Maren continues, her voice thoughtful, "what if the necklace I found at St. Mark's was a fake? Just a decoy?"

He meets her eyes and nods, implacable. "Then let's find out where the true Talisman is hiding."

Night has fallen by the time Alexander and Maren pull into the courtyard of his mother's house.

Earlier, before they'd left Rue de Grenelle, a uniformed maid had shown Maren upstairs to a beautiful bedroom adjoining Alexander's. Her suite boasts its own sitting room and a luxurious bath finished in creamy marble. In the blush and beige dressing room off the bath, to her astonishment, she had found all her clothes from the Orient Express. All the pieces she'd thought lost for good, freshly pressed and hung neatly in the closet.

She had showered quickly and changed into camel wool trousers and a navy cashmere sweater, knotting a silk scarf quickly around her neck before pulling on a navy blazer and dashing downstairs. Alexander had been in the main hall, deep in conversation with his butler, Gaston Bouchard, when Maren appeared at the landing. Both men looked up as she descended the staircase. She wished she had a camera to capture forever the way Alexander looked at her in that instant. Gaston glanced from Alexander to Maren, then back again, a hint of a smile tugging at his lips before he bowed and slipped discreetly from the hall.

In Alexander's car on the drive over, Maren had asked him about Gaston. "I thought French butlers are traditionally addressed by their last names. I noticed you called him Gaston."

Alexander had smiled, eyes on the road. "He was with me at Eton, and then when I read law at Christ Church. He managed basically everything—except classes and girls. Kept me presentable, sane, and mostly on time. It was a comfort to have someone so steady in the background. Back then, to avoid drawing attention to my having a valet, we got in the habit of using first names. When I moved into this house, he came with me. Formality has its place, but old loyalties have a way of softening rules. To most people," he'd said, "he's Monsieur Bouchard. But to me, he's Gaston."

She had hesitated. "How should I address him?"

His smile had been reassuring. "Monsieur Bouchard is perfectly appropriate. But if you'd prefer, Gaston is fine too. I'll leave it to you; and let me know if you'd rather I speak with him."

Now, as they enter the upstairs sitting room, Maren and Alexander greet Camille and find their mothers sharing a nightcap by the fireplace's glow. After the round of kisses, hellos, and first pleasantries; drinks ordered and jackets shrugged off, they settle together on the loveseat, just as Edwards enters.

"Hello," Maren says. She and Alexander both rise, and Alexander greets him with a cordial nod; the two men shake hands.

"Please, Miss Bennett, call me Alistair," Edwards replies.

She smiles. "Thank you, but then you must call me Maren."

On the sofa, Geneviève reaches for Alistair's hand, giving it a gentle squeeze as she smiles at him.

Maren wonders at what goes unsaid between Alexander and Edwards. She remembers the chill at the train station, the careful politeness. Geneviève intimated last night that there was some disagreement over sending her after the Talisman, but she wonders if it might also have something to do with Alexander's mother. She decides not to ask unless someone chooses to offer an explanation. Every family deserves its privacy, and she senses that matters deeply to Alexander.

After conversation about travel and the state of the gardens at Le Cœur, as the family calls it, Alexander turns the discussion to the real reason for their visit. He tells them about Maren's observation that the necklace she found was missing the Nur hallmark.

Geneviève says sadly, "The last time I spoke with Maren's father, he told me he had a hunch it might be in Istanbul, though he was still investigating. That's one reason when I hired Maren... after... that I arranged for a train ticket from Paris to Istanbul. That ball is such an important event during the Season. I hoped there might be someone aboard with information or connections."

"I wonder if he discovered the same thing I did," Maren says. They all turn to her. "The first time I visited Saint Mark's, right after my father died, a woman standing beside me pointed-ed out the blue-green tiles and said, 'It's a map if you know how to see it.' For a long time, I thought it meant following the tiles to the stone wall, finding the lion, and the crevice where the necklace was hidden. I assumed the river of tiles was just a path. But on my last visit, I started thinking—what if the tiles are, quite literally, a map?"

"In what way?" Alistair asks.

"Well, I wasn't sure, so I took a photo." Maren pulls out her phone, scrolling through as she explains, "I'd been thinking how, on fifteenth- and sixteenth-century maps, rivers were often used as reference points for orientation."

Alexander leans in. "You mean they used rivers as landmarks."

She nods at him and smiles. "Exactly. Sometimes those images were stylized, but they encoded real geography."

She hands her phone around, showing the overhead photo of the river of tiles.

Elaine Bennett, fascinated, says, "These representations were meant to endure over time and help people identify important or sacred places."

"So, at first, I assumed the tile river at Saint Mark's must show a Venetian canal," Maren adds, "but when I compared it with aerial maps of the city's waterways, I couldn't find a match."

"That's the Bosphorus," Alistair says quietly.

Maren's face lights up. "Yes!" she beams. "I think this is what Dad discovered."

"Why," Alexander asks, "would there be a map in Venice pointing to a hiding place in Istanbul?"

Elaine answers, "Venice had close and sometimes rather opportunistic relations with Constantinople for centuries. Venetian merchants, diplomats, even crusaders, moved between the two cities, and Venetian art and architecture were deeply influenced by Byzantine styles."

Alistair nods thoughtfully. "Saint Mark's itself was modeled on Byzantine churches."

"And much of its treasure, including mosaics and artifacts, came from the East through trade or conquest," Elaine adds.

Maren continues, "After 1453, when the city became Istanbul, Venice continued trading with the Ottomans, especially in jewels and luxury goods."

Geneviève leans in. "So, if a valuable talisman necklace had ties to the East, it would make perfect sense for someone to note its hiding place using the visual language of trade and geography."

Alexander studies the photo, understanding dawning. "A pattern of tiles shaped like the Bosphorus would be a subtle but powerful clue."

Maren grins, her excitement growing. "Only an insider would recognize it as a real map, pointing not only to a place but maybe to an entire world of hidden connections."

She sinks back into the loveseat and notices Alexander watching her with an expression somewhere between wonder and devotion.

"Istanbul is a big place," Alistair says.

"Yes it is," Maren says. "But we have this text Dad sent me when he asked me to come to Venice." She shows it to Alexander.

Alexander reads aloud:

Where east and west meet, a shadow waits behind the lion's gaze.
What glitters at the heart of the lion is but an echo.
A faithful twin for curious eyes at the city of the Evangelist.
Seek the true flame where continents divide.
Its doors unbar only when the crescent dances with the rose
And masks fall away in music and light.
The Chosen follow the path when they pause and reflect.

Elaine says, "*A shadow waits behind the lion's gaze.* Could that refer to the decoy necklace in Saint Mark's Basilica? The lion is its symbol."

Alistair nods. "And *true flame*... perhaps that's a metaphor for the real Talisman. *Where continents divide*. That's Istanbul, where Europe and Asia meet."

"*Doors unbar only when the crescent dances with the rose*," Maren says aloud. "The crescent is the Ottoman symbol, and the rose could stand for Venice. Maybe that means the hiding place can only be reached during a special event, when these two worlds come together."

"Like the ball?" Geneviève suggests. "*Masks fall away in music and light?*"

Alexander looks around the room. "It sounds like we need to be in Istanbul. When is the ball?"

"Tomorrow night," Geneviève replies. She turns to Maren with a smile. "And you, my dear, will need your dress." Her eyes twinkle. "I'll make some calls in the morning."

Back at Rue de Grenelle, Maren feels silly that she is so tentative and nervous about spending the night in Alexander's house. She changes out of her clothes and into a silk nightgown, takes a breath, and sits on the edge of her bed. Wondering. She doesn't have any idea about his habits or evening rituals. Does he read before bed? Does he floss? There is something almost more intimate about spending the night here than being with him earlier in the study.

There's a soft knock on the walnut door that connects their rooms.

She opens it to find Alexander, barefoot, in pajama trousers and an old Oxford t-shirt, more boyish and endearing than she's ever seen him. A softness in his eyes that makes her heart skip. He smiles. "Would you like some company tonight?"

Relief and happiness sweep away her nerves. "Yes. I'd love that." I really have to calm down, she thinks. He can probably tell I'm a bundle of nerves.

He studies her face for a moment, something thoughtful and reassuring in his eyes, then he seems to make a decision and holds out his hand. She takes it, letting him lead her, trusting that he knows exactly what she needs. Their fingers fit together so warm and perfect.

Maren thinks, with a little chuckle of amusement, of the floating drama of her nightgown as he leads her down long corridors, past closed doors and old portraits gazing out from the darkness. She feels like a heroine in a Victorian novel, sweeping barefoot through shadowed halls, crossing places where silvery shafts of light stream through tall windows and across marble floors. The hush of the house feels sacred, as if they are the only two souls awake in the world.

"Are we allowed?" she whispers.

"I don't know." He stops suddenly, considering. "I think so."

She hesitates, looking at him.

He laughs, rolling his eyes. "Yes, silly, it's my house. Do you think I make a habit of breaking into strangers' houses and making love in their libraries?"

On the main floor, the house on Rue de Grenelle is quiet, half the lights dimmed for the night. He tugs her hand as she trails after him, their footsteps nearly silent on the ancient floors. They pause at heavy oak doors. Alexander pushes them open to reveal the music room. High-ceilinged and elegant, it's bordered on one side by windows that look out onto the formal gardens at the back of the house.

A pale glow slants along the herringbone floor and across the polished body of a grand piano. Alexander releases her hand just long enough to lift the piano lid, then slips onto the bench. He pats the seat beside him, and she joins him, careful not to let her nightgown tangle around the pedals.

"You play?" she asks, enchanted by how much there still is to learn about him.

"At times," he says lightly, flexing his hands in a way she finds unexpectedly charming. "But not often for an audience."

He starts in a low register, a few notes, hesitant, and then gathering confidence. The melody emerges, unmistakable: "Someone to Watch Over Me." Maren sighs. She looks at him, and he smiles with the memory of Budapest.

She leans against his shoulder, letting the music wash over her. When he finishes, neither hurries to speak. The silence is comfortable.

He turns on the bench, straddling it to face her, so close she can feel the warmth radiating from him. "You know," he murmurs, "I never liked this house much until now."

She laughs, a soft, delighted sound. "Why now?"

He brushes a strand of hair from her cheek. "Because you bring it to life."

His lips find hers, gentle at first, then hungry. He lifts her nightgown, guiding her bare legs around his waist until she's straddling his lap, pressed close. Meeting her eyes, he slowly slips the gown over her head and lets it fall behind her. She wraps her arms around his neck, letting herself be gathered in, cherished and desired all at once.

When they finally part, flushed and breathless, she buries her face in his chest, listening to the steady beat of his heart. "Let's stay like this," she whispers.

He nods. For a while, they just sit, barefoot, wrapped in each other, moonlight spilling softly across the piano and the old parquet floor. The house is quiet around them, waiting to be filled with love, laughter, and something entirely new. Something neither of them has ever known before.

Twenty-Three

CUSTOMS OF THE COUNTRY

"GOOD MORNING, MA CHÈRE." Geneviève's voice carries warmly through the phone, despite the early hour. "Your gown is ready at Dior. They've agreed to open the atelier early so the seamstress can make any final adjustments. Shall I come and collect you? I suspect this will be delightful for us both."

Alistair is just pulling into the gravel courtyard when Maren descends to the forecourt, her steps quick and light. Through the car window, she glimpses Geneviève in the back seat, poised and elegant as always. The moment Alistair opens her door, Maren rises on her toes and plants a cheerful kiss on his cheek.

For an instant, he looks startled. Then that familiar composure slides back into place, though Maren catches something else in his expression; amusement, perhaps even a hint of charm. She realizes how her easy displays of affection must contrast with the careful formalities that fill his days. The thought makes her smile.

Geneviève sees his expression and laughs softly. "Just wait until you see her in the dress."

When Alistair pulls to a stop in front of Dior, the city is still waking. The atelier won't open officially for another four hours. Maison Christian Dior presides over the corner of Avenue Montaigne and Rue François 1er, surrounded by a constellation of luxury, including Chanel, Louis Vuitton, and Givenchy. Normally, these flagships draw tides of stylish shoppers, but at this hour the quartier sleeps, its wide pavements nearly deserted.

Geneviève and Maren cross to the entrance together. Madame Valois, the senior vendeuse who guided Maren through her fitting weeks earlier, meets them at the door. She unlocks it with a smile, exchanges warm handshakes, then leads them to a private lift just off the boutique floor.

On the second floor, they enter the couture salon. Maren thinks of how much has changed since she first sat in this very spot with Madame Valois, discussing her new dress. Now her gown waits on a mannequin crafted to her exact proportions, while a seamstress stands nearby, ready to answer questions about construction, fit, and care.

Maren circles the form slowly, holding her breath. The fabric seems too delicate to touch. The gown is everything she imagined—and more. She looks between Geneviève and Madame Valois, hands pressed to her chest.

"How can I ever thank you both?" she whispers.

When Maren is ready, Madame Valois gestures toward an adjacent fitting room. "Mademoiselle Bennett, we are prepared. If you would like to try on your dress, I will assist you."

Maren is grateful she dressed practically—a simple blouse and skirt, easy to slip off and on. Inside the fitting room, Madame Valois and the seamstress help her into the gown and matching sapphire peau de soie pumps. Maren watches in the mirrors as she's zipped and fastened, then returns to the main salon where Geneviève waits in an armchair.

When Maren steps out, Geneviève says only, "Oh my."

The gown fits perfectly—a vision in luminous sapphire silk organza. Strapless, with a dramatic plunging V at the back, every line speaks to the atelier's artistry. The silhouette is sleek: a slim-fitting sheath that traces her figure, paired with a voluminous overskirt that gathers at the waist and trails behind like a billowing peacock's tail. The overskirt rises higher in front, allowing glimpses of the elegant sheath beneath as she moves.

But it's the embroidery that takes her breath away. The bodice and overskirt shimmer with intricate needlework in matching sapphire thread—a garden of flowers, winding vines, bees, and delicate butterflies, each motif accented with beads that catch and scatter light. The edge of the train is embroidered with lilies of the valley, Monsieur Dior's favorite flower and lucky charm. Madame Valois lifts the edge of the train to reveal a hidden wonder: beneath the bustle, the embroidery continues, ensuring that as Maren walks or dances, flashes of iridescent beadwork will glimmer with every step.

As a final flourish, Madame Valois brings Maren a short sapphire bolero jacket, crafted from the softest cashmere and adorned with embroidery that echoes the gown's design. She holds it out for Maren to admire; the embellishments shimmer in the salon's light.

"The ensemble is now complete," Madame Valois says, with evident pride in the atelier and talented petites mains. "Your dress, jacket, shoes, and gloves will be packaged for travel and delivered directly to your plane this afternoon. Please do not hesitate to contact me if I can be of assistance."

On the car ride home, Geneviève and Maren marvel over the beauty of the dress and how precisely it fit from the very first measurements. All that remains is for the seamstress to hand-stitch the hem to their chosen length.

"You looked absolutely beautiful," Geneviève says. "Now there's only one thing missing." She reaches into her bag and hands Maren a small package.

Inside a padded gray suede box, Maren finds the Talisman earrings, bracelet, and ring. She looks up at Geneviève, speechless.

"You may need these for the next part of your adventure," Geneviève says.

"Why are you being so kind to me?" Maren asks.

Geneviève pauses in that familiar way that reminds Maren of Alexander. "Because you have bravely agreed to undertake a quest that may prove daunting, perhaps dangerous. Because you are the daughter of one of my oldest friends. And above all, because my son is in love, and I am happy to see him content at last."

"Thank you," Maren says, noticing Alistair's smile in the rearview mirror. "Your generosity means more to me than I can say."

Geneviève rests her hand on Maren's. "Good luck, ma chère. We may need every bit of it this time."

At Le Cœur Fidèle, Maren dashes up the front steps and hesitates at the door, uncertain whether to knock or simply walk in. She wonders whether Alistair notified Mr. Bouchard of their arrival. Probably, she decides. In this world, communication is almost an art form. It's the silent thread that makes everything proceed without a hitch.

Unlike her usual life, punctuated by disruptions and awkward timing, here most things run smoothly. People are ready before they're needed. There's scarcely any waiting, and both staff and principals are able to carry out their work with professional calm; never appearing rushed or flustered.

At home, Maren thinks, everyone prides themselves on self-support, as if asking for help or even keeping others informed is a weakness. There's almost a stigma attached to too much communication.

Here, it's the opposite. At this level, where everyone moves with such grace, communication is expected, and it's woven into every interaction. Information flows discreetly and efficiently, ensuring that everything and everyone is perfectly prepared. Rather than being a burden, it forms the invisible framework that lets daily life for the elite unfold with seamless precision.

Alexander's butler opens the door with a slight bow as soon as she reaches the top step, ushering her into the splendid hall. "Hello, Maren," he says with a welcoming smile.

"Hi, Gaston. Have you seen Alexander?"

"I saw him last in the breakfast room," Gaston replies.

"Thank you." Maren laughs. "Um... Can you point me in that direction?"

"Of course. If you would follow me," Gaston says, leading her down the hall. At the breakfast room door, he nods to Maren, then to Alexander. "Sir." With that, he departs, leaving them alone.

Earlier that morning, with Alexander fielding office phone calls before dawn, Maren had slipped on jeans, a sweatshirt, and suede driving mocs before wandering, bleary-eyed, to the kitchen in search of coffee. Gaston was there tidying up. Her request caught him off guard for a moment, but he quickly recovered, showing her where to find cups and cream, his manner softening with her gratitude.

"Mr. Bouchard," she had asked as she poured her coffee, "do you have a preference for how I address you?"

Gaston paused, then gave her a kind smile. "When we are alone, I would be honored if you would call me Gaston. But with the public, I must retain a certain intimidating reputation. Sometimes it's useful when we have a full house." He winked, and Maren couldn't help but laugh.

"Would you consider doing the same for me?" Maren asked, smiling. "Maren, when it's just us, Miss Bennett or Mademoiselle Bennett in public. I'll leave it to you to decide the boundaries, whatever feels right, and I'll follow your lead."

He nodded. "A pact, then, Mademoiselle Maren. For now, let us have our coffee as friends, before the rest of the house wakes."

Alexander looks up from his laptop as Maren enters, then stands.

She beams at him, kisses him hello, and settles into the chair he pulls out for her.

"Did you have a good time?" he asks.

"The dress is spectacular," she says. "And your mother says hello. The Dior courier will deliver it to the airplane this afternoon as soon as the hem is finished."

Alexander refills his coffee. "I found something interesting about the night of the ball in Istanbul. Would you like coffee?"

Maren perks up. "Oh? No, thank you."

"There's going to be a total lunar eclipse that night. Not here, but in Istanbul. It peaks just after midnight," he says.

Maren raises her eyebrows. "An eclipse?"

He turns the device to show her a chart. "The moon will pass through the very center of Earth's shadow. It's the deepest kind of total lunar eclipse."

She looks at him, impressed. "And let me guess—it will be above the palace."

He nods. "The maximum aligns perfectly with the view from the Topkapi Palace."

"Interesting timing," Maren says thoughtfully.

"Yes," he says. "And rare. A central eclipse like this isn't uncommon globally, but it might only happen directly above the palace once in a generation."

Maren smiles. "So that's when it happens. When the ballroom is full of guests."

"I think that's the event your father was trying to tell you about in his text."

"Do you think," Maren wonders, "that's what he meant by 'masks fall away in music and light'?"

"It could be," Alexander says. "Masks are traditionally removed at midnight at a masquerade ball."

Maren shakes her head, worry creeping into her voice. "Alexander, we have no idea where to find the Talisman, or what we're supposed to do. It took me an hour to find the necklace at Saint Mark's, and at least then I arrived with clues. If the eclipse is our only chance, we may have only minutes."

Alexander replies, "Then we'll have to trust our instincts—and each other. Whatever happens, we can't let that moment pass."

"We've assembled three pieces of the parure," Maren says, her voice low. "It's more powerful, and more vulnerable now than it's been in a century. The stakes have never felt higher, and the countdown to midnight feels impossibly short."

They arrive at Paris–Le Bourget just after one. The car pulls them onto the sunlit tarmac, where their jet is waiting. Boarding is swift as their bags are stowed. Inside, the cabin is all pale leather and polished wood, with every comfort anticipated.

As promised, Maren's dress is already on the plane, carefully stored in a wardrobe built into the cabin wall rather than tucked away with the luggage below. She runs her hand over the protective cover, feeling a thrill of anticipation.

Alexander shakes hands with the pilot and first officer, whom he knows well. The pilot tells them the flight should be about three and a half hours, with a car waiting when they arrive at Atatürk Airport. A VIP coordinator will meet them at the plane to assist with immigration and customs.

Within minutes, the engines purr to life. As the plane climbs over the city and turns east, Alexander tells Maren that the evening will start with a cocktail hour at eight, followed by dinner, dancing, and entertainment until the wee hours. "That gives us four hours to find the necklace. It may be a long night. You might want to rest on the way."

By late afternoon, the domes and minarets of Istanbul signal their arrival. It was such an easy flight, Maren thinks, and she's grateful to have slept the whole way because she feels refreshed and excited for the evening ahead.

They check into their hotel and are soon settled into a two-bedroom suite on the second floor. The hotel occupies a restored nineteenth-century building, part of the Atik Pasha Palace. Fittingly, Maren thinks, it's a waterfront mansion from the Ottoman era. At one time, the guest manager explained, there was a whole series of grand palaces and summer residences along the Bosphorus. Maren grins, thinking about how this particular palace was essentially the Sultan's guest house. The view is incredible, and Alexander smiles as he makes phone calls while watching Maren go from window to window.

The Bosphorus Strait stretches out in both directions. She looks across the expanse, crisscrossed by vessels large and small, and imagines what it must be like to be in a boat on one of the world's busiest waterways. She can also see the hotel's lushly landscaped waterfront gardens and jetty, and beyond that, the Bosphorus Bridge.

Alexander orders snacks and wine from room service, and Maren goes into one bedroom to shower and dress. But she's constantly distracted by Istanbul's golden domes and the sun setting in a fiery blaze.

As she does her hair and makeup, she thinks about what Alexander had said about how tonight's lunar eclipse will create a long-lasting deep red color called a "blood moon." She thinks that sounds quite dramatic and mysterious in itself, and wonders how the eclipse figures into the discovery of the Talisman necklace.

Maren slips on her robe and pads out to Alexander's room, seeking a refill for her wine. Alexander emerges from the steam of his bathroom, a towel slung low around his hips. He pauses in the marble doorway, arms crossed, leaning against the frame as he watches her. She sets her wine glass down and walks over to him. She lifts her hand and traces a bead of water along the side of his neck and across his shoulder. Standing close, she kisses her favorite spot just below his ear. "That's a promise," she says as she picks up her wineglass again.

"Good," he says. "Don't think I won't hold you to it."

A short time later, Maren emerges from her room, transformed. The sapphire gown skims her silhouette, and the beaded flowers, butterflies, and winding vines sparkle madly in the room's low evening light. The overskirt trails regally behind her, lending every step a queenly grace. Catching Alexander's gaze, she laughs, gathering the overskirt in one hand and turning slowly so the dress can shimmer and flare.

Alexander stops mid-fastening his cufflinks, transfixed. For a moment, he only stares, taking her in from head to toe before crossing the room and offering his hand with a playful bow. "Forgive me, Your Majesty. I wasn't informed I'd be escorting royalty tonight."

Maren's laughter rings in the air as she takes his hand. He draws a little closer, lowering his voice. "You're gorgeous, Maren."

She moves her train aside and sits at the table, watching Alexander finish dressing. He stands in front of the mirror, focused on tying his bow tie. When he sees her watching, he smiles and turns. "Yes?"

"I was just thinking about your reputation as a 'French lothario,'" Maren says.

"Oh, that," he replies.

"Do you realize, Alexander," she teases, "that according to People magazine, you're number 27 on the World's Most Eligible Bachelor list?"

He grins. "Really? Only twenty-seven?"

"Well," she says, "there are about four billion men in the world, and if half of them are unmarried, that's two billion. So, being number 27 out of two billion is... pretty impressive."

"I suppose when you put it that way, I'm quite the catch." He rolls his eyes and makes another attempt at his bow tie.

She rises and slips between him and the mirror. He catches her around the waist and pulls her in for a kiss.

"Do you know what I love most about you?" she asks softly.

"I can't imagine," he says, "I'm just thrilled that you do."

She smiles, her hands going to his tie. "I love that you rise when I enter a room. Also that you don't make a big production of it. It's just natural for you."

He watches her. "It's not a difficult thing, Maren. All I have to do is stand up."

She flips the ends of his bow tie, expertly looping one over the other. "It's charming that you acknowledge my existence."

He laughs. "Well, maybe that's why I made the list. Women must have a pretty low bar. Standing up doesn't require talent. Or looks. Or even brains."

She laughs. "I don't normally like to make comparisons, but not one other man I've ever dated has done that. Most of the time, they didn't even look at me when I talked. Some of them didn't even look at me when *they* talked."

He pauses, admires her handiwork in the mirror, then takes her hands in his, suddenly serious. "I sincerely hope you're kidding."

"Sadly, no." She shakes her head. "But here is why I love you: your kindness and courtesy actually speak more to the man you are at your core than to anything I might inspire. And somehow, that makes it all the more alluring."

He gives her a look, equal parts tenderness and amusement. "Alluring. Hmm... that may be the best compliment I've ever received. From now on, I'll do my best to remain dangerously polite."

She leans in, brushing her lips against his cheek. "If you climb any higher on that list, I'll be in trouble. I'm not sure I'm up for fending off that much competition."

TWENTY-FOUR

DANCING WITH DANGER

T OPKAPI PALACE HAS CROWNED the hilly promontory of Seraglio Point, where the Bosphorus meets the Golden Horn, since the 1460s, its courtyards and pavilions nestled within ancient walls that once defended Byzantium. The domes, tiled corridors, and hidden passageways were designed for both imperial grandeur and profound seclusion. Topkapi became the pulsing heart of Ottoman ambition—the sultan's seat, his court, and the stage where ceremony, policy, and drama intertwined.

Tonight, the palace, transformed for the annual Golden Heritage Gala, shimmers in the November darkness. The highlight of the international social season, the philanthropy supports the preservation of world art and cultural heritage through major grants from the celebrities, dignitaries, and billionaires it attracts. Gardens, usually subdued in autumn, have been reborn for this single evening. Masses of fragrant white flowers, grown in private greenhouses and coaxed into bloom, line every path and glow in the moonlight. Within the pavilions, blooms of every hue cascade from marble urns and climb carved screens: rare orchids in one salon, clusters of midnight-blue iris in another, crimson roses trail alongside moonlit terraces. Each space is a unique world of sight and scent, enticing guests to wander and discover.

By the time they arrived, the pavilions were already vibrating with activity, music, and color. Maren noticed the intriguing variety among the guests: some hidden behind ornate masks, savoring the anonymity, while others moved about with bare faces, intent on conversation or simply preferring ease over mystery. Her own mask, sequined and feathery, had been set aside after the first dance so she could breathe and see more easily. Alexander had eschewed a mask altogether.

As they walk to the dance floor, Maren leans in. "I think the parure is awake."

He glances at her. "Awake?"

"We have three pieces of the parure, so I thought they would be powerful together, but when I put them on at the hotel, I was worried they weren't working," she says with a laugh.

He cocks his head. "So they're just picky about location?" Then, he gallantly whirls her into his arms. "Our first dance," he says.

"Second," says Maren

Alexander smiles. "Of course."

How could he forget that? Maren thinks, a little disappointed. That dance will be burned into her memory forever.

"You know," Maren says, gliding with Alexander in another waltz, "you really are a remarkable dance partner."

Alexander smiles, looking down at her. "I just try not to step on anyone's toes."

She laughs. "No, really, where did you learn to dance like this?"

He hesitates, then says, "It was important to my parents that I have a classical education."

You mean... classical, like conjugating Latin verbs at a blackboard?" Maren grins as she steps with him through a turn. "Translating Horace, fencing lessons, learning to waltz?"

Alexander smiles. "All of that, and plenty more."

She tilts her head. "So, you spent years in libraries and lecture halls?"

"Yes and no," he says. "At one point, I realized no university could teach me everything I wanted to know. So after graduating, I created my own syllabus."

"Your own syllabus?" Maren says.

He nods. "I made a list: languages I wanted to speak, books I wanted to read; history, philosophy, astronomy, art, music, even some basics of mapmaking and cryptography. Then I found ways to learn them."

He chuckles when he sees the look on her face.

"Don't be impressed. Anyone can do it," he says, "and for free. There are podcasts, lectures, and public libraries. Even online courses from Yale and your very own alma mater."

"You make a convincing case for continuing education."

Alexander grins. "I did meet more girls at university," he says, and Maren laughs.

"Is it hard to be in the public eye?" Maren asks. "You are remarkably patient with people."

Alexander laughs. "Again, you give me too much credit."

Maren looks up at him and thinks how interesting he is. "You're always positive," she says. "And so generous with me."

"I make a point of surrounding myself only with people who are optimistic and open-minded."

"That's great advice."

"I have to," he replies. "I have only so many hours in a day, and a great deal I want to do. To that end, I'm more fortunate than most: I have a staff who are diligent about protecting my time. And I have a close inner circle. No one enters that unless they are positive and generous as well." He smiles.

"Seneca would approve," Maren says before she can stop herself. "He said we should associate with people who are likely to improve us."

Alexander's gaze sharpens, pleased. "You read Seneca?"

She lifts a shoulder. "I've always chosen people I could help, as if being needed were the same as being loved. I'm only now realizing he might call that dangerous."

He considers her for a moment. "Aristotle would say the same, in his own way. There are pleasant friendships, useful friendships... and then the highest kind, where both people care about each other's character. Those are the only ones worth building a life around."

Alexander takes her hand, and they make their way from the dance floor to a table set up with refreshments.

He's very deliberate, Maren thinks. What comes across as endless equanimity results from intentional choices. Alexander curates his closest relationships so that only optimism and generosity surround him. Maren has never even considered the possibility of doing that in her own life. She always wishes she had more time. Alexander's boundaries create that, so he can do what's important to him. He doesn't place the responsibility on others to make those decisions for him.

Feeling both nervous and hopeful, she asks, "Do you ever let someone into that inner circle by accident, Alexander? Or does it always have to be earned?"

He gives her a long look, mischief in his smile.

"It's never an accident, Maren. I don't choose my friends for proximity. I choose them for their quality of spirit. And you definitely qualify."

He lifts her hand to his lips, brushing a kiss across her knuckles. "Now, if you'll excuse me for a few minutes."

She watches Alexander walk away, weaving deftly through the crowd. Tonight, she's seen him move easily among old friends, colleagues, and new acquaintances much the same way, always friendly and humorous, yet holding firm to a polite barrier around his private life.

Maren sips her champagne, wishing her connection with Alexander could bridge every barrier. She wants to be more to him than a fleeting love, and the thought unsettles her; love alone has never promised anyone a lifetime. After all, he loved Simone once, too. The stakes feel impossibly high. She dreams their story might last, not only as a romance but as something enduring and truly mutual.

After a few minutes, a familiar voice interrupts her thoughts. "Care to dance?" Lucien asks, extending a hand.

"Try not to bore her," Alexander says as he returns, just loud enough for Lucien to hear.

Lucien's expression doesn't shift, but he answers anyway. "Don't worry, I haven't left a woman unsatisfied in years."

As Lucien takes Maren's hand, the music changes, and Maren feels the parure respond to Lucien's arrival.

"I see you've grown quite cozy with the playboy," Lucien says, eyeing Maren with his usual predatory interest.

Maren looks at him, amused. "He's not as reckless as he looks."

Lucien gives her a fleeting, offhand smile. "Pity."

Maren studies his profile in the candlelight. "You don't strike me as the domestic type, Lucien."

He looks down at her. "Darling, I'm whatever type the moment requires."

The ball, Maren realizes, is only just beginning.

"Are you here to help me, or help them?" She says, looking toward two Turkish gentlemen leaning on a column who don't appear to be interested in dancing.

He gives her a half-smile. "I'm here because the job pays well, and you're interesting." He glances at the Talisman jewels. "I'm also here because I'd hate to see all of your hard work be lost to people who are less lucky, but more aggressive."

She looks up at him. "You believe in luck?"

"I believe in talent, Miss Bennett. The rest you figure out as you go."

"Is the Brotherhood that aggressive, Lucien?" She asks.

"Depends on who you meet. Your father stirred up a bees' nest when he found that ring." He glances at Maren. "The Brotherhood has never been monolithic, Miss Bennett. There are zealots who want the necklace at any cost, and others who just want it protected. The trouble is—you won't know which is which until it's far too late."

Lucien looks into Maren's eyes, voice low and dry: "If you're going to make a habit of trusting people who hire thugs, you may want to invest in sturdier jewelry next time."

She smiles disarmingly at him. "And yet, here I am, risking it with you."

He inclines his head, "It's either bravery or appalling judgment, and I've seen both win the day, given the right circumstances."

Maren tilts her head, searching Lucien's face as they move across the floor. "If you know so much about the pieces of the parure, why don't you just use them to find the necklace?"

Lucien doesn't answer her. "I'm pleased you saw through the decoy necklace at Saint Mark's. I wondered for a while if you were going to be able to keep up."

She arches an eyebrow, riposting his parry. "I'd have expected you to know by now that the jewelry pieces are only powerful when a woman wears them. Try to keep up, Lucien."

Lucien shrugs, "The earrings don't really suit me, anyway. Besides, magic doesn't respond well to cynics."

Maren studies him, lowering her voice. "So, you're all just using me to find the authentic Talisman necklace? Would I be correct in assuming the Brotherhood has no idea where it is either?"

Lucien doesn't answer directly. "Let's just say, tonight you're the one with all the right accessories."

Maren lets Lucien guide her into the next turn, the music swirling around them.

She narrows her eyes at him. "That explains why they haven't taken the jewelry from me yet. I'm just a tool for the job."

He shrugs, "We all have our purpose, Miss Bennett."

"And what is yours, Lucien?" Her voice is soft, looking into his eyes.

Lucien smiles, "I'm simply planning to keep you in one piece until the moon does its trick."

Before she can retort, he leans in slightly, lowering his voice. "For what it's worth, I did spot something in the pavilion... a tile with a symbol that matches the one on your father's journal. Two circles."

Maren is surprised. "The two intersecting circles? The vesica piscis?"

"Funny how things show up when you least expect them, Miss Bennett."

Just as Alexander reappears, Lucien spins her elegantly, releasing her with a wink.

When Alexander takes her in his arms again, Maren says, "Lucien said there's a tile with the interlocking circles symbol in the main hall, but it is filled with people dancing. We'll draw too much attention if we walk around looking for it."

"Then we'll dance our way there, Miss Bennett," Alexander says dryly.

Alexander guides Maren through the open doors from the moonlit terrace into the Imperial Hall as the music changes to the tango. The ballroom is a kaleidoscope of movement as couples turn and spin in measured steps between the outdoor and indoor spaces.

The pavilion is marvelous: Venetian mirrors reflect and multiply the light from candles and crystal chandeliers, while blue-and-white tiles gleam along the walls in intricate patterns. The domed ceiling soars above them, creating a magical atmosphere.

"Over there—" Maren breathes as they move into an elegant caminata, their feet stepping in perfect rhythm like cats stalking through the room. She spots the interlocking circles symbol on an emerald green tile among the ornate tilework on the far wall. "Just like Lucien said."

Alexander leads her through a graceful figure-eight pattern that allows her to scan both sides of the room as they turn. On the opposite wall, another green vesica piscis tile catches her attention. Identical to the first, but positioned directly across the room.

"Alexander," she whispers, as they continue their tango in a flowing giro around the pavilion's perimeter, moving counter-clockwise like all the other couples. "There's another one."

Maren circles around Alexander in the traditional windmill movement of a subtle molinete. Alexander remaining at the center, her gown swirling as she pivots. She spots a third green tile on the eastern wall, then quickly finds the fourth on the west. Her heart races as the pattern becomes clear.

"They're on every wall," she whispers against Alexander's ear when he draws her close into their abrazo—that intimate embrace where partners move as one body. "Four tiles, not one. What are we supposed to do with four of them?"

Alexander's brow furrows, and he guides her through another elegant half-moon turn that brings them face-to-face again. "They must work together somehow. But how?"

Other couples move around them in their own passionate tangos, sharp movements and dramatic pauses punctuating the music, completely unaware that Maren and Alexander are solving a centuries-old puzzle right there on the dance floor.

Just then, Maren feels a subtle vibration against her finger—a gentle pulse that matches the rhythm of her heartbeat. She glances down at her ring and gasps softly.

The four emeralds positioned around the perimeter of the ring are catching the light from the chandeliers, but more than that—they seem to respond to something in the room. Each emerald appears to glow faintly, pointing outward like tiny green compasses.

"Alexander," she breathes, lifting her hand between them as they continue to dance. "Look."

He follows her gaze and sees the four emeralds positioned at perfect cardinal points around the perimeter of the ring—north, south, east, west.

"The emeralds..." Maren's voice is quiet but urgent. "Four points. They're arranged just like the tiles on the walls."

Understanding flashes in Alexander's eyes as he looks from the ring to the four vesica piscis symbols positioned around the pavilion. "The tiles aren't just decorations—they're compass points."

"My father didn't mean a flower rose," Maren realizes, her pulse quickening. "He meant a compass rose. When the crescent dances with the rose..."

"Then the center is—" Alexander looks down at the marble floor beneath their feet as he guides her through a flowing ronda that gradually spirals them inward toward the exact center of the Imperial Hall.

There, inlaid in the polished marble and so subtle it would be invisible unless you were standing directly over it, is a tiny bronze crescent no larger than her thumb. At its heart, barely visible, is the smallest keyhole Maren has ever seen.

"The compass rose," she whispers, her ring still pulsing gently against her finger. "And we're dancing right over it."

Alexander's eyes meet hers, and something passes between them—a shared understanding that this moment belongs to them alone. The other couples continue their own rondas around the pavilion, maintaining their lanes like dancers at any proper milonga, but it feels as though time has slowed just for the two of them.

"No one else would have noticed," Maren whispers, her heart racing as Alexander draws her closer into their abrazo. "If I were here with anyone else..."

"But you're not," he says softly, his voice warm against her ear. "You're here with me."

The intimacy of the moment, the way they've had to work together, trust each other, move as one body, makes Maren realize how perfectly they complement each other. Her knowledge of her father's clues, his quick thinking and charm, their natural rhythm together on the dance floor. It's all been necessary.

"I need to use the key," she breathes, glancing down at the bronze crescent beneath their feet.

Alexander nods, understanding immediately. "On three?"

The music swells around them as Alexander prepares for the most important corte of the evening—the dramatic pause and dip that would normally punctuate their dance. Other dancers move past them in the flowing line of dance, completely oblivious to the ancient puzzle being solved in their midst.

"One," Alexander counts softly, his hand firm at her back.

"Two," Maren whispers, feeling for the small gold key in her hidden pocket.

"Three."

Alexander sweeps her into a dramatic, perfect quebrada—the classic tango dip that makes other couples pause and smile at the obvious romance. As Maren arches back gracefully in the time-honored pose, her hair nearly touching the marble floor, she slips the tiny key into the bronze crescent and gives it the slightest turn.

As Alexander lifts her back up, spinning her once more, they both wait, listening, watching. But nothing happens. No click, no sound, no visible change in the surrounding room. The music continues, other couples dance past them, and the four vesica piscis tiles remain as still and silent as ever.

"Did it work?" Alexander asks quietly, his arms still around her as the music changes once again, now a foxtrot.

Maren frowns, glancing down at the bronze crescent beneath their feet, then up at the walls around them. "I don't know. Nothing seems different."

They continue dancing, but uncertainty creeps in. Had they solved it wrong? Was there more to the puzzle?

"What now?" Alexander wonders, guiding her through a turn.

Maren thinks back to her father's note, running through the lines in her mind. "What was the next line of the text?" Alexander asks, as if reading her thoughts.

She closes her eyes for a moment, remembering. "The chosen follow the path when they pause and reflect."

Alexander's grip tightens slightly on her waist. "Pause and reflect." He looks around the Imperial Hall. "What if we need to literally pause... and reflect?"

Maren follows his gaze to the mirrors lining the walls, their silvered surfaces throwing back the movement of dancing couples.

"The mirrors," she breathes. "But which one? We need to stop dancing and look."

They dance toward a mirror directly under the eastern-most tile, and glide to a stop, trying to look casual while examining it more closely.

"Admiring the craftsmanship?" Lucien appears beside them, champagne glass in hand, looking every inch the sophisticated party guest. But his eyes are sharp, assessing.

"It has something to do with the mirror. I think it opens." Maren whispers, the parure warming on her skin.

Lucien glances around quickly, noting the positions of other guests, then gives an almost imperceptible nod. "Indeed. Venetian work."

Alexander catches on immediately. "We were just appreciating the historical significance."

"Of course." Lucien moves to position himself between them and the nearest group of dancers, creating a natural screen. He raises his voice slightly, addressing them as if making polite conversation. "The restoration work here has been quite extensive. Some of the original features have been preserved in the most ingenious ways."

Under cover of his casual chatter, Lucien adds quietly, "On my mark, see if it has a hinge. I'll keep our friends occupied." He gestures subtly toward two men in dark suits who have been circling the room, clearly the Turkish Brotherhood agents they noticed earlier.

"The mirror work in particular," Lucien continues in his normal voice while moving slightly to block the agents' line of sight, "shows remarkable ingenuity. The original craftsmen built in some fascinating features."

As Lucien begins an animated discussion about Ottoman renovation techniques, Alexander gently presses against the mirror's edge while Maren appears to study the frame details.

The mirror swings inward silently.

"Fascinating," Maren says, a little too loudly, then drops her voice. "We should examine this more closely in private."

"An excellent idea," Alexander agrees, and they slip through the opening.

Just before the mirror closes behind them, they hear Lucien smoothly redirecting the approaching agents: "Gentlemen! Have you seen the remarkable tilework in the east wing? Far superior to what we have here, in my opinion."

TWENTY-FIVE

A GOLDEN ROAD

THE MIRROR SEALS SHUT behind them, silencing the distant strains of violins and plunging them into total darkness. Alexander steadies Maren as she teeters on the edge of a narrow step, nearly losing her balance in the sudden blindness.

"Where are we? I can't see anything," Maren whispers, tucking the beaded train of her dress over her arm.

Alexander pulls out his phone and activates its light. The weak glow reveals a passage barely wide enough for one person, its walls lined with the same blue-and-white İznik tiles that decorated the Imperial Hall, though here they are dulled by centuries of dust. They stand at the top of a precarious stairway, stones tilted at odd, treacherous angles disappearing into endless black.

Maren whispers, "This must be part of the Golden Road, the sultan's private passageway system. Historically, it connected his chambers to various parts of the palace and beyond."

They descend slowly. Down, and down, and down they travel. "Careful," Alexander whispers, running his hand along the tiled wall for support. Maren counts the steps—twenty, thirty, forty. When the path finally levels out, Maren feels warmth and looks at her ring, surprised. One of the four emeralds is glowing with a soft, pulsing light, like a captured firefly.

"Alexander, look." She holds up her hand, and the green glow illuminates their faces in the darkness. The passage ahead branches in three directions. "It's pointing that way," he says, indicating the left passage. "It's guiding us," Maren realizes, her voice filled with wonder.

They move forward tentatively, Maren in front, following the glowing emeralds as they show her which way to turn in the passages.

"Where do you think it's taking us?" Alexander asks, ducking slightly as the ceiling lowers.

Maren feels the familiar tingle of the parure responding to something, and she hears faint voices somewhere behind them.

"Let's move," Alexander says quietly.

The passage ahead splits in three directions again, each disappearing into inky blackness. Maren holds up her ring, and the northern emerald pulses brighter, pointing them left again.

"This way," she whispers, and they move deeper into the ancient labyrinth.

The walls here are rougher and older. Possibly pre-Ottoman stonework, Maren thinks, that speaks of Byzantine foundations. Their footsteps reverberate despite their efforts at silence, and the air grows heavier.

After what feels like an eternity of following the ring's guidance through the twisting maze, they encounter their first obstacle. The tunnel ends abruptly at a large, circular bronze disk set into the stone floor, decorated with astronomical symbols.

Alexander kneels to examine it, running his fingers along its ornate edge. "Civilization's first manhole cover," he says.

Together, they grasp the heavy bronze ring embedded in its surface and heave upward. The disk slides aside with surprising smoothness, revealing a circular opening that yawns into darkness below. From the depths comes the distant, musical sound of water dripping, resonating, almost melodic.

Alexander shines his phone light down into the hole. "Fifteen feet, maybe more," he says grimly, "No handholds."

"We need to go down," Maren says, her ring pulsing on her finger, "but I don't think I can drop that far without breaking something important."

Maren looks down at her ball gown, then at Alexander with sudden determination. "Help me with my train."

"Your what?"

"The train of my gown—it detaches." She turns, showing him the intricate fastenings. "It's at least six feet of silk."

Working quickly, they unfasten the elaborate train from Maren's dress, the sapphire silk pooling in their hands.

"Do you think it will hold?" Maren asks, testing the fabric's strength.

"I think so," Alexander says.

Alexander wraps the fabric around his wrist and grips it as he helps position Maren at the edge of the opening. "Careful. We don't know what's waiting down there." He hands her his phone, and she tucks it into the bodice of her dress. "I can pull you up if necessary."

She grasps the silk rope, sliding down and dropping the last few feet. Moments later, her voice echoes up with wonder.

"Alexander—you have to see this!"

"My turn," Alexander says. He tears the silk into two strips and ties them in a knot in the center, then feeds the length through the bronze ring.

Maren shines the light upward and watches him work; sudden understanding dawning on her face. "Of course! That's why a manhole cover is round, so it won't fall through the opening no matter how it's turned or moved. You're brilliant!"

Alexander tests the knot a final time, then, holding on to both pieces of silk, begins his descent. As he reaches the end of his tether, he shifts his hands to one side, lets go of the other, and drops the rest of the way, the silk falling with him and landing in a sparkling heap.

"Brilliant!" Maren whispers again, kissing him. Above them, the voices are getting closer.

"It's a Turkish bath." A magnificent one, she thinks. Its dark blue ceiling is decorated with gold stars, the walls covered floor to ceiling in exquisite turquoise İznik tiles. A stark contrast to the cold stone passages above.

The steaming wall to wall pool, fed by natural hot springs, is lined with swirling iridescent mosaics. The air is warm and sultry and seems scented with some kind of spice. Shafts of light from unseen prisms drape the vast chamber in a soft, otherworldly aqua haze. The sound of water reverberates all around them, cascading from ornate bronze spouts into carved marble basins, a lullaby of falling rivulets.

"This must be an ancient bath," Alexander says, his voice filled with awe. "Look at the craftsmanship."

"I guess we can swim," Maren says, taking off her shoes and hiking up her gown.

Alexander sweeps his light over the water and stops. Just beneath the surface, white marble stepping stones rise, arranged in the shape of the vesica piscis—the very symbol they have trailed all night.

"There," he points. "We can follow the pattern across."

She turns, and their eyes meet. He smiles, draws her close, and kisses her, warm and unhurried.

"God, I love your lips," he murmurs.

She steps carefully onto the first marble stone, warm beneath her feet, heated by the thermal springs below. The Turkish bath was a place created for sensual rituals. Every breath Maren takes in the humid air, each touch of heated stone and shimmer of pale blue-green light, feels dreamlike within those misty, starlit walls. Slowly and deliberately, she crosses from stone to stone, Alexander's quiet presence close behind, the aqua glow draping around them as they vanish into the fog.

They reach a small tiled courtyard on the other side, surrounded by four elegant marble arches. Maren's ring pulses urgently toward the eastern archway, but when they approach, they find only a blank wall.

"It wants us to go forward, but there's nothing here," Maren says, studying the seamless stonework. "Maybe it was sealed over."

She pauses, remembering something. "Or maybe it's like the wall at Saint Mark's," she says, almost to herself, "maybe we just need the proper key." She looks at Alexander. "Help me search the ground for something that might be a keyhole."

They kneel at the base of the wall, brushing away centuries of dust and debris with the silk train Alexander carries. Finally, Maren's fingers find it—carved into the marble at the wall's base, almost invisible beneath the accumulated dust.

"Here," she breathes. "The interlocking circles again. Our vesica piscis symbol. But look, one circle is carved out completely."

They look at each other with understanding, and Maren slips off his mother's golden bracelet, placing it into the circular depression. It fits perfectly, and immediately the wall responds. A hidden door pivots open in the tiled stone, revealing a passage beyond.

As they step through into the darkness, Maren pauses to retrieve the bracelet. She lifts it from its resting place and steps back quickly. The wall pivots closed behind them, sealing seamlessly once more.

They move forward into an endless corridor. Alexander leading now. The only illumination comes from the light on his phone, casting an eerie glow just a few feet ahead of them.

"Stay close," Alexander says, reaching back to take Maren's hand. The ring's emeralds pulse—brighter when they move in the right direction, dimming when they veer off course. Left turn, right turn, straight ahead through narrowing walls that are closing in around them.

"How far do these passages go?" Maren whispers, her voice echoing strangely in the confined space.

"The Golden Road was said to connect the palace to strategic points across Istanbul," Alexander replies quietly. "We could be anywhere under the city by now."

The darkness is complete, pressing in on them like a living thing. The air grows staler, older, as they move through undisturbed passages. Another right turn, left turn. Straight ahead again through a corridor so narrow now they have to walk sideways.

Then, suddenly, the ring flares brilliant green, and they emerge into a magnificent circular chamber, walls entirely encrusted with precious stones set into gold. Emeralds, rubies, sapphires, and diamonds form intricate geometric patterns across the curved gold walls.

"Unbelievable," Alexander says, turning slowly to take it all in. "Maren, it's nearly midnight," he says grimly, looking at his watch. "The eclipse reaches its maximum in minutes." They've been navigating these passages for what feels like hours, and time has been slipping away as they solve each puzzle.

Her ring and the bracelet pulse stronger now, together. The warmth from the bracelet has spread up her arm. The three pieces are responding to something nearby, something powerful. "We have to keep going," Maren says. "The eclipse has already begun." Maren feels the pull of celestial forces through her jewelry. "The moon is moving into the earth's shadow right now."

The emeralds on the ring urge them forward into another pitch-black corridor, directly to a dead end.

Maren's heart sinks as she studies the seamless stonework around them. Above, they can hear the faint shouts of Brotherhood agents trying to figure out how to follow them.

"We're trapped," she whispers, panic rising. "We've come all this way, and there's nowhere to go."

Alexander continues searching the walls for any sign of a hidden mechanism, but finds nothing. "There has to be something—a lever, a keyhole, anything."

The eclipse reaches its peak overhead, and all three pieces of the parure pulse with urgent energy.

Maren closes her eyes, trying to think. "What did my father mean? What am I missing?" She runs through his message in her mind and suddenly remembers his closing line to her: the same phrase Professor Antonescu had said; the same one she'd written in the bookshop; the one that had somehow called to her—"What you seek is seeking you."

"Alexander," she blurts. "Stop searching."

"What?"

"The necklace isn't hidden," Maren breathes in wonder. "It's waiting."

"Stand still." Maren takes a deep breath, lets it out slowly, and wills herself to stop moving. Stop searching. Stop trying to solve this like a puzzle. "The last line of my father's text—your mother said the same thing to me—*Stand still for once and see what comes to you.*"

Alexander stands beside her and takes her hand.

Maren closes her eyes and slows her breathing. The moment they both become completely still, something extraordinary happens. The parure's pulsing synchronizes, creating a steady rhythm that matches their heartbeats. In response, thin lines of light begin to appear in the stone walls around them—not mechanical seams, but something far older and more magical.

The lines form the shape of a door directly in front of them, glowing softly with the same green light as Maren's ring.

It's not about finding the Talisman, Maren thinks, suddenly clear. It's about being worthy of it. The door finds us.

The eclipse reaches maximum totality above them, and the glowing door swings open on hinges of pure light, revealing the chamber that has waited a century for this moment.

Twenty-Six

THE ESCAPE

MAREN AND ALEXANDER STEP into a small, shadowed alcove. At its center stands a smooth, round columnar plinth, about four feet high, carved from a solid block of gold-flecked royal blue lapis lazuli, veined with pale limestone. The display once held something precious, surely the necklace, but now only an etched gold disk remains atop it, with a notch marking where the treasure had rested. A faceted crystal prism glows faintly overhead, but otherwise, the chamber is empty and unremarkable.

Realizing her mistake, Maren pivots just as the stone door grinds shut behind them. The sound echoes through the chamber before fading to an ominous silence. There is no handle, no visible seam—just cold, unyielding stone, sealing them within.

"No! No, no. Oh, come on!" Maren slams her fist against the wall where the door had been. Her voice fades away, swallowed by silence.

Alexander says nothing. He traces the chamber's edges, searching for a crack or puff of air. He crouches, inspecting the floor, scanning for seams or fissures.

"We're too late," panic rising in Maren's voice. "Someone beat us to it—if the necklace was ever here at all."

Her fingers move across the surface of the plinth, then she kneels and breathes on the stone, fogging the surface. No hidden marks appear. She rises, throat tightening. "What have I done?" she whispers. "What if we're trapped this time—really trapped?" She shakes her head, fighting the thought. "No. There has to be a way out."

Alexander joins her at the plinth, running his hands carefully over the surface, just as she had. In the stillness, the parure pulses, stronger now.

She steps back, breathing hard. "Light," she whispers, looking at the ring. "Nur. The key is the light. Where love and light meet..." You're going to have to help with this. "What? What are you telling me?"

Maren closes her eyes. In her mind, she sees the moon slipping free of the eclipse, the celestial event creating the interlocking circles of a perfect vesica piscis in the sky above the palace. She looks up instinctively as light from the newly unveiled sliver of moon passes through the prism in the ceiling, concentrating into a thin, brilliant stream of light shining directly onto the center of the plinth.

"Hurry!" Alexander calls out, suddenly understanding.

Maren yanks off the ring and slams it into the golden slot atop the stone pedestal. The focused beam strikes the ring's smooth cabochon turquoise stone and its diamond compass rose, sending countless stars spinning across the curved walls. The emeralds blaze to life. Ancient mechanisms grind awake, and the gold disk lifts slowly, revealing a hidden compartment. The necklace rises into view—an explosion of emerald fire, luminous gold, and rose-cut diamonds. Maren and Alexander stand transfixed, watching centuries of legend become reality before their eyes.

Alexander is first to move. He looks behind them at the stone door. It is still shut tight. "I don't see another way out." Maren circles the plinth, her shadow moving on the walls. "Is it a trick? Is this the actual necklace?" She reaches toward it, then hesitates. She half-expects it to vanish if she touches it.

Alexander studies the ceiling and the prism. "The mechanism stopped. That... might have been our one chance."

Maren takes a deep breath and lifts the necklace from its cradle. The gold feels strangely warm, alive. She fastens it around her neck.

Nothing. Then, the world shifts.

Colors sharpen. The chamber ripples with faint lines of light along the floor and walls. The seams of the stone blocks now glow gently. Maren gasps. "Alexander—I see it. I see where the exit is."

She stumbles back, nearly dropping the ring as she retrieves it. The glowing lines pulse and draw her to a narrow seam on the wall behind the plinth, a crack too faint for the naked eye until now.

Alexander comes to her side. "What do you see?"

She points, already moving. "There!"

With the ring back on her finger, all of the parure working as one, Maren feels a path open in her thoughts. Her palm touches a barely there depression in the stone. Light jumps from the necklace to her hand, a mechanism slides aside, and a slim door grinds open, revealing darkness beyond, but this time, a way forward.

The narrow passage stretches into nowhere, but wearing the parure, Maren can see lines of light threading through the ancient stone like veins of gold. It's as if the jewels recognize these tunnels from the dawn of an empire.

"This way," she whispers, her voice barely audible above the distant sound of voices echoing around them, maybe from above. Maybe outside the Talisman chamber. She doesn't know, but it seems the Turkish Brotherhood has found another route. The voices are urgent and commanding. Maren doesn't need to understand the words to know she and Alexander are not home free. They are running out of time.

The necklace pulses against her throat, and suddenly she can see more than just the escape route; she sees men moving through the passages they've already traveled, spreading out like hunters tracking prey.

Alexander's hand finds hers in the darkness. "Can you see where we're going?"

Yes." The word comes out steadier than she feels. The parure shows her the path ahead, but not just the physical route through these Byzantine passages. Images flash through her mind: Ottoman courtiers escaping through these same tunnels; her great-grandmother and Alexander's, young and determined, hiding the bracelet during the war; all the women who have worn these jewels before her, each adding their own courage to the collection.

In her mind, she sees the princess, tragically forced to use the parure for a purpose that was against her nature and against the nature of the jewels themselves. Maren feels the devastation of that legacy—a reminder that true guardians understand what must be protected, and why.

"We did it. We actually did it." Maren says, amazed. She stops walking and turns to face Alexander. For a moment, they just look at each other. She thinks about the magnitude of what they've accomplished. He looks as if he's thinking the same thing.

"The necklace," he says. "How does it feel? Wearing all of it together?"

Maren considers the question. The complete parure feels like coming home to herself, not overwhelming, but clarifying. Like she's finally seeing the world as it really is, not just how she thought it was. It's not what I expected," she says. "I thought it would be more... dramatic. But it's not about power, Alexander. It's about clarity. Understanding. Love."

She reaches for his hand. "I can see why our great-grand-mothers protected it. And why so many have wanted it. But most will never understand what the parure truly is—not after what happened to... her. The princess. No woman should ever again be forced to use the parure to act against her own nature, against love."

An urgent need wells within her to bring the parure to safety and preserve it for the women who will come after her.

"This way," she whispers, ducking into a narrow opening and turning sharply to the right.

This passage is different from the ones they've navigated so far—even older, perhaps, carved directly from the bedrock beneath Istanbul. The walls are damp with centuries of seepage, and the air smells of salt and age. But the parure keeps urging her on, the emeralds on her ring pointing like a compass toward safety.

They run, and the air grows fresher as they follow the glowing lines, and Maren realizes they're moving upward now, toward the surface. The earrings bump softly against her neck as she stops and turns her head, listening for pursuit.

"I don't think... they can follow us... this way at least...," she pants, relief flooding through her. "The chamber sealed itself after we left."

But even as she says it, Maren knows their troubles are far from over. The jewels show her flashes of what's happening above ground: several men in dark suits, their faces grim. Lucien standing alone on a terrace, speaking into his phone. Other agents spreading through the palace grounds.

The passage opens into a wider tunnel, this one with fitted stones and proper drainage—part of Istanbul's ancient cistern system, she realizes. They're under the city now, running through the Byzantine waterworks that supplied Constantinople and Istanbul for over a thousand years.

The sound of their footsteps echoes off the arched ceiling as they follow the tunnel. Moonlight filters down through grates far above, creating pools of silver light on the slick stones.

The passage curves upward again, and suddenly they find themselves at a dead end, gasping as they try to catch their breath, looking up at hand and footholds leading to another round bronze cover. Maren climbs up and Alexander follows. Together, they balance on a step and push at the cover. It moves an inch at a time.

"It's making a terrible racket," Maren whispers.

"Let's just take a chance," Alexander says, bracing himself and shoving the cover hard to the left with a grunt. They squeeze through and emerge behind a wooden screen, blinking as their eyes adjust. It appears to be some kind of storage room. Moonlight streams through a high transom window.

Stepping carefully over stacks of folded rugs and tarnished brass urns, they approach a solid wood door. Alexander holds up a hand, and they both freeze, listening. Through the weathered wood, Maren can hear the sounds of Istanbul at night. Alexander slides aside the heavy iron bolt with deliberate care, mindful of any sound. The door opens, and cool night air touches their faces as they step into a narrow alley.

"Where to next?" he asks. She can see concern in his eyes as he takes in her exhausted state in the dim streetlight.

Maren wonders what he's looking at, then sees her reflection in a shop window and winces. Her once-elegant gown hangs in tatters, streaked with dirt and what might be centuries-old spiderwebs. A leaf clings stubbornly to her hair.

"Toward the water, I think," she says, closing her eyes and letting the parure guide her. "But Alexander, I'm not certain. I'm sorry."

"Maren." His voice is gentle but firm. "Look at me."

She opens her eyes, expecting to see disappointment or frustration. Instead, his voice is impossibly tender.

"If I tell you something now," he says, then pauses, taking in their surroundings, "in this strange place, being chased by God knows who, after we just found a magical necklace in someone's five-hundred-year-old basement..." He glances down at his own torn shirt and dirt-stained jacket and laughs. "Looking absolutely nothing like people who attend fancy balls—will you believe me?"

"I'll try," she whispers.

He reaches up and gently extracts the leaf from her hair.

"I've never needed you to be certain about anything. I'm not trying to fix you. I'm not waiting for you to transform into someone else. Even if we do look like we've been cleaning out a barn."

Despite everything, Maren smiles.

"My love for you isn't conditional on your having all the answers, or your composure, or how you look in a ballgown—though you do look rather magnificent, even covered in cobwebs." His thumb brushes away a smudge on her cheek. "I don't need you to be 'resolved' or emotionally tidy. What I've realized over these past crazy weeks is that I love you because of the whole, shifting, beautiful mystery of who you are. Right now. Exactly as you are tonight."

Maren feels tears threaten. "Even when I'm leading you through drainpipes based on nothing but feelings?"

"Especially then," he says, and kisses her forehead. "Though next time, maybe we could try dinner and a movie."

Maren just smiles.

"The hotel," Alexander says. "I don't think we can go back there."

"No, we can't." The necklace is warning her, showing her images of men waiting in their hotel lobby. "You're right. They're waiting for us."

They make their way through Istanbul's winding streets, staying in the shadows. The parure helps Maren navigate, showing her which alleys to avoid, which corners hide watchers. She's felt nothing like this power—not overwhelming or frightening, but like having the whispered advice of every brave woman who came before her.

There is a private pier just ahead, tucked between two larger marina complexes. Maren has a sudden vision and spins to find Lucien, backlit by the sleek glow of a yacht's lights. Gone is his formal wear; he's changed into dark trousers and a charcoal peacoat, blending with the night.

"Cutting it rather close, Miss Bennett," Lucien says dryly, his gaze going immediately to the necklace resting at her throat.

"How did you know we'd be here?" Maren asks astonished.

"I didn't," he says. "Word travels fast in certain circles. You might think you've been subtle, but apparently half the city's criminal underworld got the memo about your little treasure hunt."

Maren's brow furrows with worry. "How many are following us now?"

"Well, let's see... there's your original admirers, palace security, local police responding to noise complaints, plus every treasure hunter and black-market dealer in Istanbul who's gotten word of your discovery," he shrugs. "Quite the guest list."

"Are you helping us or helping them?" Alexander asks bluntly.

Lucien's mouth quirks in that familiar half-smile. "That depends entirely on your definition of 'help,' doesn't it?" He glances between them. "Though I will say, standing here in the open debating my loyalties probably isn't your best tactical choice right now."

Maren exhales, tension easing slightly despite the circumstances. Even in a crisis, Lucien's wit is oddly reassuring—like finding a familiar landmark in unknown territory.

As if summoned by his words, shouts echo from the street above the pier. Flashlight beams cut through the darkness, sweeping closer across the water.

Lucien nods toward the yacht. "I think it's time to take our leave."

They break into a run toward the boat, but Maren stops short when she spots two men in dark suits standing on the back deck. "Lucien! How could you?"

He turns back with that maddeningly calm expression. "Come now, Miss Bennett, you're rather committed at this point, unless you fancy a midnight swim through the Bosphorus."

Alexander's hand finds Maren's elbow, steadying her as the flashlights draw nearer. They have no choice but to board.

A woman emerges from the cabin and takes her place beside the men in suits. She looks composed and studious, clearly not hired muscle. The yacht's captain, a weathered man with kind eyes, nods to them without speaking and immediately begins casting off the lines.

As the boat pulls away from the pier, Maren sees the first flashlight beams reach the spot where they'd been standing moments before.

Lucien says, "May I present Maren Bennett, Alexander Girard, Dr. Helen Stewart." Maren recognizes the woman's face from photographs in her mother's papers.

"Helen, please," the woman says, extending a steady hand. "From the Sorbonne. Your mother asked us to see you safely home."

Maren looks from Dr. Stewart to Alexander in surprise. "The Sorbonne Society? You still exist?"

Dr. Stewart smiles. "We evolved, but yes. We've been looking for the parure as well. Her eyes go to the necklace at Maren's throat, and her expression becomes almost reverent. "This is the first time it's been complete in a very long time."

"Are you here to take it?" Alexander asks, courteous but stepping slightly protectively in front of Maren.

"Take it?" Dr. Stewart looks genuinely surprised. "No, Mr. Girard, we're here to help you decide what to do with it."

One man steps forward. "There's a car waiting to take you to Atatürk Airport. We have resources for expediting your departure, and Mr. Girard's jet can have you back in Paris by morning."

Dr. Stewart explains that the modern Sorbonne Society works not as a secret organization any longer, but as a network of scholars, historians, and art experts dedicated to protecting significant artifacts.

"The Turkish Brotherhood that has been chasing you is a splinter group," Dr. Stewart explains. "The legitimate antiquities society in Turkey contacted us weeks ago, concerned about treasure hunters. They want the parure to be protected but separated."

"I can understand that," Maren agrees, her hand unconsciously touching the necklace. "It would be a shame to keep it from public view entirely, but it can't stay together. That would be too dangerous."

"What happens now?" Maren asks, turning to Dr. Stewart.

"We'll take this yacht to a private pier outside the city. Somewhere your pursuers won't think to look," Dr. Stewart says, glancing toward the captain, who nods in acknowledgment. "From there, a car will take you directly to Atatürk Airport, where Mr. Girard's jet is waiting. Fresh clothes, proper security, and you'll be back in Paris this morning."

Alexander looks relieved. "And the parure?"

Dr. Stewart's expression grows thoughtful. "That decision belongs to Miss Bennett. The parure is complete again, which means its protective powers are at their strongest. But it also means it's at its most vulnerable. There will always be those who want to claim it for the wrong reasons."

Maren's hand goes instinctively to the necklace at her throat again. The responsibility settles on her shoulders, but it doesn't feel burdensome. It feels right.

"I need to talk to my mother," she says. "And Alexander's mother, and Professor Antonescu. The three families who've protected it all these years."

The yacht cuts through the dark waters of the Bosphorus, past the sleeping palaces and under the great bridge that spans two continents. Istanbul looks peaceful from here, giving no hint of the chaos they've left behind. Maren stands at the railing, Alexander's jacket around her shoulders. She recalls Professor Antonescu's words—that love makes things endure. Surrounded by centuries of courage resting against her skin, watching Alexander's profile in the moonlight, she thinks the professor was right.

Love is worth the risk.

Behind them, Istanbul shimmers against the night sky, its minarets and domes keeping their ancient vigil. Ahead lies their plane, Paris, home—and the daunting question of what happens when legend becomes real.

But for now, on these dark waters between past and future, Maren allows herself a moment of pure gratitude. They're alive. They're together. Whatever comes next, they'll face it as the parure intended, not alone, but bound together by something stronger than danger and older than time.

TWENTY-SEVEN

THE FAITHFUL HEART

T HEIR DEPARTURE FROM ISTANBUL had been unexpectedly smooth, thanks in no small part to Dr. Stewart and the men from the Brotherhood. Once on the Girard private jet, they had cleaned up, changed into fresh clothes, and had something to eat. As soon as the plane cleared the runway, both Maren and Alexander breathed a deep sigh of relief and dozed the entire three and a half hour flight to Paris.

Mid-morning, the bare arched branches of linden and sycamore herald their arrival at Le Cœur Fidèle. Leaf litter that had gathered in clumps along the gravel lane swirls and settles again as the car goes by. Maren looks out the window as they pass the bronzed lawn that wraps around the forecourt.

Autumn has always been one of Maren's favorite seasons. There's a particular peace in this time of year, the way nature, after the exuberance of spring and summer, settles into a well-deserved rest, silently restoring itself for what comes next. She finds comfort in the reminder that vitality between seasons doesn't disappear; it merely gathers strength.

As the car slows near the front steps, Maren sees Alexander's posture unwind with palpable relief. In all the time she's known him, she has never once heard him complain. She suspects that this kind of composure is rooted in his upbringing.

Refusing to speak ill of circumstances seems woven into his personality.

Everyone is uncomfortable at times; everyone gets tired, hot, cold, frustrated, and inconvenienced by life. It is fairly easy to be cheerful when things go well. Maren is beginning to believe that perhaps it is the way one carries discomfort—and whether one announces it—that reveals more about a person's bearing than almost anything else. With Alexander, that steady endurance is both a habit and a statement. He's a presence she enjoys being near and finds deeply reassuring, as constant as the November landscape itself.

Once they have bathed and changed into comfortable clothes, Maren and Alexander make their way down to the breakfast room. It is decorated in a joyful array of coordinating checks, stripes, and florals in blue and yellow. The French windows that open onto a stone veranda are dressed in a delicate floral print cotton chintz in ivory, scattered with clusters of pink and yellow roses, their petals softly blurred as if just brushed open. Wisps of green leaves curl naturally among the blooms, giving the pattern a sense of life and inviting the outdoors in. Intertwined throughout the design are slender blue ribbons, their length tied here and there into graceful bows, weaving in and out among the flowers and adding a playful, feminine touch.

Maren smiles. "This room is beautiful. Do I see Geneviève's hand in this?"

"Of course," Alexander replies, a grin lighting his face. "She redecorates it every few years, but I think these are her favorite colors. The fabrics might be refreshed, but the patterns never really change."

On the sideboard, Gaston has arranged a light, simple lunch: a platter of cold roast beef, slices of crusty country bread, a selection of mild and sharp cheeses, a dish of unsalted butter, and a glass pitcher of sparkling water with thin rounds of lemon.

"I wasn't sure what you would like for lunch," Alexander says. "What do you usually have?"

Maren laughs. "Honestly? A sandwich and soup, or some-times a sandwich and salad—almost every day of my life."

"You're a creature of habit, I see."

"And convenience," Maren says, reaching for a slice of bread. "Soup and salad are available in some form or another in every museum in the world, which is where I spend most of my days. Also, I don't enjoy cooking, so I can have half for lunch and take the rest home for dinner. It's efficient, if not exactly inspiring."

Maren knows there is an entire unspoken conversation lingering between them. She has a job, an apartment, and a carefully constructed life waiting for her across the ocean. As much as she would love to have lunch with Alexander every day, just like this, neither of them has said anything about what happens next. He hasn't mentioned the future, and she hasn't either.

If there's anything she's learned in these past weeks, it's that no matter what happens, she will be fine. She has found happiness and contentment within herself and in her life. She loves her job and finds it fulfilling, just as career counselors promise when they tell you to find something you'd gladly do for free.

She is comfortable in her own skin now, être bien dans sa peau, as her mother calls this characteristically French way of being. For now, there are a few loose ends to tie up with the parure, and while they do, she's determined to enjoy every minute here and every minute with him.

Alexander interrupts her daydream, his tone teasing. "Would you like to see the house this afternoon? The official tour, as opposed to the midnight tour?"

Maren feels a flush rise to her cheeks. "The midnight tour was pretty great, as I recall," she says. "You're an excellent... tour guide."

Alexander grins and leans in just a little closer, lowering his voice. "Thank you. I strive to be thorough."

"I'm assuming the daylight version comes with slightly more clothing?" Maren says.

Alexander meets her eyes. "For now."

After lunch, Alexander excuses himself to make a call, leaving Maren to explore on her own. She remembers Gaston mentioning that he would be in the flower room, arranging a new delivery. Curious, she makes her way through the warren of back corridors, past the butler's pantry and the old servants' hall, toward the north wing. The flower room is tucked discreetly beside a glassed-in conservatory.

The flower room feels almost like a secret retreat, and Maren thinks it's her favorite room in the house so far. It is long and narrow, and lined on both sides with broad, waist-high worktables of thick, white Carrara marble, their surfaces bearing the patina of decades of bumps, leaf stains, and water rings. Above them, open shelves display rows of baskets of every shape and size, their liners, and an assortment of porcelain orchid pots. There are glass vases, a few slender and modern, but many in heavy, old Georgian crystal, its deep cuts refracting the light. There are gleaming copper watering cans, antique clay pots, and old French jardinieres. The walls are tiled in serene white and soft Delft blue, easy to clean after a busy day of arranging stems. One wall holds a bank of deep drawers for twine, cutters, floral tape, and ribbons in every shade. At the far end, large windows look out onto the walled kitchen garden. In grand houses like this one, the flower room, a sanctum both practical and beautiful, is usually located near the rear service entrance and the greenhouses, a crossroads of indoors and out.

Maren finds Gaston at a wide, deep stone sink that is clearly original to the house, arranging an armful of blush-pink Ecuadorian roses that have just arrived, their scent lush and heady.

"Hi," Maren says. "Would you like some help?"

He glances at her, a rare smile softening his usually reserved features. "Hi Maren. Yes, always. If you don't mind cold water and thorny fingers," he says, passing her a slim-handled pair of shears.

She grins, rolling up her sleeves. "I'll risk it."

The atmosphere is easy, companionable. Gaston shows her how to strip the leaves and thorns, and cut each stem at an angle, setting the roses in a bucket of water "to recover from travel," as he calls it. As they work, he tells her about the gardens at his mother's house in the Loire Valley: the tangled lavender hedges, the trellises weighted with white climbing roses, a fig tree that never quite produces enough for jam.

"You have a good eye for it, Maren," Gaston says, his voice warm with approval as he watches her assemble a simple arrangement.

She laughs. "You're the true artist, Gaston. I'm just trying not to get water everywhere."

He gives her a gentle, old-fashioned nod. "Even the grandest garden has room for new hands."

They lapse into comfortable silence, the only sounds the snip of shears, the clink of glass, and the distant calls of birds. Sunlight slants across the counter, warming Maren's bare arms as she works.

Footsteps tap across the marble of the adjoining hall. Alexander appears in the doorway, lingering for a moment, smiling at the scene.

"Hello," he says. "I hope I'm not interrupting?"

Gaston straightens as he sets the vase aside. "Good afternoon, sir." Then, turning to Maren, he asks, "Miss Bennett, would you prefer the roses in the entry, or shall I use hydrangeas instead?"

Maren sees from the subtle shift in his manner, that formality is back in place now that Alexander is present. She understands all at once that this is more than tradition or pride; it is Gaston's way of showing respect—for Alexander, for this house, and for her place in it.

Matching his gravity, Maren smiles and replies, "Thank you, Mr. Bouchard. I think the roses will be perfect in the entry."

Maren is looking forward to seeing the house with Alexander, as he takes her hand and leads her through the cavernous rooms on the ground floor. "The house was commissioned in the early eighteenth century, at the height of Parisian elegance. In its day, it was renowned for soirées that blended a great deal of both political intrigue and artistic glamour. It was constructed for my eleven-times-great-grandmother, the formidable Élisabeth-Alexandrine de Bourbon, a marquise by marriage but also with her own royal connections."

Maren nods. She knows that in France, a monarch could grant a woman a title in *suo jure*, her own right, which made her a titleholder rather than just receiving a title as a spouse. When a special remainder was added, she was able to pass the title to her daughters.

"When did they add the mansard roof and ironwork?" Maren asks. "That must have been in the mid-nineteenth century?"

"You're right," says Alexander, continuing as they stroll through hallways, occasionally stepping through French windows onto verandas or down into small, secluded courtyards.

"As you know, the city transformed during the Second Empire. A descendant married into the Lenoir family—wealthy bankers with ambitions of making Paris their permanent home. It was during this era that the iconic mansard roof and ornate ironwork balconies were added."

"Making Le Cœur Fidèle, even then I'm sure, a model of classic French architecture," Maren says.

Alexander nods and leads Maren into what appears to be a ladies' study on the near side of the orangerie. "Fast-forward to my great-great-grandmother, Marguerite Lenoir, another in a long line of resolute custodians. She survived the tumult of both World Wars within these walls. During the Occupation, she used the grand salons to hide precious art and shelter those at risk. After the war, she restored the house and filled it once more with laughter and music. She also had a passion for collecting rare books and paintings. She left it to my great-grandmother, Mathilde de Sévigny.

Mathilde was the one who named the house 'Le Cœur Fidèle,' to honor the love and courage of generations. From Mathilde, the house passed to my grandmother, Clementine D'Orléans, and when she died, she left the house and all its labyrinthine archives, secret gardens, and echoing galleries to her sole grandson." Alexander smiles, remembering his beautiful and flamboyant grandmother.

"I have the legacy now," he says.

"Of care, and tradition," Maren says, looking at him with love, "and a faithful heart."

Alexander twirls her around and pulls her in for a kiss. "Yes," he says. "Always."

"This was the study used by, well, all of my grandmothers," Alexander says.

On one wall is a life-size and quite dashing painting of Mathilde by the society painter, Philip de László. In it, she is standing with one hand resting on an elaborate mahogany desk scattered with books and flowers. Her head is turned as if she's just looked up from writing a letter, her blue-green eyes bright with intelligence and a touch of mischief.

She wears a tailored tweed suit with a cinched waist and a double strand of pearls at her throat; the soft sheen of her ruffled blouse catches the painter's light. Her dark, elegantly coiffed hair frames high cheekbones and a determined chin. Alexander's chin, Maren thinks. There is both grace and audacity in her bearing—a woman of style and substance, utterly at ease in her world.

The background of the painting is filled with the muted greens and golds of a sunlit garden glimpsed through tall windows, lending the portrait an air of invitation and subtle drama, a fitting tribute to one of the house's most legendary matriarchs. The carved, gold-leafed frame is nearly a foot wide. The painting itself, by Maren's estimation, spans an impressive ten feet by five, making it a striking presence on the wall.

"The vault is this way," Alexander says, activating a hidden latch. There's a soft click behind the portrait. The painting is mounted on two horizontal bars, one at the top and one at the bottom. Alexander reaches up to unfasten two additional latches, then carefully slides the portrait to the left, the massive frame gliding smoothly along its track.

Behind the painting is what appears to be a steel door with a keypad. Alexander enters a thirteen-digit passcode, then follows it with another code from an app on his phone. The vault door swings open smoothly, and as lights flicker on inside, Alexander steps through the opening and gestures for Maren to follow.

"It's been modernized over the years," he says, chuckling at Maren's expression of amazement.

The vault is as large as a room, about fifteen by twenty-five feet, filled with furnishings, rugs, and tapestries. Paintings are hung on metal racks that swing out for viewing. A large flat file holds what appear to be drawings, etchings, and watercolors. Shelves display Oriental vases and French porcelain. A column of shallow, velvet-lined drawers houses jewelry.

Alexander pulls out one of the wide drawers and reveals the necklace, bracelet, and earrings of the Talisman parure. When Maren sees this, she hesitates, then slips the Talisman ring from her finger and places it alongside the other pieces.

"You don't have to do that, Maren," Alexander says gently. "That belongs to you now."

"I'm just the current guardian," Maren replies with a small smile, unconsciously rubbing the spot where the ring had been.

As Alexander rummages through a large horizontal filing cabinet, Maren trails her fingers along the spines of books lining the far wall of the vault—leather-bound volumes smooth with age. She pauses at one with a cover of worn blue velvet and delicate Ottoman gilt work, tracing the intricate designs as she carefully pulls it from the shelf. The title, tooled in faded gold, reads: *Trésors de l'Empire Ottoman*, Treasures of the Ottoman Empire.

She settles onto a nearby stool, opening the book with reverence. Carefully hand-gilded illustrations illuminate the pages: intricate tilework, jeweled turbans, court intrigues rendered in vibrant color and gold.

As she turns a thick, crackling page, a detailed rendering captures her eye. The scene is one of courtly splendor, the sultan's wife seated beneath a canopy of silks and lantern light. Maren's pulse quickens as she studies the jewels: a necklace, bracelet, earrings, and ring, each a part of the very Talisman parure resting only a few feet away from her in the vault.

"Alexander," she says, intending to show him the illustration.

But then she sees something else: crowning the woman's dark hair is an elaborate headpiece, alive with the same motifs and gems as the rest of the set. Emeralds, diamonds, and turquoise, with gold filigree across the brow. This piece is undeniably part of the parure, but new to Maren.

She lifts her eyes from the page, heart hammering. At the back of the book, she notices a slip of folded, yellowed paper tucked behind the endpaper. Opening it, she finds a single line written in looping, old-fashioned script:

Where the heart watches, the crown rests.

Maren gasps and stares at the words. The message is cryptic, but one thing is clear—the parure isn't complete, and she guesses the missing headpiece is hidden somewhere within the very walls of this house.

Alexander glances over from the filing cabinet, noticing Maren's silence and the intent way she holds the book. He crosses the vault to see. "What did you find?"

Maren doesn't look up immediately, her eyes lingering on the illustration. "I think you need to look at this," she says, tilting the book so he can peer over her shoulder.

He bends to examine the page. "Is that—?"

She nods. "The Talisman parure. The necklace, bracelet, earrings, and ring, all exactly as we have them. But look here." Her finger traces the woman's ornate headpiece, set with matching emeralds and diamonds. "There's a crown or diadem. We don't have this piece."

Alexander frowns, studying the artistry, then glances at her, thoughtful. "It's so detailed."

"It gets stranger," Maren says, carefully unfolding the note and handing it over. "This was tucked in the back."

He reads the line aloud, brow furrowing: "Where the heart watches, the crown rests." He's silent for a moment, then smiles. "That sounds like one of Mathilde's riddles."

Maren's lips curve. "I think it's a clue. The headpiece must be here, somewhere in the house."

Alexander exhales slowly. "Well, Le Cœur Fidèle is nothing if not full of secrets. Ready for one last treasure hunt?"

She meets his eyes, delight mixed with determination. "Absolutely."

TWENTY-EIGHT

GENEVIÈVE

THE NEXT MORNING, WHILE Maren and Alexander are having breakfast, Geneviève texts to invite Maren for coffee. Alexander encourages her to go, as he has early calls, adding that he will join her there later so they can all discuss the parure.

A short while later, Maren stands in her dressing room, uncertain what to wear. She imagines Genevieve will be dressed as she always is, in a tailored skirt falling just below the knee, a coordinating blouse or sweater, a long rope of pearls, sheer stockings, and high-quality low-heeled pumps. It's a style almost indistinguishable from Maren's mother's: polished and understated, pieces chosen with deliberate care and with the idea of keeping them for a very long time.

Her mother often says she doesn't know how anyone manages to dress well with too many clothes. True style, she insists, isn't about variety but about restraint—knowing when and how to say no. She's fond of quoting Gabrielle Chanel: "Elegance is refusal."

It has been difficult for Maren to say no to what she doesn't truly love or need in clothing, in food, in companionship, even in the way she spends her free time. Possessing the clarity to pass over distractions that don't bring genuine joy requires surprising strength, she thinks. When someone lives with such discernment, Maren is often impressed by the discipline and confidence that underpin their choices. Elegance, she feels, isn't about opulence or excess; it's about careful selection and the conviction of knowing what suits her and what doesn't. In her most private moments, she longs to live that way herself.

Maren wonders if her admiration for her mother and Geneviève is rooted not only in their outward polish, but in the assurance with which they navigate the world, guided by personal certainties and a hundred little refusals. Perhaps, she muses, that is the essence of style. For now, it feels to her like riding a bike with training wheels, but in her own tentative way, she is beginning to practice it too.

Later, at Geneviève's, Camille leads Maren across the marbled hall and into the library. Geneviève is already there, her back to the shelves, exchanging a tender moment with Alistair Edwards. He leans in, pressing a slow kiss to the back of her hand, his thumb tracing the inside of her wrist. There is so much intimacy and devotion in that subtle gesture that Maren feels momentarily awkward at intruding on their privacy. But she is delighted to see the affection Alistair and Geneviève share.

Alistair doesn't notice Maren's entrance, and slips from the room through a side door, disappearing into what Maren guesses is a private study or office. Only after he's gone does Maren step fully into the library. She loves this room and imagines that this beautiful space is a sanctuary for Geneviève, where she retreats and recharges.

As Geneviève pours the coffee, Maren admires the dark blue and gold fishnet pattern on the cups. "This is a beautiful service," Maren remarks. "I've never been to Limoges, but I've always admired the porcelain. It's been produced for centuries."

Geneviève nods. "Louis XIV purchased one of the local factories so he could have porcelain wares made for his court.

That truly put Limoges on the map. And thank you," she adds, "this set actually belongs to Alistair. The pattern is one of the rarer designs, and he's especially fond of it because it reminds him of his childhood." She pauses, affection in her voice. "Alistair comes from a diplomatic family. His family name and connections afforded him an excellent education at Harrow and Cambridge, and after university, he worked in private security."

Maren considers this. "That would explain his technical skills: protection, negotiation, driving under pressure."

"Yes," Geneviève continues. "He left England twenty years ago and came to France to work for high-profile clients. His discretion, fluency in several languages, and dignified presence made him both inconspicuous and invaluable. My husband hired him a year before he died, after a series of high-profile kidnappings raised concerns for our safety. When Etienne, Alexander's father, passed away, Alistair stayed on."

"For all that we try to navigate gracefully, families are always a tangle, aren't they?" Geneviève says with a rueful smile. "Alistair and I have a special connection, though he's quite a bit younger than I am. We discovered how naturally we fit together after Alexander's father passed away."

Maren hesitates for a moment. "It's charming that he still drives for you."

Geneviève's eyes warm. "He insists. He worries about me. And, well, this is new for both of us, so we're still considering how to proceed. Our families know, of course, but we haven't made the relationship public just yet."

Maren nods, understanding. "Is that the source of the tension between Alistair and Alexander?"

Geneviève glances into her coffee, thoughtful. "They are both good men. I'm certain they'll find a way to work things out. But yes, there has been some discomfort. Looking back, I realize that distance crept in between myself and Alexander's father, and Alexander sensed it, even as a boy." She looks up, her expression candid and a little sad. "I never felt I could tell his father about the parure. I didn't think it was my right to share those secrets."

Maren says, "And you feel now you can share it with Alistair."

"I do," Geneviève replies, her voice touched with regret. "I should have told Etienne. There's a part of Alexander that may never understand how fully I'm able to share my life now with Alistair. I suppose I learned too late that marriage can't thrive in silence."

She smiles. "But a good marriage also has a kind of accord, a harmony, that seems to need fewer words. As we say, le cœur a ses raisons que la raison ne connaît point. The heart has its reasons, of which reason knows nothing."

"Yes," Maren replies, smiling. "My mother says that all the time. That, and 'Plus le cœur grandit, moins les paroles sont utiles.' The more the heart grows, the fewer words are needed.'"

Maren sits back, recognizing the truth in her own life. "Sometimes, that kind of peacefulness just doesn't exist for two people, no matter how much one tries to talk it into being," she says, recalling past relationships. "Ethan, my former fiancé, and I always tried to create compatibility by talking about it, but it never worked. No amount of words can create harmony if it isn't already there."

Just then, the click of the library door breaks their conversation. Alexander enters, pausing at the threshold, his gaze falling first on his mother, then landing on Maren.

Geneviève smiles, "Come and join us, cher."

"Bonjour, Maman," Alexander replies, touching her hand before turning to Maren. He meets her eyes, a smile passing between them. Maren feels a giddy lift of happiness at his arrival, warmth blooming in her chest.

Settling into an armchair, Alexander leans forward. "We need to talk about the parure, Maman. As you know, we found the necklace in Istanbul and thought the set was complete. But Maren discovered something at Le Cœur—an old book that shows the parure included a headpiece at one time. And there's this note suggesting, we think, that the missing piece could be somewhere in the house."

He shows Geneviève the note and says, "There are more people who know about and want the parure now. Some may know only about the necklace, while others might know about the entire set. We need to find that missing piece—and soon."

Geneviève leans in, her attention sharpened by concern.

Alexander continues, "Keeping the jewelry in the vault at Le Cœur is risky. As long as the parure remains in private hands, it will draw anyone with knowledge or ambition. I'm convinced that the only way to keep everyone safe is to donate the parure to a museum, somewhere with proper security and the expertise to protect it."

He glances at Maren, then back at his mother, his tone urgent. "My security detail just notified me that the cameras picked up two suspicious lurkers outside the property walls. The police have been informed. We're in good hands for now, but we only have a short time before things could become dangerous."

Geneviève's brow furrows, understanding the gravity.

Alexander leans forward, fingers tented, his expression thoughtful. "If we donate the parure, we must consider where. The Smithsonian, perhaps. That would offer American protection and the benefit of international scrutiny." He glances at Maren, clearly seeking her opinion.

Maren nods. "The Smithsonian would be possible. But the parure's history spans borders. There's the Topkapı Palace Museum in Istanbul, since the jewels once belonged to the

Ottoman court. Returning them there would mean restoring them to their original home."

Geneviève adds, "And Venice shouldn't be overlooked. The Museo Correr has an exceptional collection that reflects Venice's centuries of trade and diplomacy with the Ottomans. And of course, the Louvre—its Galerie d' Apollon once held some of the parure. Each of these museums could offer both honor and necessary security."

Alexander nods, considering. "Or perhaps we disperse the pieces among several museums, to ensure no single person or entity can ever claim the complete set again."

Maren picks up her coffee cup, her tone resolute. "There may be resistance. Each museum will have its claims. Each nation will have its arguments. But none of us, nor the jewels, will ever be safe unless they're truly out of reach and entrusted to hands that can protect them."

They are silent for a moment as they consider the options, knowing the decision is as complex as the parure itself. Maren knows that their next move must be both wise and swift.

"If the two of you agree," Alexander says after a moment, "I'll contact the Louvre and the other two museums. Maren, perhaps you can make arrangements with the Smithsonian. We'll find out which pieces they're interested in, and my staff can coordinate with them and arrange secure transport as soon as possible."

"Alexander, cher," Geneviève asks in her considerate but direct way, "I'm sorry to ask you this, but what do you think Simone will do when she realizes she doesn't have the real Talisman necklace?"

Maren knows Alexander's first instinct is silence; he looks down and adjusts his watch. But then, almost imperceptibly, he simply sets the armor aside. Maren sees it and feels the significance.

"She may never realize," he says at last.

Maren feels a bright reassurance. Alexander is choosing to build a less guarded relationship with her than either of their parents had. The mark of a man who might at last believe that letting Maren in will make his life richer than his careful defenses ever could.

"She thinks the real necklace is the one she has, the one hidden at Saint Mark's, that Maren found. Every clue pointed there. For all she knows, we lost it to her that night."

Maren exhales. "Will she try to sell it?"

Alexander shakes his head. "No. Selling it was never her aim. She wanted to possess it—to keep it from me. If she sells it, she knows I will just buy it, and that would defeat her purpose."

Maren narrows her eyes slightly. "Which is?"

He looks at Maren and shrugs, but then grins. "Lifelong revenge."

Geneviève takes a deep breath with a grateful smile. "Thank you, Alexander. I feel better knowing where we stand."

Between them, the moment is small but profound, and perhaps the beginning of a new closeness.

Alexander shifts the conversation. "Now, there's only the matter of the tiara. The headpiece. Any idea what the note means?"

Geneviève leans back, reflecting. "'Where the heart watches, the crown rests,'" she repeats. "Yes, I think I do, Alexander. In the music room at Le Cœur, above the fireplace, there are hearts carved into the plaster molding."

"I always thought those were flowers," Alexander says.

"They are," Geneviève replies with a smile. "Heart-shaped flowers known as bleeding hearts."

Maren leans in, fascinated by the many layers of this story.

"And with them," Geneviève continues, "are roses and violets interwoven in the design."

"Bleeding hearts, roses for love, and violets for remembrance," Maren says, reflecting on the symbolism.

Geneviève nods. "They were always Mathilde's favorite motifs for some reason. They are even painted in her portrait."

"The flowers on her desk in the painting. She's writing a letter," Maren breathes.

Alexander glances between them, curious. "Do you really think the tiara is hidden somewhere in the music room?"

"It would make sense," says Maren, "if the note is a clue."

He stands. "Shall we see if the crown truly rests where the heart watches?"

Maren says with excitement. "Let's find out."

The music room is one of the loveliest spaces at Le Cœur Fidèle. A massive marble fireplace anchors one end, flanked by bookcases that soar from the floor to just below the crown molding fifteen feet overhead. The walls and ceiling are adorned with deep plaster moldings—carved fruit, flowers, cupids, and musical instruments—while fluffy clouds float across a painted summer-blue sky above, giving the room a feeling of light and openness. Hand-painted garden scenes bloom across the walls between the moldings. Through a row of ten-foot French doors, draped in pink, coral, and gold striped silk, the view extends into the garden beyond, merging indoors and out in a seamless, airy atrium.

Throughout the room, scattered groupings of chairs, settees, and tables rest atop richly colored, threadbare Aubusson rugs that Maren suspects are original to the house. They give the room a perfect balance of refinement softened by an offhand effortlessness that her mother calls *désinvolture*, which invites comfort as much as admiration.

At the heart of it all stands the centerpiece: a gleaming grand piano crafted by the renowned Érard makers, with a polished burled walnut cabinet and gilded bronze ormolu legs.

Alexander, Geneviève, and Maren stand in front of the fireplace, studying the intricate plaster flowers woven into ornate patterns along the molding, framing a large portrait of a de Sévigny ancestor with her dogs.

"You're right. Bleeding hearts," Maren says, peering more closely, "but what are they pointing us to?" Her eyes follow the trail of flowers, bound with a carved ribbon just above the mantel.

Beneath the medallion, resting on the marble mantel, the steady swing of the pendulum inside an oversized eighteenth-century clock commands their attention. The piece stands three feet tall and eighteen inches wide, and about a foot deep, crafted in the typical Louis XVI style, with elegant marquetry, fine gilded accents, and graceful proportions. There, in the smooth woodwork just above the clock face, is a garnet heart set in gold.

Alexander and Maren exchange a look. "Could it really be that easy?" Alexander asks with a laugh. Geneviève, arms crossed, tilts her head and gives a slight shrug.

Maren says, "There's only one way to find out."

Alexander calls for Gaston. Maren marvels at how Gaston manages to materialize almost instantly, always with his unruffled, unhurried air, as if he takes secret delight in confounding everyone about how he can be everywhere at once. He seems perfectly aware of the effect and enjoys it. Together, they slide the library steps over to the mantel, and with great care, lift the clock from its place and carry it to a table nearby.

On the back of the clock is another garnet heart set in gold. Alexander presses it. With a click, the back panel swings open, and everyone crowds in, peering at the clock's interior. The works are an intricate cluster of brass gears, the coiled mainspring, slender rods meant to move the hands, and a boxlike chamber likely protecting fragile components from dust. But no tiara.

Among them, there's a sigh and evident disappointment. Gaston asks if he may take a closer look, and Alexander nods. Maren watches as Gaston's fingers feel around the rim inside, concentration etched across his brow as he skirts the moving escapement and gears. He holds the top of the clock lightly for balance, glancing up toward the ceiling as he reaches farther back. Then Maren hears a click as Gaston presses something she can't see.

The inner panel opens; and Geneviève brings her fingertips together in a delighted little clap. Inside, there is a large linen pouch and a smaller one tucked just behind. Gaston straightens, handing one pouch to Alexander and another to Maren, then feels carefully around the recess once more to be sure nothing's been missed.

There's a chorus of praise: "Well done, Gaston," Geneviève says warmly, and Alexander adds, "Excellent work," as he opens the larger pouch. His eyes widen as he lifts out a gold circlet set with lapis, diamonds, turquoise, and emeralds, matching the headpiece they had seen in the old book. "Do you think this is real?" he says.

Maren opens the second pouch and removes a bracelet. She scrutinizes it and says, "If it's not the Talisman bracelet, it's a perfect replica," then shakes her head and hands it to Geneviève. "No inscriptions. But that," she says, looking over Alexander's arm at the circlet, "that's genuine. It says Nur, just like the other pieces. That's Roxelana's crown."

At first, there is only silence and the sound of the ticking pendulum.

"Where the heart watches, the crown rests," Geneviève says softly. "Mathilde left these for someone to find someday.

But how did the tiara end up here, and why would a fake bracelet and necklace have been made?"

Neither Alexander nor Maren has an answer. The four of them stand together in the golden autumn light, silent and contemplative, with the jewels gleaming between them. The mystery only deepens, leaving them to wonder about the secrets, choices, and loves of those who came before, knowing that some truths might remain hidden forever.

Three days later, an express delivery arrives addressed to Alexander and Maren, and Gaston delivers it as they come down the stairs for breakfast. Maren tears open the cardboard sleeve and finds a worn, yellowed envelope alongside a folded note. "It's from Florian Descălu," Maren says, handing the note to Alexander, who reads:

"'I found this among my father's things years ago. Considering recent events, you should have it.' It's signed, 'FD.'"

Mystified, Maren slides her finger beneath the seal of the envelope and carefully unfolds a letter, the paper delicate with age, Mathilde de Sévigny's elegant script looping across the page. Alexander leans in, silent. Maren translates:

My Dearest Xavier,

If you are reading this, then somehow we have both survived. There are choices we make for the sake of love, and others for the sake of survival. I still carry both.

My marriage to Charles de Sévigny had been planned since childhood. It was a match woven of fortune, not devotion. They could never have understood the heart's revolt, or the love I found with you.

Your gifts of protection, should I ever have to choose between my safety and my duty, became my salvation one night, as you must have known they might. I would never have been able to spirit Elisabeta out of France with both necklaces in her possession were it not for your genius. When I was stopped and searched, it was the decoy tiara I handed over in exchange for our lives. Perhaps they are still out there somewhere.

Had I been able, I would have chosen another path for us. But in those darkest days, what we sacrificed—our love, our future—ensured others would have a chance at theirs. When I hid the true tiara away inside the clock today, it was with tears of gratitude and heartbreak, thankful for your devotion, aching with all I can never say to you aloud.

I hope that those who uncover these secrets one day will understand that the bravest actions are sometimes born in deepest silence, and in the longing that le cœur fidèle leaves behind. The greatest thing I have ever done is to love you. My greatest sorrow is all the years we will not have.

I will hold you in my heart forever, in that place where love and light meet,

Mathilde

"Le Cœur Fidèle," whispers Maren. "The Faithful Heart. You said Mathilde is the one who named this house. Xavier made the decoys to protect the Talisman, and to save her life. She named it for him."

Maren looks up at Alexander, and for the first time, sees tears in his eyes. All she can do is wrap her arms around him, as if this embrace could bridge all of the years, and lives, and secrets that came before.

TWENTY-NINE

LEGENDS

THE SMITHSONIAN MUSEUM OF Natural History stands regally on the National Mall, having occupied its prominent address on Constitution Avenue since 1910. Tonight, its classical façade is illuminated by evening floodlights, creating drama and grandeur for this marble temple to curiosity and memory at the very heart of Washington, D.C.

The Smithsonian is a cabinet of wonders, expansive enough to contain the story of the world. Its labyrinthine galleries hold everything from ancient fossils and dazzling gemstones to meteorites and artifacts of vanished civilizations. Well, almost everything, thinks Maren.

Maren stands in a gold lamé evening gown beneath the towering glass dome in the entrance hall, a flute of champagne in hand. She is flanked by Alexander, Geneviève, Alistair and Camille, all dressed in gala finery. The priceless Ottoman parure with its historic emeralds, lapis lazuli, turquoise, and diamonds has finally been divided. Now the Smithsonian, the Louvre, the Topkapi Palace Museum, and the Correr Museum in Venice each hold part of the parure, protecting it from any one person's reach. Only a single piece was withheld.

As Maren puts it, bemused, "It's probably the first time in history four museums have agreed not to squabble over jewelry."

Alexander, adjusting his cufflinks, adds, "We've achieved diplomatic détente by keeping everyone equally dissatisfied."

They share a laugh, relieved that for once, bureaucracy and compromise have kept the past right where it belongs: safe, admired, and just mysterious enough to keep the story alive.

Geneviève sips her champagne. "As long as the paperwork says *custody arrangement* and not permanent loan, no one's pride is irreparably damaged."

When her mother arrives, Maren gives her a hug and a glass of champagne and strolls with her, Geneviève, and Camille through the special exhibit that has been prepared for this singular night. Velvet-lined cases hold Ottoman miniatures, filigree daggers, and hand-painted tiles. Curators from the National Gem Collection, the Arthur M. Sackler Gallery, and the Freer Gallery circulate among the guests, talking about the artifacts and, Maren notes with a wry smile, practicing the ancient art of subtle fundraising—equal parts scholarship and persuasion. At the center of it all is the Talisman necklace called Roxelana.

After cocktails and canapés, the museum director approaches the podium and raises his voice slightly above the room's contented buzz. He adjusts his glasses, smiling out at the distinguished array of foreign dignitaries, university scholars, museum curators, corporate sponsors, a handful of celebrities, and even a few influencers glittering at the edge of the crowd.

"This extraordinary Ottoman necklace was generously donated by a personal friend of mine and a longtime friend of the museum. A collector, a scholar, and, I have always suspected, something of a romantic."

There is a polite ripple of applause. Maren smiles, lifting her glass. And then, something tugs at the edge of her awareness.

She turns.

There, at the back of the room near the exit archway, stands Lucien. He is half in shadow, his hands folded lightly in front of him. Still elegant. Still wolfish around the eyes. Elusive as ever.

He meets her eyes. With the smallest, familiar smile, he offers his rakish two-fingered salute. The same gesture she remembers from the Orient Express.

When she looks back a moment later, he is gone.

She knows they could not have recovered the Talisman necklace without his help; that's why she and Alexander had decided its donor should be Lucien. The Brotherhood will be satisfied now that he has done his job. There are no speeches left to give, no debts left to pay. But she knows what his being here means. Lucien chose to see it through, and perhaps, just this once, to witness the happy ending he never allows himself.

She shouldn't have been surprised by Lucien's ties to the museum; it's just another secret belonging to a man made of mysteries. But when she had discovered his Turkish-European heritage, everything suddenly made sense. Beneath all that cynicism, Lucien believes in protection and peace. Maren has a feeling she will see him again one of these days.

The director continues, "And we are deeply honored to be the stewards of this extraordinary donation. A priceless necklace, whose beauty and historic importance will now be preserved for generations to come. Please join me in thanking its remarkable benefactor, Mr. Lucien Demir-Altan, patron of the arts... and, clearly, a man who understands the power of legacy."

There is polite applause, then genuine applause.

Lucien, of course, is not present.

After the ceremony, Maren walks past the display once more, pausing before the necklace glowing in its spotlight. She feels that familiar pull and closes her eyes. She sees herself walking the lawn at Le Cœur Fidèle with Alexander, and holding her hand is a little boy who looks just like him. She opens her eyes and smiles at the necklace. "Don't think I won't hold you to that."

She thinks about the portrait of Mathilde and understands what she saw in that painted gaze: elegance and defiance, sorrow, yes, but above all, love. Maybe Mathilde's legacy is that we must search for what truly matters. And perhaps she reminds us that not every secret needs solving.

Now, as chamber music fills the hall, Maren drifts toward Alexander, weaving between guests and docents. She reaches his side, and he takes her hand, a gesture natural now.

No ring. No talisman.

Just the two of them.

As they walk away, hands entwined, Maren glances back. A secret at last unburdened. Love and light, kept hidden for so long, now sheltering them both, strong and shining amid the many treasures of the world.

Alexander asks, "Do you think you'll wear the ring again someday?"

Maren looks up at him. "Yes. Someday. But for now, we all deserve a rest."

The End

THIRTY

EPILOGUE

THE BEGINNING.

In Washington, D.C., Maren and Alexander made the social rounds—a handful of glamorous Christmas parties, a little work for each, and one unforgettable evening at the Kennedy Center. Alexander had been fascinated by Maren's apartment. "You realize this place is roughly the size of my walk-in closet, yes?" Maren only laughed, tossing a cushion at him. "Cozy is the new chic," she declared, and Alexander, with no argument, had promptly made himself at home.

One morning, as Maren was making a pot of coffee, Alexander told her he needed to be back in Paris for a meeting in two days. The words slipped out before she could stop them. "Gosh, I'll miss you."

He looked up from an article in the sports section, genuinely surprised. "What are you talking about? I'm not leaving without you. Who would tie my bow ties?"

He opened the paper again and said, "Besides, I hear there's an urgent shortage of art restoration experts in Paris this week. You can't let France down like that."

Maren smiled and set a cup of coffee on the table.

Then he looked at her over the paper and said, "Pack your bags, Maren. This was always a round-trip ticket."

They arrived in Paris to gently falling snow, frosting Le Cœur Fidéle like a wedding cake, Maren thought.

Later, while Alexander was making calls, Maren changed into a pair of gray sweatpants, thick, cozy socks, and her old Harvard sweatshirt. She brought a cup of hot chocolate, a stack of work, and her laptop into his grandmother's study, settling in at the desk.

By the time Alexander found her an hour later, a pencil was tucked behind one ear, and she was making her way through a pile of work requests and contracts, scribbling notes on a yellow legal pad. It seemed the Tate in London wanted her to lead the upcoming restoration of "The Turkish Bath," one of Ingres's monumental works slated for exhibition.

"Hi," he said, standing in the doorway, looking at her oddly.

"Hi. She said, glancing up. What are you doing?" She cocked her head at him and wondered if it was okay to walk around his house in sweatpants.

"I'm just taking in the view," he replied, not moving. "Would this be a good place for you to work when you're in Paris?"

Maren looked around the room, taking in the fire glowing in the fireplace, the lofty ceiling with its 18th-century painted medallions and gilded moldings, the parquet floors, and the tall windows draped in silk damask.

"Yes," she said. "I think it would be perfectly adequate."

She wondered if he remembered what he'd said that morning in Budapest.

He laughed, crossed the rug, and pulled her to her feet, circling an arm around her waist and taking her hand in his. He danced with her slowly around the room, humming "Someone to Watch Over Me."

"I think you should just stay," he murmured in her ear. "So I can watch over you. Forever."

As snow fell softly outside and blanketed Paris in a veil of white, he drew back just enough to meet her eyes. "Will you marry me, Maren?"

And Maren, knowing that sometimes the best adventures begin with a simple yes, said, "Yes."

THE ROSES OF
AINSWORTH MANOR

L ADY NELL AINSWORTH IS not your typical noblewoman. A
successful—if reclusive—romance novelist living in the
vast halls of Ainsworth Manor, the Georgian estate she unexpectedly inherited, along with a somber dog named Roger
and a tangle of family secrets. Nell prefers the company of
fictional rogues and literary dukes to the predictable socialites
of modern-day England. But her quiet life of plotting love
stories and avoiding the real thing is turned upside down
when a mysteriously coded letter from the continent hints at a
long-buried family secret involving lost treasure, betrayal, and
a centuries-old vendetta.

Enter Henry Templeton: former MI5 desk analyst turned
reluctant valet after a very public scandal cost him his career
and his reputation. When Lady Nell, in dire need of someone
capable (and discrete), spots his quietly efficient resume in
a stack of applicants for the live-in handyman position, she

hires him on the spot—though his loyalty comes with a healthy dose of sarcasm and an eyebrow permanently raised.

Together, they uncover a trail of cryptic clues, dating back to Napoleonic times, that sends them on a wild chase across windswept moors, shadowy libraries, and glittering European cities.

As danger circles closer and the lines between fact and fiction blur, Nell must step out from behind her pen and face a story far more thrilling—and threatening—than any she's ever written. In the process, she and Henry will be forced to confront not just the secrets of Ainsworth's past, but their own guarded hearts.

Romance, riddles, and rifle fire await in The Roses of Ainsworth Manor—a sharp, witty, and heart-racing adventure that proves real love is the most dangerous plot twist of all.

THE ROSES OF AINSWORTH MANOR IS AVAILABLE NOW ON AMAZON.

ABOUT THE AUTHOR

Nina Gates is an American author of upmarket romantic suspense whose novels are praised for their cinematic style, emotional depth, and elegantly profound insights. Her stories transport readers to glamorous settings around the world, where love and mystery intertwine. She lives in Texas and is currently at work on her next novel.

BOOK CLUB QUESTIONS AND AUTHOR INSIGHTS

Hello Friends!

If you haven't finished the novel yet, you might want to pause here and return when you're ready. What follows includes details from the ending! For everyone else, welcome to the conversation.

Use the questions that appeal, skip the rest, or come up with your own. There are no right or wrong answers. The author notes are from my story log, while planning and writing the book.

For more adventures, we're building a romance community on Substack, and you'll find fun extras. You can get in touch with me directly, chat with fellow romance fans and more. Can't wait to see you inside!

Love and Romance, Nina

Q: Two prominent themes in the novel are the power of saying yes and that a single decision can change a life. Do you believe that's true? How do these themes apply to Maren's journey?

Author Notes: Maren's story begins (and ends) with a literal "yes"—Each critical step in her journey comes from her willingness to step out of her comfort zone and choose an uncertain path. By saying yes, she doesn't just unravel the mystery; she also invites new love, friendship, and growth into her life. Maren's experience affirms that one decision can change everything, not because it magically solves all problems, but because it unlocks the possibility of growth and opportunity.

Q: One theme that weaves through the book is the idea from the poet Rumi, that "what you seek is seeking you." Do you believe that's true? How do you think this idea is reflected in the plot and the characters' journeys?

Author Notes: The plot and character arcs both consider this concept: Maren searches for closure, and a sense of belonging, but in the process, she discovers those things are also searching for her—through unexpected allies, uncovering family secrets, and even love. The motif appears literally, as with the map and clues that seem tailored for Maren, and metaphorically, as characters repeatedly encounter the person or knowledge they most need just as they're ready to receive it. Ultimately, for Maren and Alexander, what they're truly seeking is self-acceptance and genuine connection, and those arrive only when they have the courage to be vulnerable and open to possibility. The theme reminds us that the journey is reciprocal: our desires and questions shape the world around us, and if we're open to saying "yes" to life, we just might find that what we've been looking for is already making its way toward us.

Q: Lucien is an interesting character. How do you think he became the way he is?

Author Notes: Lucien is an elegant person. He displays impeccable manners despite his cynicism. He is fluent in a kind of old-world behaviour—traits typically forged through an elite education, frequent travel, and distance from ordinary domestic life. When I imagined him, I imagined he's worked on both sides of the law: as a protector, a rival, and one who understands the world's gray areas. Lucien hints at betrayal, missed opportunities, and the necessity of self-reliance. His attitude emerges from an early betrayal or foundational relationships where trust was broken, especially in childhood or young adulthood, prompting emotional reserve and strategic detachment. He places distance, not necessarily physical, but definitely emotional, between himself and others.

Q: What is it about Maren that seems to soften Lucien's cynicism and attract him to her?

Author Notes:

• Authenticity and Vulnerability: Maren is open about her uncertainties, losses, and desires. She doesn't posture or play games, which stands in stark contrast to the guarded, world-weary figures Lucien is accustomed to. Her honesty invites him to drop his own defenses, at least for moments.

• Adaptive Strength: She is resilient and willing to reinvent herself. Lucien observes this as Maren tries on new identities, admits when she's misjudged, and grows in self-awareness and confidence. That quality earns his genuine respect and sparks his curiosity, as it's something he admires but perhaps struggles to access in himself.

• Intelligence and Curiosity: She approaches the world—and her quest—not with a hunger for power, but with curiosity, thoughtfulness, and care. Lucien responds to people who seek knowledge for its own sake; Maren's desire to solve the mysteries of the parure is motivated not by greed but by understanding and even love.

• Wit and Playfulness: She can banter, laugh at herself, and meet Lucien's playful remarks with her own—creating a rare sense of equality and chemistry. He's challenged (and delighted) by her willingness to trade stories and explore ideas, rather than simply react or retreat.

• Capacity for Trust and Forgiveness: Despite her wounds, Maren is willing to seek help, to offer trust (even cautiously), and to recognize the humanity in others—including Lucien. This quality is unfamiliar to a man used to cynicism and betrayal, making her presence disarming and hopeful.

Q: How does Maren soften Lucien's cynicism?

Maren represents for Lucien a chance at authentic connection and a reminder that truth and love are worth protecting. She navigates shadows without losing her sense of self or joy. For Lucien, her optimism and willingness to believe in what endures, even in adversity, speaks as a quiet challenge to his detachment, suggesting that even in a world of secrets, beauty and meaning persist for those willing to risk openness.

Q: For Maren, putting the ring into the vault at the end, after developing such a unique relationship with it was a significant moment. What does this reveal about her character growth throughout the story?

Author Notes: Placing the ring in the vault marks Maren's realization that she no longer needs it as a guide. Earlier in the story, she relied on the ring's presence or vibrations to affirm her instincts about people and events, sometimes longing for it to give her more specific advice—like in the Budapest bathtub scene, where she wishes it would "speak in complete sentences." By the end of the book, Maren understands that perhaps the actual power of the ring is not that it guides her, but that it encourages her to trust her own judgment, emotions, and intuition. Setting the ring aside for a while to give them both a "rest," as she says, signifies her newfound confidence and independence.

Q: The story opens with Maren's father sending a cryptic message from Venice. How does this inciting incident shape the events that follow?

Author Notes: The message is both a call to adventure and a puzzle—its ambiguity propels Maren into action, forces her to revisit her relationship with her mother and her late father, and sets the tone for the novel's blend of mystery, grief, determination and reinvention.

Q: Why did the author choose to make the talisman a parure (a set of jewels) rather than a single object?

Author Notes: A parure allows for multiple layers of mystery and a sense of history passed through many hands. It gives the quest scope and lets various characters possess or lose different pieces, making the chase more complex and emotionally charged.

Q: The Orient Express journey features shifting alliances and hidden agendas. How did the author use this setting to advance the plot?

Author Notes: The train provides both glamour and confinement, forcing characters into close quarters where secrets can't stay hidden long. Each stop and passage creates new revelations, betrayals, and moments of vulnerability.

Q: Every character in the novel lies or withholds information from Maren. What are some of these instances? How do these deceptions drive the suspense, as well as Maren's evolution as a character?

Author Notes: Every lie or half-truth raises the stakes and keeps Maren—and the reader—guessing about each character's real intentions. Each character, like real life, has their own reasons that make sense—at least to them. It also underscores the realistic theme that perception and reality often diverge between people experiencing the same events, especially in matters of the heart.

Q: The ball in Istanbul is a major turning point. How was it significant to both the plot and character arcs? How do the ball and the escape effect Alexander and Maren's relationship?

Author Notes: The ball is where glamour and danger collide—relationships are revealed, betrayals unfold, and Maren is forced to choose whom to trust. It's a staged, beautiful event masking deeper currents, much like the plot as a whole. Both events allow Maren and Alexander to "try out" this new relationship under unique, sometimes stressful circumstances.

Q: The coded maps and riddles left by Maren's father form a subplot. What role do these mysteries play in her journey?

Author Notes: They force Maren to use and, just as important, trust her own skills, be observant, think critically, as well as confront emotional truths tied to her parents—the mystery isn't just external, but threaded through her identity and family legacy.

Q: Why did the author weave in historical elements about Ottoman jewels, the Silk Road, and Venice's ties to Istanbul?

Author Notes: It grounds the plot in authentic details, making the stakes feel real and giving the story a sense of layered time and cultural complexity. These ties allow for a richer narrative tapestry and deeper thematic resonance. Plus, it's interesting.

Q: How did the author balance action sequences (such as thefts, chases, and confrontations) with quieter moments of introspection?

Author Notes: I structured the plot to alternate suspense and reflection—after each thrilling or dangerous moment, Maren is allowed to process, making her choices feel more lived-in and her growth more believable.

Q: The novel's ending leaves some threads open. Why do you think the author did that? Did she intend for ambiguity, or is there more to the story?

Author Notes: Some mysteries are left unresolved to reflect real life and to give readers room for their own interpretations. For Maren, who has a tremendous urge to figure things out and solve mysteries, she realizes that not every mystery needs to be solved. Sometimes she can just exist within it. I wanted to end on a note of hope and new beginnings, but also with the sense that Maren's story could continue.

Q: How does Maren's initial decision to walk away from Alexander in the Saint Mark's Square scene reflect major personal growth on her part?

Author Notes: I love this scene. Maren's choice to walk away from Alexander is a turning point for her. Ultimately, her willingness to let go of control opens the door for a more authentic and equal relationship later in the story. It gives Alexander the opportunity to come forward.

Q: Many romance novels end once the characters get together, but The Gilded Talisman continues for several chapters after Maren and Alexander become a couple. Why do you think the author did this, and did it enhance your experience of the story?

Author Notes: Continuing the story after Maren and Alexander unite was deliberate—I wanted readers to experience not just the formation of a relationship, but how love matures when tested by adversity and the unknown. It's even more fun for the reader because it's like getting two books in one. Just when you think the emotional arc is resolved, the story shifts, and the couple must now unravel new challenges together. This gives readers the satisfaction of both a romance and an evolving partnership, letting them see how trust, teamwork, and love can grow stronger through real trials long after the "happily ever after" moment.

Further Discussion

- What was your overall impression of the book?

- Did you enjoy the book? Why or why not?

- How would you describe this book in one sentence?

- Were the characters believable, and what motivated them?

- In what ways does Simone weaponize her knowledge

of Alexander?

- How does Alexander's willingness to talk about Simone with Maren and his mother reflect a change in him?

- What about the relationship between Mathilde and Xavier? Did you suspect early on that he had made the necklace? Were you surprised by their relationship?

- Light and darkness appear frequently—from the inscriptions on the parure, to the eclipse, to hidden tunnels to brilliant revelations. How does this motif reflect the characters' emotional journey?

- The novel explores the tension between preserving artifacts and keeping them accessible to the public. How should society balance protection with sharing cultural treasures?

- Did the book make you feel any particular emotions?

- Can you connect any of the characters in the story to your own life experiences?

- How did the settings contribute to the story?

- If you could change one thing about the book, what would it be and why?

- The novel suggests that "love makes things endure." How do different kinds of love: romantic, familial, between friends, and cultural, manifest in the story?

- What does Maren's expertise in art restoration bring to the story beyond plot convenience? What does it tell you about her personality?

- How does the novel portray the relationship between past and present? Are the characters prisoners of history or empowered by it?

- How do clothes play a part in the novel? How does Maren's changing personal style reflect her changing ideas?

- What does the story suggest about courage? How do different characters show bravery in their own ways?

- If you discovered a legendary artifact with mystical properties, what would you do? How do you think the characters' final decisions about the parure reflect their values and growth?

- Often the very traits we see as neutral or ordinary in ourselves are the ones that set us apart: quirks, intellect, kindness, authenticity, etc. What traits have you been surprised to learn that others admire, or consider a strength of yours?

www.ingramcontent.com/pod-product-compliance
Lightning Source LLC
Chambersburg PA
CBHW031605240626

47153CB00002B/642